Raghu is an ⟨...⟩ ⟨...⟩ and a hobbyi⟨...⟩ ⟨...⟩ finance at the Indian Institute of Management, Ahmedabad, for nearly two decades before turning a banker as the president of ING Vysya Bank in Bengaluru. He is currently the CEO of GMR Varalakshmi Foundation. He is also an adjunct professor at the University of Bocconi in Milan, Italy, and Schulich School of Business, York University in Toronto, Canada.

Raghu has probably the largest collection of antique locks in the country, has played chess at all-India level, and was briefly a cartoonist for a national daily. He has been writing extensively for leading newspapers and magazines and currently blogs for the *Times of India*. His books include *Locks, Mahabharata and Mathematics*; *Ganesha on the Dashboard*; *Corruption Conundrum*; *Don't Sprint the Marathon* and *Games Indians Play*.

Visit him online at www.vraghunathan.com.

Genealogical table of the Kurus in Mahabharata

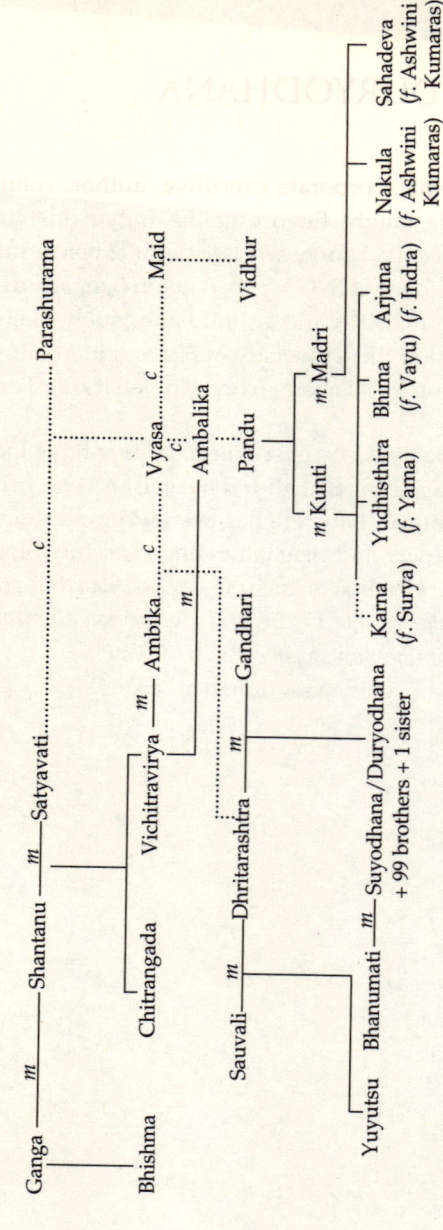

```
Ganga ─── m ─── Shantanu ─── m ─── Satyavati ············c············ Parashurama
                   │                     │
                   │                     │                              Maid
                Bhishma                  │                                │
                              ┌──────────┴──────────┐                    │
                         Chitrangada            Vichitravirya ··c·· Vyasa ·c· ·····
                                                    │ m              c
                                                    │                 │
                                               Ambika ·········· ····· ···········
                                               Ambalika
                                                    │ m
                                                    │
                        ┌───────────────────────────┼─────────────────────┐
                        │                           │                     │
                   Sauvali                      Pandu                  Vidhur
                        │ m                         │
                        │                    ┌─────┴─────┐
                  Dhritarashtra ── m ── Gandhari    Kunti  m  Madri
                        │                    │        │         │
         ┌──────────────┴──────────┐     ┌───┼───┐  ┌──┴──┐  ┌──┴──┐
         │                         │     │   │   │  │     │  │     │
      Yuyutsu  Bhanumati ─ m ─ Suyodhana/Duryodhana   Yudhisthira  Bhima  Arjuna  Nakula  Sahadeva
                            + 99 brothers + 1 sister  (f. Yama)  (f. Vayu) (f. Indra) (f. Ashwini  (f. Ashwini
                                                                                      Kumaras)    Kumaras)

                                                      Karna
                                                    (f. Surya)
```

Notes:

- Bhishma is the half-brother of Chitrangada and Vichitravirya
- Ambika is married to Vichitravirya, but has a son with Vyasa after she is widowed
- The Kauravas and Pandavas have no blood relationship
- One of the Kaurava brothers, Yuyutsu, is born to Dhritarashtra's second wife, Sauvali
- Kunti has three sons: Yudhisthira, Bhima and Arjuna – all born outside wedlock; she also has another son, Karna, born before her marriage to Pandu
- Madri has two sons: Nakula and Sahadeva – also born outside wedlock
- Dhritarashtra, Pandu and Vidhura are half-brothers, all born of Vyasa
- Ambika and Ambalika are sisters, both married to Vichitravirya
- Bhishma or the grandsire (grand-uncle) is also a half-brother-in-law to Ambika and so a grand-uncle of sorts to the Kauravas and the Pandavas
- f = fathered by; m = married to; c = copulates with; dotted line: out of wedlock

DURYODHANA

V. Raghunathan

HarperCollins *Publishers* India

First published in India in 2014 by
HarperCollins *Publishers* India

Copyright © V. Raghunathan 2014

P-ISBN: 978-93-5136-330-9
E-ISBN: 978-93-5136-331-6

2 4 6 8 10 9 7 5 3 1

V. Raghunathan asserts the moral right to be
identified as the author of this work.

On the cover, Duryodhana has been depicted in the unorthodox
Javanese tradition to denote the uncommon representation
of the character's personality in this book. The woman next
to him could be his wife or his love – the two women
he is torn between, as portrayed in the work.

This is a work of fiction, though based on the Mahabharata, and many
of the incidents described in this book are the product of the author's
imagination. Any resemblance to actual persons,
living or dead, is entirely coincidental.

All rights reserved. No part of this publication may be reproduced,
stored in a retrieval system, or transmitted, in any form or by any
means, electronic, mechanical, photocopying, recording or otherwise,
without the prior permission of the publishers.

HarperCollins *Publishers*
A-75, Sector 57, Noida, Uttar Pradesh 201301, India
77-85 Fulham Palace Road, London W6 8JB, United Kingdom
Hazelton Lanes, 55 Avenue Road, Suite 2900, Toronto, Ontario M5R 3L2
and 1995 Markham Road, Scarborough, Ontario M1B 5M8, Canada
25 Ryde Road, Pymble, Sydney, NSW 2073, Australia
31 View Road, Glenfield, Auckland 10, New Zealand
10 East 53rd Street, New York NY 10022, USA

Typeset in 10.5/14 PalmSprings Regular at
SÜRYA

Printed and bound at
Thomson Press (India) Ltd.

To the memory of my father

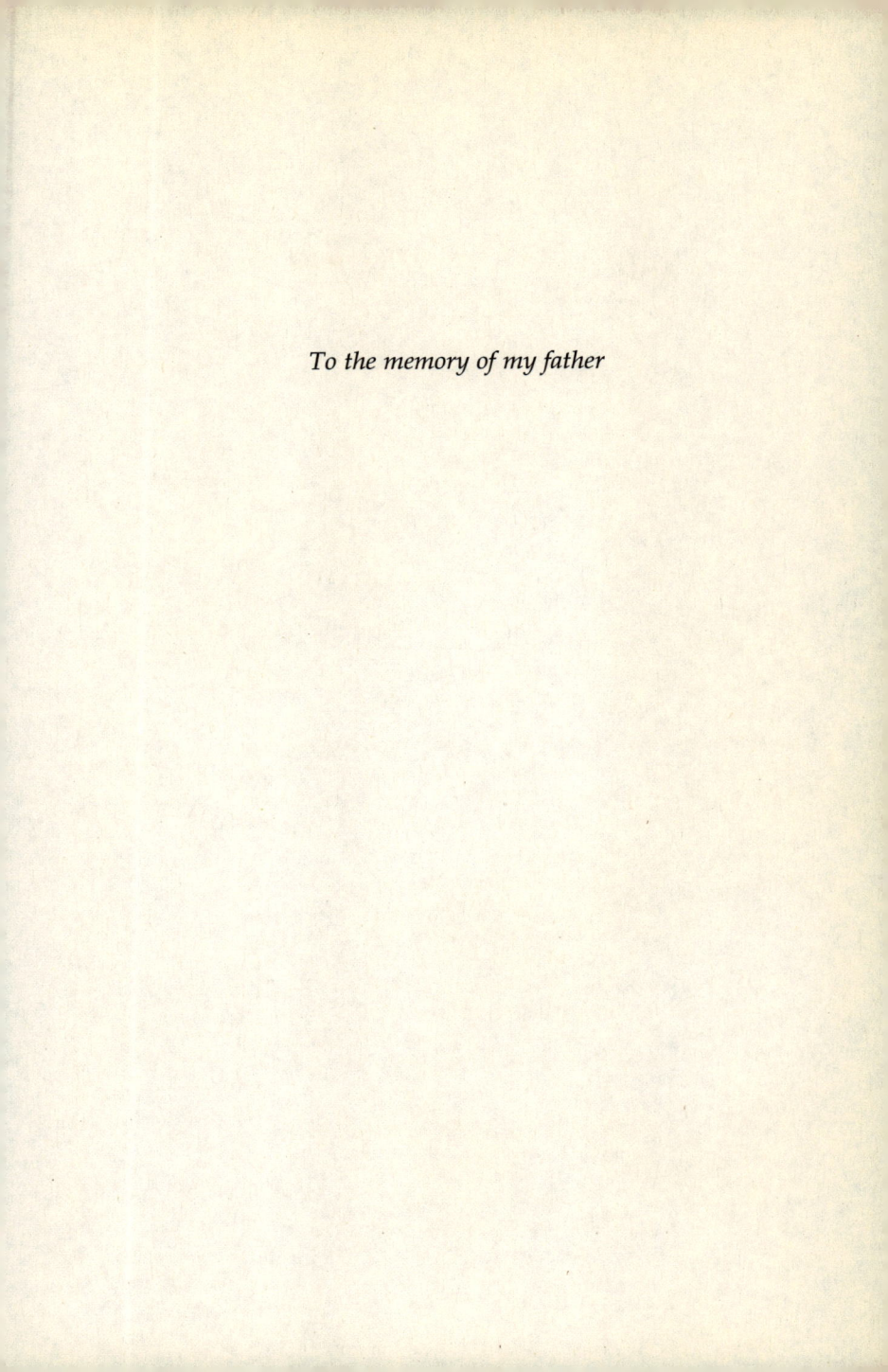

Author's Note

The Mahabharata, along with the Ramayana, ranks among the greatest epics of ancient India. Set some five millennia ago, the Mahabharata is a collection of nearly 100,000 shlokas or double that number in dual verses – which is about seven times the length of the Illiad and Odyssey combined. It evolved over a period of nearly a millennium, through contributions by innumerable and anonymous contributors. However, the origin of the epic is traditionally ascribed to Sage Vyasa who, as the grandfather of the Kaurava clan, himself plays a significant part in the epic. Apparently, Vyasa, who is said to have dictated the verses to Lord Ganesha, meant the text to be itihasa, which in Sanskrit means 'this is what happened'. In other words, the text is intended to be 'history' rather than 'mythology'. While several references to early Vedic times and practices give the epic a history-like credibility, the lack of verifiable historical facts places the text in a distinctly mythological space.

This real and surreal character of the epic makes it one of the most important ancient texts of mythology painted in historical hue, while the segment of Gitopadesha – a didactic sermon about dharma (higher duty) – gives it a moral character.

The epic captures the story of two sets of paternal cousins – the Pandavas and the Kauravas – in the Kuru kingdom of Hastinapura. The sum and substance of the story is the heroic struggles of the Pandavas against the excesses of the evil Kauravas, leading to the ultimate victory of the heroes. The Kauravas are the sons of King Dhritarashtra, who is blind, while the Pandavas are the sons of Pandu. Dhritarashtra and Pandu are half-brothers, sharing the same father. Since Dhritarashtra, the elder of the two, is blind by birth, the reins of the kingdom are handed over to the younger brother Pandu following the death of their father. However, as Pandu cannot beget children, he abdicates the throne and leaves the kingdom accompanied by his two wives Kunti and Madri, repairing to the Himalayas to undertake rigorous penances. At this point, Dhritarashtra ascends the throne. Duryodhana (originally named Suyodhana), the eldest of the Kaurava brothers, is hoping to succeed his father.

However, in a few years, Kunti returns from the Himalayas with five sons, the Pandavas. In time, she claims the throne, or at least a share of the Hastinapura kingdom, for her eldest son, Yudhisthira, who is also the eldest of the Kaurava and Pandava cousins put together – the Kurus.

From here on, Duryodhana spares no effort – fair or foul – to thwart the exertions of the Pandavas to secure a share of the kingdom. In due course, Dhritarashtra prevails upon his eldest son to let the Pandavas have the wild end of their kingdom, namely the forest of Khandava. By dint

Author's Note

of hard work and sagacity, the Pandavas establish their capital city of Indraprastha and turn the land into a powerful kingdom and go on to conduct the rajasuya – the declaration of sovereignty over the surrounding kingdoms, including Hastinapura. This, Duryodhana is unable to stomach.

Together with his maternal uncle Shakuni, he invites Yudhisthira for a game of chance – chaupar. Yudhisthira ends up wagering and losing not only his kingdom, but also himself, his brothers and wife, Draupadi, aka Panchali. In a climax of the dark deeds ascribed to the Kauravas in the usual version of the epic, Draupadi is sought to be disrobed by one of Duryodhana's brothers in the court of Hastinapura.

Following these losses, the Pandavas are exiled for twelve years, followed by one year of incognito existence, with the promise that Indraprastha would be handed back to them upon their return, provided they are not discovered during the last year of living undercover.

When the Pandavas return after thirteen years, Duryodhana refuses to meet his end of the bargain on the grounds that they violated the conditions of the thirteenth year. This inexorably leads to the end-game, which culminates in the epic war of Kurukshetra in which brothers, uncles, teachers, cousins and friends fight each other, and the lives of millions of men, women and children are lost, and many others widowed and orphaned. In the ultimate vindication of their dharma, the great war is won by the Pandavas.

It is as a prelude to the war – when one of the Pandava brothers, Arjuna, refuses to fight his cousins, teachers, uncles and grand-uncles who are arrayed on the other side against him and his brothers – that Lord Krishna gives the Gitopadesha, which contains an ocean of wisdom relating to choices that one is constrained to make in life.

That's the usual version of the epic.

Quite apart from the place it holds among Hindu texts, the Mahabharata is a veritable minefield from which one may quarry a rich haul of wisdom relating to virtually any and every aspect of human nature – moral fibre and foibles alike. The Gitopadesha too is an ocean one may trawl for wisdom in matters relating to the highest duty of man.

Developed over a millennium before the birth of Christ, in the format of telling a story within a story within a story, mimicking a Matryoshka doll, the Mahabharata, in short, portrays humanity in all its glory and gore, and has examples of virtually every conceivable human dilemma, big or small, and provides sage guidance for resolving those.

However, there are as many variants of the epic – both ancient and contemporary – as there are authors. Modern scholars have often given their own interpretations to the works of ancient scholars. Some have challenged the translations or interpretations of the original Sanskrit shlokas and provided their own interpretations or translations.

Duryodhana is written against this backdrop of narratives that have arisen as alternatives to the mainstream version of the epic. While most popular versions of the Mahabharata portray Duryodhana as the perpetrator of all that is wrong, it seems to me that there is a good reason to view him as the wronged party instead.

Author's Note

As one who likes to side with the underdog, I thought it would be interesting to play advocate to Duryodhana and see the Mahabharata from his perspective. The book is not a scholarly interpretation of any version of the Mahabharata. As a matter of fact, I am hardly a scholar of Hindu texts, including the Mahabharata. Nor do I claim to have read every major work on the epic in the market or libraries.

I have borrowed about 75 per cent of my story from the usual available texts and some 25 per cent has been derived from my own imagination in order to come out with what I fancy would make a good case for Duryodhana being as grey a character as any of the other major heroes in the epic, and not as dark as he has been painted in the average version of the epic. I would like to describe the book as a novel simply because I have introduced episodes that are purely fictional and not part of any version of the Mahabharata that I am aware of.

As usual, I am most grateful to my best friend and wife, Meena, who always helps with the editing of my early manuscripts. I am also deeply grateful to my good friend and literary agent Priya Doraswamy who gave me some very useful inputs and advice that the book has enormously benefited from. I am grateful to Nilofer and Shaan for most graciously designing the cover of this book and to Shilo for her design inputs. I am equally grateful to my friends Manish, Nilofer, Shweta, Shobha and Sushma, who gave me very encouraging and useful reviews on the early version of my manuscript. I am indebted to Krishan Chopra, my editor at HarperCollins, whose invaluable suggestions have indeed found their way into the final result; I can't be sure if I have done full justice to them. And finally, I am extremely grateful to Prema Govindan for the copy-editing support, which has added significantly to the quality of the text.

V. RAGHUNATHAN

Prologue

The human race is not so much black or white as grey

The title of the chief villain of the Mahabharata belongs unequivocally to me.

Why? Could it be because that's how Sage Vyasa, aka Krishna Dvaipayana – also ironically my biological grandfather – presented the chronicle to you? Or could it be that Vyasa wrote much of the epic ex post facto, and not as matters were unfolding, so that his narration – and therefore the words of those who told and retold the stories after him – swayed way too much towards how the victors of the climactic war at Kurukshetra wanted it told? After all, it is human nature to find everything about the victors virtuously rosy and everything about the vanquished a vicious black.

Victors always paint themselves as larger than life; they can do no wrong; their sweat smells sweet; their breath is fragrant … why, they can walk on water! The vanquished are forever the whipping boys of posterity, as we Kauravas ought to know better than most. That is why our so-called cousins, the Pandavas, have forever been adorned with divine halos, and we the Kauravas with demons' souls.

Before I proceed with my account of our story, let me make a comment – a sort of a disclaimer. The problem with our complex family history, which is as far flung in geography as in time, is that we can often tell you nothing about any *one* episode in our lives without telling you about *another* episode at another time or place that caused the first episode, and then something else again that caused that second episode, and so on, so that touching on any single story from our lives ends up setting off a whole chain reaction, like so many dominoes. By the time you return to the story of your original interest, you may well have lost track of it. So every now and then, I may need to make excursions away from the main story, and the onus shall be upon you to keep track of the main line of my narration.

For example, if I am to convey to you why sage Vyasa could have had a burr under the saddle about us Kauravas, I need to go back a little and tell you a story. The story is that of my grandmother, Ambika, and her husband Vichitravirya – not my grandfather, though – who were childless when the husband died. If you are a tad confused about my grandmother's husband not being my grandfather, that's because there is yet another story explaining this one.

The two stories telescope back to the time of the Kuru King Shantanu of Hastinapura and Queen Satyavati, who were parents to two handsome sons – Chitrangada and Vichitravirya. When Shantanu passed away, his elder son Chitrangada succeeded him to the throne. Unfortunately, he died a young man not yet married, fighting a powerful Gandharva chief, so that his younger sibling, Vichitravirya, succeeded him. But the gods do play dice, and merciless are their throws. So the next of their manoeuvres ensured that the younger brother too died without progeny, leaving behind a young widow with no child and the Kuru clan with no successor to the throne, so that continuation of the Kuru race hung in balance.

After Vichitravirya's death, in a bid to somehow fashion a successor for the clan, the desperate Queen Mother, Satyavati, asked her daughter-in-law, that is my widowed grandmother Ambika – to marry her half-brother-in-law, Bhishma.

I need to take another little diversion in my stories here.

Before marrying Satyavati, Shantanu was married to the gorgeous Ganga, from whom he had a son, brave Bhishma. One day, owing to Shantanu violating a pre-nuptial agreement, Ganga walked out with her son, to bring him up single-handedly. Bhishma grew up into a learned young man, well-versed in the Vedas, and highly skilled in the use of a variety of weapons, especially the bow and arrow. Ganga restored the youth to his pater Shantanu, and then left again, never to return. Shantanu, who had always missed his son, and the son, who had presumably always missed his father, grew unusually devoted to each other. It goes without saying that brilliant Bhishma, being the only son, was poised to take the reins from his father when the time came.

But fate had other plans, and the time never came, because one day during one of his royal hunts, a single and lonely Shantanu fell head over heels for the unusual charms of nubile Satyavati, the daughter of a chieftain of the fishing community, when he saw the piscatorial princess drying her hair delicately in the sun. When Shantanu sought her hand from her father, the wily chieftain – familiar with the affairs of royalty – refused, unless Shantanu agreed to make the first born of his daughter the king. This, fair-minded Shantanu could not bring himself to agree to, dote as he did on his son Bhishma.

But such is the plight of the lovelorn that one may live, but not be lively; one may walk, but like a somnambulist; nibble at food, but hardly eat. What is more, even as they keep their lips sealed, their plight speaks eloquently. So Bhishma didn't have to move heaven and earth to divine the cause of his father's dolefulness. And no sooner did the son realize it than he vowed never to ascend the throne, hoping it would clear the way for his father to marry Satyavati. But still, the far-sighted fisherman demurred, querying what prevented Bhishma's future offspring from staking a claim to the kingdom, endangering the claim of his daughter's progeny. This is when Bhishma vowed to remain celibate, thus clearing the last obstacle for Shantanu to marry Satyavati.

Now connecting the dots backwards, you will realize that Bhishma was a half-brother of Vichitravirya, and hence half-brother-in-law to my grandmother Ambika, whose husband Vichitravirya had died young. Thus Bhishma, who was respectfully referred to as the grandsire, was my grand-uncle of sorts.

So where was I? Ah yes, Queen Mother Satyavati asked my grandmother Ambika to marry the grandsire Bhishma –

and simultaneously pleaded with Bhishma to accept the alliance for the sake of the continuity of the Kuru clan. Bhishma, wedded to celibacy as he was, refused to budge.

Here we need to go back to another story, which is that, unknown to the world, the Queen Mother had another son back from a casual fling with Parashurama – the great sage dedicated to relieving the earth of the burden of Kshatriyas by separating their heads from their bodies with some surgical wielding of his axe.

And this formidable Parashurama, in a rather licentious stage of his life, had used his authority and aura to seduce an impressionably young Satyavati. The son born of the union was none other than my biological grandfather, sage Vyasa, who, as fate would have it, was quite unpleasant to look at, with a face only a mother could love – but didn't or couldn't, being unmarried. Thus it was left to Parashurama to bring up the first born of Satyavati on his own. But in time, what with few distractions from Vedic studies in the dense forests where Parashurama mostly lodged, the child grew up to be a renowned scholar.

To cut a long story short, when the grandsire refused to oblige the Queen Mother, she managed to convince my grandmother to copulate instead with her cast-away son Vyasa, so the clan could at least beget a Kuru successor (though how a child born of such intercourse would be a legitimate Kuru heir is a mystery to me, as Vyasa himself was not a legitimate son of Satyavati, and no royal either). This – finding no escape from a demanding mother-in-law – my poor granny agreed to, unaware of what lay in store for her.

When Satyavati sent for her son and explained what

was expected of him, my grandfather, with the detachment befitting a bearded hermit, and without much ado, marched in the direction of my grandmother's bedchambers. And when the reclusive Vyasa, all dreadlocks and dreadful looks, suddenly appeared before my young grandmother, she was so frightened by the apparition that she refused to let the sage into her chambers!

When a peeved Vyasa reported the developments to his mother, a resolute Satyavati pleaded with him to pay another visit to Ambika who, still unwilling to allow the sage anywhere near her, got one of her pretty ladies-in-waiting to proxy for her. Apparently, my grandpa realized the substitution only after his seed had already been planted inside the maid.

Not one easily deterred from his mission, he turned once again to Ambika to do his mother's bidding – some mummy's boy that – only to see her shut her eyes tightly and go through the formalities of copulation, not once opening her eyes.

This upset the sage so much that he cursed my grandmother and any baby that may be born of that intercourse. This in turn shocked poor Ambika so much and stressed her out so thoroughly during her ensuing pregnancy that she ended up begetting a blind baby, the accursed child being my father Dhritarashtra. Not only did Sage Vyasa walk out on my grandmother, leaving her holding the blighted baby, he also cut off all further contact with the mother and the innocent child. The child *could* not see its father ever and the father did not *wish* to lay his eyes on it ever. As a matter of fact, trawl through the epic as much as you will, and you are unlikely to dredge any reference that my grandfather ever showed any paternal affection for my poor father.

So I ask you, should it come as a surprise that Vyasa mirrored that ancient prejudice against Dhritarashtra and his offspring in his account of the Mahabharata? Now do you realize what I meant when I said that Sage Vyasa may have had good reasons for according me the hot seat in the epic that he authored?

I can think of other reasons that could possibly explain why the Kauravas emerge as the vilest brothers in human history. One could be that Sage Vyasa had taken it upon himself to narrate his version of the Mahabharata to Maharishi Shukracharya and that roving sage, Narada, for word-of-mouth transmission of his version of the epic. Vyasa probably considered them dependable broadcasters, because both were renowned for their prodigious memories. Now that you are familiar with our family background, which has more twists than a hemp rope, I am sure you will no longer be shocked if I tell you that Maharishi Shukracharya, or Shuka, was my grandfather Vyasa's own son from a lady of the Shuka tribe, and thus ironically my half-uncle! If you say my grandfather led an interesting life, well, you could say it again. Be that as it may, Shuka was a great scholar who would go on to become the presiding guru of the Asuras. As for Muni Narada, I am sure you know him for the gossip-monger that he was. The peripatetic sage was famed for minding everybody's business but his own.

This duo may have had prodigious memories, but they seemed to have an even better talent for theatrics and declamation. They wasted little time in spreading the story far and wide, with the enthusiasm of gossiping mothers-in-law. From the image they have accorded me through their storytelling, I can only believe that, if it helped tell a good story better, the gentlemen weren't beyond embellishment. I am sure the duo generously anointed every sub-plot with every spice they could muster, if only to make my character less than palatable. In my more contemplative moments I wonder if I should not be more charitable to the Kuntiputras who were my enemies, considering the amount of damage my own grandfather and uncle did me!

In short then, the two, in my opinion, completed the assignment for tarring the Kaurava reputation, diligently filling such gaps as Vyasa may have unwittingly left. If so, perhaps the entire credit for besmirching the Kaurava name in general, and mine in particular, cannot be monopolized by Sage Vyasa; some credit must accrue to the Shuka–Narada duo too.

Besides, when it came to spreading stories, Narada was in a class of his own. It was as if he knew that a story was hardly entertaining if all its characters came in shades of grey, even if that's how most humans actually are. So the roving snitch craftily threw in a bunch of all-white heroes; a dusky heroine in a sexagonal love story; a horde of sinister villains, headed by a moustachioed rogue Duryodhana with sidekicks like Shakuni the Infamous Gambler who specialized in dice-sharping and Dushasana the Notorious Molester whose specialization was to pull at the loose end of saris; a blind father; doting mothers; scheming mothers-in-law; bachelor uncles; and assorted

Duryodhana

kings and godmen in cameos. And thus he told the story as a series of skirmishes between presumed good and bad guys, culminating in a climactic Armageddon in Kurukshetra. And he embroidered story after story about all of us and our ancient families in a fine brocade of sundry hues, and told them to any idler who had a pair of ears and the time and inclination to listen.

As for Shuka, I mean him no disrespect but, truth be told, his tongue was as loose as his control over his daughter Devayani, who ultimately led him to let out the vital secrets of his clan to the Suras, their enemies. In case I have piqued your curiosity, let me digress a bit.

Ours were times when people in Bharatavarsha belonged to two distinct races: Suras (or Devas) and Asuras (or Rakshasas). The Devas were fairer in appearance with sharper features, while the Asuras were of darker complexion but built big. Both controlled their kingdoms and powers zealously.

The Devas had pre-eminence in weather prediction. They had not only mastered the art of making fire, but had also learnt to put it to a variety of uses. They had also learnt to control water resources by taming rivers and could harness solar energy. And, of course, they considered themselves more righteous than the Asuras.

Asuras, on the other hand, considered themselves more moral; they made excellent friends and had conquered the art of healing, trade and commerce. They also commanded the art of taming wind power to their advantage.

You may have read accounts of Deva gods Indra (king of the gods and also the god of weather), Agni (lord of fire), Usha (the god of dawn), Surya (the sun god), Apas (the one who ruled water) and Yama (the god of dharma and death) as the ruling Devas of the time. Likewise, you would also probably be aware of the gods of morals, such as Mitra (the god of contract), Aryaman (the guardian of guests, friendship and marriage), Bhaga (the god of sharing) and Varuna (the god who controlled the sky and wind), who were the reigning Asuras. Well, now you know where they came from.

The only problem with them was that rather than complement each other's powers for the common good, the two groups were perennially at loggerheads. At some stage in the Vedic times, it suited the Devas (who held an upper hand in the affairs of the world and were probably in control of writing the mythological history of the times) to demonize the Asuras as Rakshasas, while the truth probably was that there were as many bad eggs as good ones in both the clans.

Now, Brahaspati was the patron guru of the Devas, and Shuka that of the Rakshasas. Shuka, pottering about medicinal plants, had found the formula for a secret concoction of herbs that could all but bring the dead back to life, thus providing the Asuras with not only a vibrant public health system, but a clear advantage in war over the Suras. No matter how many Asuras the Suras hacked away, Shuka would speedily bring them back to health, while the Suras could do no such thing for their wounded and dying.

Seriously concerned, the Suras brewed an elaborate scheme to even their odds against the Asuras. The plot involved Brahaspati's son, Kacha, finding his way into the sanctum of Shukracharya as his student, somehow winning his confidence and stealing the secret formula. So Kacha wormed his way into Shuka's ashram and from there into the heart of his daughter, Devayani. Soon, the girl was besotted with Kacha, who put her infatuation to good use and exploited her naiveté to wrest her father's secret formula. So infatuated was the lass that she would emotionally blackmail her pater into reviving Kacha every time he was killed by the Asuras for the double agent that he was. But once Kacha had laid his hands on the formula, he claimed that his feelings for Devayani were fraternal and not romantic, and left the ashram post-haste.

Now I have nothing against naïve Devayani – she was I am sure a comely enough lass. After all, she had nothing to do with what her father did to my reputation. But I narrated the story only to let you know how the weak Shuka gave away the one competitive advantage the Asuras had over their enemies by letting out their key secret. Now, how much weight can you put upon the words of such a man?

I am not trying to insinuate that Vyasa, Narada or Shuka harboured any specific ill-feeling towards me. The truth is, they hardly knew me. After these thousands of years, my memory may be playing tricks but, unless I am seriously mistaken, their paths hardly ever crossed mine, at least never directly. So they could not have had any reason to hold a personal grudge against me. I am not a big fan of any of the three, though none of them did me any harm when I was alive. The damage they have done to me, or rather my reputation, making me out to be the vilest of the villains in history and mythology combined is, as I said, mainly posthumous.

How serious is this damage to my own or to the Kaurava clan's good name? Look at it this way: you must have come across dozens of people named Arjuna and Krishna in your daily interactions, probably an occasional Bhimsen, and even an odd Yudhisthira or a Panchali. But ask yourself, how often do you bump into even an urchin named Duryodhana, Dushasana or Durmukha? That's how serious the damage to our reputation has been. Worse, our given names were actually Suyodhana, Sushasana, Sumukha, Sushala, etc. Take just three of our names, for instance. Suyodhana, Sushasana and Sumukha mean one who is adept at wielding weapons, one who rules well and one who has a handsome face respectively. On the other hand, our distorted names Duryodhana, Dushasana and Durmukha mean one who makes wrong use of weapons, one who is a bad ruler and one who is ugly!

Be that as it may, after all this time, I have more or less forgotten my real name, and those of my siblings, and have learnt to answer to Duryodhana, and refer to my siblings as Dushasana, Durmukha, Dushala, etc. Can there be a bigger tragedy for a man?

Regarding Vyasa's possible motivation to malign the Kaurava name, I have already spoken of his curse upon my poor father even before he was born. But if Shuka and Narada harboured no grudge towards me personally, why would they too besmirch the name and reputation of the Kauravas? I don't know for sure, but let me make another conjecture: the five nitpicking brothers and their scheming mother were always the kind who, whatever their persona in private, always presented a goody-goody picture to the world at large. Me? I was the kind from whom you got what you saw. So I wouldn't be surprised if even Vyasa was taken in by the façade of great gentility put up by the Pandavas and their cohorts. And the brothers never missed an opportunity to badmouth me, albeit subtly, for reasons that will become self-evident later in this narration. So again, Vyasa – viewing me through the prism presented to him by the Pandavas – must have been suitably biased about me, a prejudice which he must have passed on to Shuka and Narada.

And from there on, it was as if transmission distortions took charge. Every positive anecdote about the Pandavas was sugar-coated and exaggerated, while comparable accounts pertaining to Kauravas suppressed and snuffed out. Similarly, every little defect and mistake of the Kauravas was painted with tar and parallel accounts of Pandavas white-washed. After all, reputations, good or bad, when told and retold, get exaggerated like the length of a serpent one may have killed. So no wonder in due course these carefully crafted stories acquired a reality of their own, gaining random limbs, making monsters of us Kauravas and angels of the Pandavas. And if you came to swallow all that baloney, I can hardly blame you for your gullibility. After all, you are the same person who is ready to believe that a stone resemblance of Ganapati drinks milk, aren't you? So I am not exactly devastated by your belief that people can be all white or all black!

Why else would you imagine the Pandavas – who were trying to wrest a good chunk of a kingdom over which they had no right – as all good, and us Kauravas – who were merely trying to protect what was legitimately ours – as all bad? Why would you believe an Arjuna who killed Karna unethically, or a young Bhima who killed an ageing Jarasandha by cunning, to be virtuous, and still consider reprehensible the Kaurava princes' attempts kill the Pandavas craftily in order to protect their kingdom? Before I am done, I intend to straighten out some of these distortions.

You will agree that the Mahabharata will be a much lesser epic, far less fascinating, if it was only about pure good pitched against pure evil. I beg your pardon, but we hardly need a man, leave alone a godly man like Vyasa, telling us that Good must fight Evil. The truth is that the Mahabharata ought to hold its fascination because the epic is about grey versus grey; not white versus black.

Nor am I prepared to buy the argument that just because Krishna fought on the side of the Pandavas, they must have been in the right. If Krishna, being Arjuna's close friend, sided with the Pandavas, don't forget that Krishna's own brother Balarama always remained on my side. So did virtuous Karna. For that matter, hundreds of kings and princes, many of them close friends and well-wishers of the Pandavas, and in no way beholden to us, also fought on our side. Why would they have done so if I was pure evil and if there was no case in my favour?

Speaking of Krishna, in the Kaliyuga, he may be good enough to be deified as Lord Krishna and be worshipped by you. With due respect, after all, Kaliyuga is the age ruled by one-quarter virtue and three-quarters sin. But Dwaparayuga, in which we lived, was governed half by virtue and half by sin. That's why in our time, everybody – be it Krishna, Arjuna, Drona or I – was considered to be a mere mortal, and all of us were tinted in more or less similar shades of grey; roughly fifty-fifty. So pardon me if I speak of Krishna as my contemporary with his share of moles and warts.

If Krishna commanded a larger-than-life image in our time and thereafter, it was mostly a result of his careful brand-building exercise, executed through his own exaggerated references to his sundry exploits, which posterity fell for, hook, line and sinker. After all, he had made a fine art of being famous for being famous, using the little time he could spare from chasing all the Gokul girls.

Even in our time, we were aware of Krishna's boasts of slaying a particularly ferocious she-demon Putana, even as a toddler, or the cruel king Kansa – his own maternal uncle – as a mere teenager, or having lifted Mount Govardhana, no less, to save his people in Vrindavan from torrential rains, and such. If I am less than enthusiastic about accepting these tall claims at face value, it is because I for one never came across anyone I knew who had witnessed these feats first hand. But, as usual, there were many who had a distant cousin, or aunt, whose friend's nephew or brother-in-law's uncle had witnessed these feats, if you know what I mean. So, as Krishna's contemporary, I never knew how much credibility I could actually assign to his boasts.

As for the glamour associated with his heroics, well, look at what has been made of Kansa's villainy. Kansa was known to be a cruel king. It is said that he learnt through a prophecy that the eighth child of his sister Devaki would be the cause of his death. So, received wisdom has it that he imprisoned both his sister and brother-in-law, Vasudeva, in his dungeon, and proceeded to kill every child born to them, until the unfortunate parents managed to smuggle away Krishna, the eighth-born, to safety. When Kansa discovered the truth, he made many attempts to find and kill the child. Finally, Krishna as a teenager turned the tables on Kansa and slew his uncle instead.

Nice as that story is, it does not smell right. While Kansa may not have been your model brother – and I hold no brief for him – he loved his sister enough not to execute her or her husband summarily, though killing either could easily have put paid to any danger of any of their offspring killing him. Given such compassion for his sister, one is tempted to wonder why he would kill the first seven children of Devaki, rather than just wait it out for the eighth one to arrive and then kill it. No sir, he did the exact opposite. Come to think of it, why not just keep Devaki and Vasudeva in separate cells so they couldn't copulate, and save all the unnecessary killings? Surely even a cruel king would be capable of such elementary reasoning, especially if he had a degree of compassion for his sister? As I see it, posterity has chosen to paint Kansa a good deal darker just so Krishna emerges that much more glorified. So what do we believe? Or disbelieve?

While I hardly contest that Krishna may have been very good to those he considered his friends, just as most of us are to our own friends, he was not beyond routinely employing subterfuge to eradicate those he considered his foes; again like most of us.

As far as I know, he was a chieftain of the Yadavas; an advisor to various kings, who successfully portrayed himself as being larger than life, even if he was as ordinary a bloke as the rest of us. I for one looked upon him as a more-than-somewhat crafty politician and never learnt to like him.

In our times, he was regular enough to die a common man's death – by a stray hunter's poisoned arrow when resting in a forest. I am happy that at least I died a brave king's death, which brought down the curtain on a war that I do not believe I started or asked for.

But don't get me wrong. It is not at all my case that the Pandavas or even Krishna weren't nice enough blokes. Maybe they were, even if I am not their diehard fan. But my brothers and I were nice enough guys too – at least that's what our friends would have told you. The likes of Karna, Jarasandha, Shishupala, Bhagadatta, Shalya or Jayadratha would not have been our friends – some even related by marriage – if we had not been reasonable enough fellows. We had many friends and were good to them, the same as the Pandavas. And we were bad to our foes and we had many of them too, just the same as the Pandavas again. We had our sense of humour. We did our share of good deeds. We committed our share of mistakes. But we were no worse, if no better, than the Pandavas. It is simply that somewhere along the long road of mythological storytelling, someone decided to paint us a dark shade and then with every coat it just got darker and darker, as the stories were repeated again and again.

Truth be told, I died a happy man. In death, as in life, I held my head high. I never lived with one eye on the future like Arjuna, whose burning desire to be hailed the greatest-ever marksman shaped most of his actions. Nor did I have any pangs of self-doubt like him at any point in my life. I was convinced of my righteousness and I found answers to my dilemmas entirely on my own. I have never apologized to anyone for what I was or what I did – nor did my ninety-nine good brothers – *ever*. Nor is it my proposed enterprise now. As a matter of fact, I regret none of my actions. If I have any regrets at all, it is just one – of which I shall speak later.

Considering I didn't set much store by what others thought of me when I was alive, it would be uncharacteristic of me to give two hoots about what the world thinks of me now, when I am long dead. All I care for is that I lived my life being true to myself and to the higher interests of my lineage and God-ordained role – that is, my rajadharma.

The Pandavas may have made it difficult for me to live in peace in my life, but posterity made it difficult for me to even remain dead in peace. As if it wasn't bad enough that the Mahabharata had placed my brothers and me on the villains' roll of honour forever, I noticed that one by one, first Arjuna, then Yudhisthira, then Bhima, and then Panchali, and finally even my closest friend and ally Karna were coming forward to give their account of the Mahabharata. Reading their accounts (save Karna's), you would think *they* were the aggrieved party who hadn't been given their due in the chronicles of the epic, and therefore needed to set the record straight. Talk of seeking attention!

Yudhisthira tried to convince the world that it is more honourable and righteous to gamble away your wife, family and kingdom than decline a gambling invite. Arjuna,

I can understand. The guy was always full of himself – besides the hot air, that is – and it should hardly strain anyone's fancy that he should have tried to enhance his image further, even beyond what the standard account of the Mahabharata accords him. And then I was surprised that the good old simpleton Bhima did it too! And how! If you believe his take on the Mahabharata, there was no soul nobler than him in the three worlds combined! And to think the fellow killed me sneakily, as in the case of Jarasandha, with some help from that milkman Krishna again! Yes, it rankles; not that I had not been equally or even more sneaky with him when I tried to drown him. But then I am supposed to be wicked anyway, right? And Panchali? After being dumb enough to reject me and even Karna in favour of Arjuna, with four brothers thrown in for free, she has been carrying on as if it was I, rather than those husbands of hers, who sold out her honour and dignity. Thank god for small mercies, Nakula and Sahadeva have spared us the ordeal of having to read their versions; but then they were always a modest enough pair with much to be modest about.

But Karna, I can quite understand. If I suffered in a hundred ways at the hands of the Pandavas, he suffered a hundred-fold more. He truly was the tallest among the men of our time, and has been since; and the original version of the Mahabharata did not do him justice at all, which is hardly surprising. So he had to tell his side of the story and correct the erroneous versions that have been passed along as gospel. He had to expose the deep-rooted caste bias in the minds of the Pandavas, who repeatedly taunted him for his 'lowly birth' (ironically unaware that he was the son of their own unwed mother). He even tried to play my advocate here and there in his account, but then the poor guy had enough of his own case to fight and to set mythological history right for himself. There was only so much he could do for me.

But to return to the point, when I saw the Pandava clan telling its tall tales, you could say I sort of turned in my grave, sat up, and here I am. If they think their stories had not been told well in the Mahabharata and needed retelling by them personally, I suppose I have more than a wee bit of a case too. In fact, you hardly need a savant to tell you that I am perhaps the most wronged party in the entire saga. It is this distorted balance that I am trying to set right.

What am I going to tell you about myself that you do not already know? Why should you invest time in understanding the real me? Isn't the epic protracted enough without my adding to it further? Such questions are likely to nag you. My only response to them is to ask you another question: Wouldn't you want to see the other part of the Mahabharata – the Dr Jekylls among the Kauravas and Mr Hydes among the Pandavas?

PART I

1

Like unwelcome guests, bad news always comes uninvited

My memory of our childhood is vivid in a dreamlike way, even if that sounds somewhat paradoxical. My earliest memory is that of my blind father, Dhritarashtra, who was the king of a vast empire. The world at large seemed to make much fuss about him. He seemed so very big, his long beard flowing, up there, atop a flight of stairs, sitting on a huge throne, at a height well above our head-level. He would raise his head with a broad smile every time one of us – and we were a full one hundred brothers (and a sister) – ran into the palace hall, hollering breathlessly, draped in our silk robes and dhotis, and shod in leather footwear, to complain to him about any of our numerous real and imagined grievances: Sushasana is cooking a fish on an open fire in the garden under a bush and has burnt some of the flowers and a sunbird's nest; Jalasha took the reins of the chariot from the hands of the sarathi for a full ten minutes and, what is more, nearly ran over a calf; Surmada told Sushala that because she had eaten his orange along with the pips, a fruit tree would grow through her stomach and Sushala is crying so hard, her eyes are the colour of blood. We would go on and on, and my father's response would always be an absent-minded 'Ah, excellent ...'

And when he stood tall, robed from head to toe in resplendent silk, with loads of pearls around his neck, his kundalas sparkling in his ears, crown extended at least one full palm-length over his head, arms akimbo, feet planted apart about four measures of an outstretched palm, he would look veritably humungous. He would spread his arms wide and say, 'Come, come you rascals ... and now which one is this?' as we ran up the stairs to his throne. And when we reached his legs, he would bend down, pat our heads and with uncanny precision name us – 'Sarasana, Chitravana, Vikatanana!' Although how he did it, we would never know!

Often, we would place boyish bets, staking generous sums from our allowances, about whether or not he would be able to name us correctly, which would often be the very purpose with which we would rush into the palace hall in the first place. We would exchange ornaments or robes hoping to confuse him, because we were always able to confuse our pet dogs in the dark using such tactics. But our father never made a mistake. Over time, he not only understood, but was well into our game, so that after he had identified us and whispered the correct name into our ears, aloud he would call out a different name, pretending to have made a mistake, in a mock attempt at helping one or the other of us win the bet! Of course, whichever of us lost the bet would not take this intentional error lying down and would make much fuss! Our father would then in mock anger give us a dressing down, hollering something like, 'What am I paying Kripa for? Doesn't he ever spend some time teaching these rapscallions? Why are they forever running about like vagabonds? Bhishma, dispense with Kripacharya's services!'

And Kripacharya, if he was sitting in the court at the time (since this would usually be after our class hours, of course), would stand up and say something like, 'Ah, thank you ever so much, Your Honour. I wouldn't mind a long sabbatical at the very least. A three-year retreat for every month of teaching these hundred mischief-mongers would do nicely!' and sit down with a satisfied smile!

Our father would warn us against wasting the court's time ever again and ask one of the attendants to escort us to the far end of the palace grounds so the court could have some peace and quiet.

I also have this image of my mother Gandhari from as long back as I can remember: Gliding gracefully around the palace dressed in light-coloured silk saris, her hair elaborately made up, bedecked in jewels, with a white handkerchief tied around her eyes, as if she too were blind, though our servants and friends assured us that she was not. Much later, piecing bits of stories together, as pried out of various gossipy maids and courtiers, would we learn the reason for this.

Apparently, when my father was still a young man, Queen Mother Satyavati charged grand sire Bhishma with the task of finding a suitable wife for my father. In response, Bhishma sent King Subala of Gandhara a *request* which he couldn't refuse – the hand of his beautiful and intelligent daughter, my mother Gandhari that is, for my father Dhritarashtra.

As soon as word reached my mother that her husband-to-be was a blind prince, she chose to simulate blindness herself so as not have any advantage over her husband. Most of us thought mother had been rather silly in her chosen course of action in this regard. Wouldn't it have been smarter to keep her eyes wide open to act as father's surrogate eyes? What was the point of both not being able to see? Whom did Mom's self-inflicted blindness help, really?

Answers to these questions were never forthcoming. But nevertheless, that bandana around her eyes made us think the world of our mother. Though young, we knew that her sacrifice, even if misplaced, must have called for a great deal of courage and resolve. Even if it wasn't the smartest thing to do, it was not something any of us could ever bring ourselves to do for someone, no matter how much we loved that person. Yes, we may have fancied ourselves smarter than Ma, but we certainly weren't braver.

No amount of our childish pleas to her to let us see her eyes – about the beauty of which we had heard a great deal from the courtiers – ever bore fruit. She was always kind and wore a beautiful smile upon her like a sparkling ornament. The only time we ever saw her angry was when one of my brothers, Durmarshana, crept up behind her silently, as a snake slithering on oil-spill, in a bid to undo the knot of her handkerchief, so we could see her eyes! But she whipped around in the nick of time, held both his hands in hers, and gave him such a 'look' that none of us dared try the stunt ever again. We all know mothers have an extra pair of eyes behind their heads. But even mothers with handkerchiefs tied over their eyes? Besides, how did she manage to convey her anger through those veiled eyes, putting the very chill into us hardy rascals?

My ninety-nine brothers and I looked more or less similar, even if I was a trifle bigger built than my brothers. The similarity and the difference grew more obvious with time. Our resemblance had a reason. Chances are, you have read one or the other account of how we were born, just as we too had heard several accounts of our birth.

My mother's ambition in her youth was to beget one hundred sons. It seems once, happy at my mother's ministrations while a guest at her father's palace in her youth, sage Vyasa (strange are the coincidences), as a parting gift, blessed her with the assurance that her wish would be fulfilled. However, it seems the union of my parents did not result in her pregnancy for the first couple of years. And when it did, it resulted in a still birth.

As providence would have it, Vyasa happened to be passing by Hastinapura on the very day of the tragic birth, and decided to pay a visit to my parents. Distraught at her infructuous delivery, my mourning mother apparently taunted the sage about his false prophecy.

Stung to the quick, Vyasa set himself to right the wrong and divided the aborted mass into one hundred parts, thus creating one hundred siblings, putting them in artificial wombs simulated by mud pots! And that's how we – the Kaurava centuplets – were born and hence looked very similar. But to be more exact, Vyasa had also thrown in a sister, whom he made with some residual mass. And I was the first to hatch out of the 100-odd barrels, like a baby crocodile breaking out from its clutch. I suspect the first portion of the apportioned mass must have been a tad larger, before Vyasa standardized the portions for the remaining ninety-nine, which probably explains why I was a bit larger than my brothers.

I recall being presented, every now and then, before my parents and teachers, alongside my brothers, especially just after our tests and examination in elementary education in the shaastras, and playful (non-threatening) forms of archery, mace and other types of weaponry that would prepare us for royal duties in later life.

Ours was a fabulous, sprawling palace, whose vastness and a million dark nooks and corners gave us an enviable spread of space to play hide and seek. It is hard to explain what fun it is to be one among a hundred same-aged and similar-looking brothers for the sheer variety of tricks one could pull on the teachers, servants, parents, friends and relatives, and even amongst ourselves, with a zillion permutations and combinations. When some of us didn't do terribly well in some or the other tests or demonstrations, it wasn't much of a problem confusing our parents – particularly my mother – and teachers, thanks to our similar build and looks. However, owing to my larger size, I often lost out on this advantage! Why, when some ten of us were away on some particularly forbidden and mischievous rendezvous in the town beyond prescribed hours, and we were expected to present ourselves before our mother or teachers for a count, it was child's play – and I am not even punning – to confuse them with some of us getting counted more than once. This wouldn't pass muster with our father though, if he was really serious.

Believe you me, we were a happy lot without a care in the world. Oh how I wish I had the memory and the time to tell you all the pranks we pulled on the world at large!

I also have some early memories of frequent references to Uncle Pandu. Uncle Pandu was one of my father's half-brothers, born to Vyasa and Ambalika, who was my grandmother Ambika's sister. After the meeting of Ambika and Vyasa had resulted in a less-than-pleasurable communion of the two, the unrelenting Satyavati had, for good measure, put her son on to Ambalika, the second wife of Vichitravirya. Having heard of her sister's frightful experience with Vyasa and Vyasa's curse upon Ambika, Ambalika was better prepared and knew what to expect. So her shock at meeting Vyasa was more muted, though not subdued enough to prevent her from turning pale as the blood involuntarily drained from her face when she set her eyes upon the aspect of the sage. Vyasa probably took less umbrage this time, being, by now, better prepared for the effect he seemed to have on widowed queens. Nevertheless, such was the effect on poor Ambalika that her paleness during the consummation resulted in Pandu being born a rather pale child – a near-albino.

In time, Uncle Pandu took two wives, Kunti and Madri, none of whom we ever met when we were young. However, I do recall that, as a little boy, Uncle Pandu's name shadowed that of my father like Rebecca shadowing Maxim de Winter. We constantly heard about him and his wives, occasionally from my parents, but mostly from our nannies, servants and charioteers.

Some of them would tell us in hushed tones that because our father was blind, it was Uncle Pandu who had ruled Hastinapura before my father. That would make me inexplicably uneasy, though I could not have been older than eight or nine, because I knew enough by then to know that my father was *The King*. He was the elder of the two brothers and it was not his fault that he was blind. Nor had he ever refused the throne, or had the throne refused to him, to the best of my knowledge. So how could Uncle Pandu have ruled the state?

We would also be told that Uncle Pandu was a great warrior who had added many a smaller realm to our kingdom, and consolidated it into the flourishing empire it was. I do recall many occasions when we would commemorate the anniversary of a particularly renowned victory of Uncle Pandu and the palace would be festooned with colourful lights and buntings, with women dressed in their best finery and men playfully flirting with them. The elders thought we little boys did not understand these things, but with two hundred eyes strewn all over, you would be surprised at how much and what all we saw and knew.

But let me not digress. On such occasions, my father, hailed as a gentle, just and kind king, if somewhat irresolute by all those who knew him, would shower fulsome praise upon our absentee uncle. Listening to him, one would never suspect Pandu to be only his half-brother. I always thought that it was rather generous of him, even if he seemed to go a tad overboard at times, extolling the virtues of Pandu as a brother, as a general, as an administrator ... Sometimes I wondered if father wasn't deliberately overdoing the hyperbole to project himself more favourably before the populace which had held Pandu in great affection during his days as an administrator.

As is true in most stories relating to our past, we would also receive different accounts of Uncle Pandu from sundry courtiers who appeared to hold a variety of views.

Some would hail Pandu as a very noble royal, though it would never escape my attention that father never referred to uncle as ever having been the king. Some others would tell us that while Uncle Pandu had undoubtedly been a great warrior and had won many battles for Hastinapura, our great uncles Bhishma and Vidhura were no less. Ah, allow me a minor digression here. Remember the seed Vyasa had sown into one of the maids from Ambika's palace? Well, Vidhura was the fruit – a great scholar of the Vedas and the shaastras and considered righteousness incarnate – and was therefore yet another half-brother of my father and Uncle Pandu. Even though Vidhura was brought up as a brother of Dhritarashtra and Pandu, he was never accorded the full status of a royal prince, for he was the son of a palace maid. This was also the reason why Vidhura, though the eldest of the three, would always be overlooked for succession to the throne.

But coming back to Pandu, yet others would tell us that he had attended to only the day-to-day affairs of the state and that he had only ever been a *regent*, and never the *king*; so the strategic decisions on when to wage a war and against whom, for example, had always remained with my father, taken in consultation with his wise counsellors like Bhishma, Vidhura and others, including Uncle Pandu.

I would keep toying with one or the other of such versions, finding some that made me happy and some not so. But this much was clear: once Uncle Pandu took early retirement from his duties and departed for the upper reaches of the Himalayas, my father had ruled the kingdom directly as the king. So it is not as if he had not been capable of being the king before uncle retired. It may be that when he was around, uncle probably functioned as the arms and eyes of my father. This view was frequently reinforced by those courtiers who would also tell us in confidence that Pandu was essentially just accorded the honour of carrying out the king's mandate. Some went to the extent of saying that the only reason my father had asked his brother to be the regent and not Uncle Bhishma was because fraternal love usually transcends love for grand uncles. Also, it is easier to exercise authority over one's younger sibling than over one's elderly uncle.

But deep down, knowing my father, I know that he would have asked Pandu, rather than his uncles, to undertake the campaigns only so as to spare the older gentlemen the gruelling demands of warfare, restricting them mainly to advisory roles as much as possible.

It is surprising how, when you hear something for the first time, it isn't long before you hear the same thing again and again from many different sources. I received these and a horde of other similar bites repeatedly from scores of other sources – that Uncle Pandu was never a fully functioning king and that whatever role it was that he had held, he had abdicated his responsibilities and walked away with his wives into the wilderness.

I had no reason to disbelieve this version of our past. And when these accounts of our history kept coming back again and again, it got set in my memory like cement – becoming a part of me as if I were born with this knowledge – that Uncle Pandu may have been a brave and good man, but he had never been the king of Hastinapura; and my father had been the only legitimate heir and king of Hastinapura after Vichitravirya. And I, his eldest son, was his natural heir.

I did not know it at that time, but over the years I realized that even as a youngster not yet into my teens, the question of whether Uncle Pandu had ever been king or merely regent had weighed heavily on my mind and I had spent much time pondering over the many stories that would waft past my ears.

The question so possessed me that once I approached one of the well-known repositories of royal secrets – our time-worn dhobi – with careful deliberation, couching my real intent in hypothetical terms, so the old fool would not be able to fathom my real intentions: 'Kaka, I have a hypothetical question for you. Suppose, in a kingdom, a younger brother is obliged to become the king because the elder brother is not available, because he is away for some reason ... then after the younger brother has ruled as the king for a few years, the elder brother returns and the younger one gives up the kingdom in favour of the elder one, who from then on rules as the legitimate king. Whose eldest son would inherit the kingdom?'

I had framed the question to cover the worst-case scenario of Pandu having been king before my father. I just wanted a random opinion and I thought I had crafted the question cleverly enough to thwart the ancient rascal from divining my real intent. But to my utter surprise, the old devil replied in hushed tones, as if grasping my real intent and trying to comfort me: 'Worry not, Crown Prince. You shall have the legitimate right. If your dear father has been dealt a cruel hand by Mother Fate, she was not particularly kind to His Highness Pandu either. Your uncle's burden of fate was that he would never be able to have children. So in this sense, your question was hypothetical all right, as the younger brother cannot have progeny. In matters of inheritance, blindness is less of a challenge than the state of childlessness. So your uncle could never have had a successor to the throne anyway, even if he had continued being the king or the regent. On the other hand, your father, though blind, has a hundred sons, with you as the eldest. So worry not, son! Your position is secure.'

I was taken aback by the old man's impertinence. But

not sure what I could do about it, especially as he had not been wrong in divining my thoughts, I considered silence to be the better part of valour and pretended that I did not much care about his response, though I was fairly happy with it.

When I later asked my parents if what I had heard about Uncle Pandu was indeed true, they simply shushed me into silence. But I was no longer at an age to be so easily deterred. So I kept fishing for tit-bits of family history and from time to time would be told by someone or the other in exchange for a promise of never revealing the source of the information that yes, Uncle Pandu did walk out of Hastinapura to the Himalayas with his two wives to carry out penance for his childless state. I heard this version so many times thereafter that I was no longer in doubt of the facts.

Given the royal traditions of those times, a king simply had to have a son to carry on his royal lineage. My father had one hundred and one (no, I am not making a mistake here, as you will learn in good time) descendants and Uncle Pandu had none; never could. At such times, I would feel reassured deep down and say to myself, 'Suyodhana, you are the crown prince of Hastinapura – the one and only – make no mistake about it. You shall rule the kingdom after your noble father.'

And I believed in my destiny.

As if to reinforce my faith in my destiny, courtiers, who perennially clung to me like barnacles to a sperm whale, were not only beginning to seriously and frequently pay me obeisance as the crown prince, but had also started treating me as one. I would, for instance, be given the right of way or pride of place wherever I went. As my brothers and I inched closer to our teens, I was being routinely treated with deference second only to that reserved for my father, and perhaps to Bhishma as well. I was old enough to know what a crown prince was. We were by now learning some basics of our shaastras and rajadharma with Kripacharya and, as crown prince, I was specifically and obviously being groomed to be the king of Hastinapura one day. I offer no apologies for confessing that the feeling was heady then and it remained heady forever.

Though our parents were highly virtuous, kind and learned, I must confess that as young princes, we weren't altogether unspoilt – but no more spoilt than your average royal. After all, we were used to having our way and, if something or someone challenged what we considered our entitlement, we were not beyond throwing a tantrum or two to get our way.

Nevertheless, we had all been taught, by our parents and teachers alike, to be kind to our subjects. I can't recall how many times it had been drummed into me that a king does not rule over his subjects – he serves them; a good king carries his *authority* well but a noble king carries out his *responsibility* better; a king who does not command the respect of his subjects for fairness and statecraft remains forever a stranger to greatness.

To my surprise, I was beginning to learn that – even though I innately agreed with all these teachings – it wasn't always possible to know exactly what was fair, correct, right or wrong. Even the definitions of correct exercise of authority or discharge of responsibility didn't always seem simple to me. For instance, I would wonder from time to time: Is it fair or right to kill a man if you were certain that killing him would save a hundred innocent lives? Is killing a man to save your own life justifiable outside of war? Is it wrong to lie if the lie saves a worthy situation? Is it right to be truthful if the truth causes only hurt?

I also found that the rules of life seemed different for individuals and states. For example, I knew it was cowardice to suck up to a big bully to save one's skin. But wasn't it high statecraft to maintain friendly relations with a mighty state to avoid being attacked? Killing and snitching were big no-nos in personal life; but weren't assassination and intrigue par for the course in statecraft and warfare? Or for that matter, take the rules that governed the common man vis-à-vis royals. Simplicity was considered a virtue among commoners, but royalty would not command respect either among other royalty or among their subjects unless they lived life king-size. True, high conduct was most important. But for a king, high conduct alone was not sufficient currency. It had to be accompanied by high living as well.

So we would constantly bounce about alternative ideas of fairness, correctness, right and wrong during our lessons. I understood soon why the rules of conduct had to be somewhat different for royals and non-royals. I realized very early that across classes as well as within, the scriptures were frequently inconsistent and, more often than not, interpretations were bent, twisted and stretched to meet the convenience of the weighty or the victors, invariably at the cost of the weak and the vanquished. It was increasingly evident to me that if you went by the book, there would always be two sets of rights and wrongs – one for the losers and the other for the winners, royals or not. So I learnt to develop my own sense of right and wrong, which was closer to an absolute. It troubled me that right and wrong could be defined depending on whom it was supposed to please.

Accepted as the eldest of the brothers and being the sturdiest of the hundred, I had a strong influence on my siblings. We were a fairly tight-knit bunch and my ideas of fairness took strong root amongst my brothers, and all of us always remained more or less scrupulously faithful to them.

We had also been taught to be deferential to our elders. While I had no problem with the principle of the instruction, at times I found it an irksome call, especially if the elders in question displayed a thought process slower than a lame sloth. Worse, I wasn't born with a lot of patience for the slow-witted – young or old. Nevertheless, my brothers and I tried our best to abide by this counsel, except when occasionally the superior status of a young royal prince seemed to conflict with the lower status of an elderly non-royal, especially a servant.

Once, my father overheard me at my sarcastic best with one of our elderly messengers. He was prompt in pulling me up for my rudeness right in front of the messenger, impressing upon me that one's position in life came with certain responsibilities of conduct, especially towards one's elders.

Another time, when some of my brothers and I were in the presence of my parents in their quarters, one of our stewards brought us the evening refreshments. Engrossed in play, I asked him in an off-hand manner to leave it on the table and leave. No sooner had he departed than my father chided me severely for my behaviour. I was taken aback, as much by a lack of understanding of what it was that I had done to offend my old man as by how it was that he had managed to catch me at whatever it was that I had done. So I asked him exactly what it was that he was flipping his lid about. He replied angrily that he was referring to the way I had spoken to *Sushant* (I had not even known that the steward's name was Sushant), saying that it was no way to speak to anybody, least of all to those attending to our very personal requirements.

'A man, especially one who fancies himself high-born, is known by how he speaks to the most humble. Someone truly high-born never speaks to anyone without looking them in the eye. When you speak to someone off-hand, without eye contact, you disregard and hurt the very soul of that person; you disrespect their very existence and hence their dignity. The attendants, the servants, the waiters, the gardeners, the janitors, the stable boys – each one of them adds tremendous value to our lives. Whatever wages we pay them for their labour are as naught if we don't dignify them with basic acknowledgement. In future, my son, you and your brothers will never *ever* speak to anyone without turning your head and looking at them. Otherwise, you will be a lesser soul, never mind what you do to the soul of the other,' he thundered.

I was taken aback. I wanted to quip, asking how he

knew I hadn't made eye contact with Sushant, considering he couldn't have *seen* me. Fortunately I didn't. But no sooner did the thought occur to me than I was ashamed of myself. It was a lesson that stayed with me. From then on, I would ensure that all my brothers followed the advice scrupulously. And rich would be the dividends we would reap in terms of loyalty and goodwill from our staff in return for this simple gesture.

I mention all this only so you would know that we were never indulged to a point where we could behave arbitrarily towards anyone, irrespective of their station in life. To us, the values inculcated in us by our parents became an integral part of the life skills and shaastras we were made to learn in the royal gurukul. Ah, you can save that smirk for the reference to the shaastras for when you have read my account fully. It is the truth that, all in all, we were fairly well-brought-up lads as royal brats go, and whatever else we had or did not have, we all – all one hundred plus of us – had great strength of character.

We were beginning to enter more advanced stages of our education, and learning that even though people were born high and low – which was primarily the social architecture of the time to facilitate the choice of people's vocations – a man was nothing but an aggregate of his actions. A person attained high station only by virtue of his deeds; so it was possible for the low-born to rise by virtue of their chivalrous conduct and knowledge. Likewise, the high-born, if they acted lowly, only diminished themselves.

These ideas helped put brakes on our conduct, keeping us more towards the centre of the road than to its edges.

Duryodhana

We knew many other princes of our time and I can vouchsafe, for whatever value you place upon my vouchsafing, that as princes went, we were by no means a bad lot. As a matter of fact, my father, my grand uncles and even teachers like Kripacharya never had a reason to doubt my strengths and potential as the future king and saw no reason why I was not a worthy crown prince who would some day prove a commendable successor to my father.

By now, there were slow but visible changes happening in our bodies as well. I recall the time when Dushaha, Dushkarna and eight of my other younger brothers who had returned in the middle of the night from a long trip to our western frontiers, looked at me the following morning and could not stop guffawing for a full five minutes, irritating me no end. They held their stomachs in exaggerated laughter and, pointing towards my face, chimed in chorus, 'Look at that little vegetation on his upper lip and those little volcanoes!'

Clearly, I was reaching manhood ahead of them. I remember rushing to our quarters and looking at my reflection in the polished copper mirror and being proud of the facial hair, but nearly in tears at the pimples. As I saw my face all the time in the mirror, I hadn't noticed the fuzzy growth all over my cheeks and chin, which was rather obvious to my brothers who were seeing me after nearly three months.

The very next morning, I went to the royal barber and left peremptory instructions for him to come to my quarters every morning at sunrise, for 'I shall need a shave every day'.

I intended to keep up this routine until I was ready to grow a respectable thick black moustache – an ambition that would incidentally come good majestically in time. As for the pimples, I could do very little. There was nothing to do but to let them pass with time, even though my brothers were having the time of their life at my expense. To make matters worse, before long, my voice cracked. And soon, so did the voices of my brothers; and every time one of us tried to sing, as we were wont to from time to time, some of the elders, including some of the more daring old servants (though they would always add 'so as to not disturb the sleeping king or queen'), would shush us up.

But one thing that distinguished my looks from most of my brothers' were my eyebrows which were always thick and had by now nearly joined together in the middle, with a slight bend on the bridge of my nose, giving the appearance of a small bow perched above my eyes, with my nose a downward-pointing arrow. There were other changes happening too, but I would spare you the low-down details, except to say that our testosterone levels were running high and our games were getting more and more aggressive and warrior-like, with mock fights frequently turning serious. But none of us was complaining. We were all entering our teens in the peak of our royal health and spirits.

All in all, life looked like a never-ending picnic. We had wonderful parents, loving citizens and obsequious courtiers to make our lives pleasant. Besides, our maternal uncle, Shakuni – not much older than us – was a fun-loving guy who would frequently head big-game hunting parties for us in the forests around Hastinapura, which made us feel we were living it up. We would organize tournaments in the middle of the jungles with real wild game as tests of our prowess. To cap it all, we brothers were extremely close to each other. In short, our life was good and we had no complaints.

Good times have a habit of not lasting. In our case, we had been happy too long and so a turn in our run of happiness was probably overdue.

This turn came when, early one morning, my brothers and I were in the deepest phase of our sleep – just before we were expected to get up and get ready for our lessons. The brouhaha was loud enough to penetrate the thick walls of our quarters and wake us up – we who could sleep through an elephant jumping about in the room. I was the first to spring out of bed and rush to the large window, part the blinds, and look down. The scene is permanently etched in my memory, like a tattoo on my soul.

Even though what I beheld was a pleasant enough sight – of a procession comprising a remarkably poised lady with five young boys (roughly our age or younger, single file) in tow, all dressed in spotless whites, without a single jewel upon their persons, like hermits – somewhere deep down, I heard a voice telling me: 'O Suyodhana! This could well be the end of your peaceful and happy existence.' The feeling was not unlike the twinge in one's knees preceding the onset of arthritic pain, which is there to stay and would only get worse with time.

To this day, I have not been able to place the source of the prophetic proclamation that rang in my ears louder than a school bell. I suppose you could only call it intuition. I had no way of knowing who the lady and the boys were. Uncle Pandu was the last association I would make in my mind with the spectacle I was witnessing. And even if the thought of my uncle had sprung to my mind randomly, I would hardly have associated the five boys with him, knowing he could not beget children.

It was obvious that the lady was of regal bearing. She had a face that signified the nobility of motherhood, and yet had an air that warned you not to cross her path. She had the sharp and sagacious look of a master tactician who could hold her own against any adversary. It was also obvious that she was not merely well known but also highly regarded, for she was folding her palms in a 'namaste', turning her neck from side to side as only the high-born know intuitively how, to the thronging masses who had materialized even at that early hour. The men and women lining the streets had snatched whatever flowers they could find – from their courtyards, from the nearest pots, from the gardens of their neighbours and even from the remnants of their early-morning puja, perhaps – to shower the loose petals upon the lady and the boys! The petals rose gently up in the air and fell down softly upon the six. It was obvious that the boys were the lady's sons.

I found myself involuntarily scrutinizing each boy carefully. There was this glow on all their faces which spoke of their noble birth. The five were clearly siblings though, curiously, they hardly resembled each other, except maybe the last two.

The first of them, walking just behind the lady, was clearly the oldest of the five, looking mature beyond his years, though he could not have been older than me. A more serene look than his, I could not recall seeing before. The second in line was a hulk, all fat and muscle, a giant of a lad, about a head taller than even me. He looked the sort I would avoid getting into a brawl with unless I had to. The third had a striking resemblance to me – the same height, the same build, the same gait – except that he was dark of complexion, almost of a bluish hue, though perhaps not as dark as Krishna. He had haughty features. Now, many had told me that I had haughty features, though I never quite understood what they meant. But if the expression on this fellow's face was also on mine, I was beginning to understand haughtiness. The fourth in line, a dark and handsome boy, had the makings of a fine horseman and a fencer, as I could tell from his bow legs and slight frame which he carried on tiptoes. The last in the line, though similar to the fourth, had a more serious face, and he seemed precocious in a young-scholar sort of way.

The boys looked sombre and well-behaved enough – if a bit awed by the grandeur around them – and yet, there was something in their demeanour that put me off. They had the air of the teacher's pet who thinks himself inviolate and invincible. Out of nowhere, a passing shadow of thought passed my mind that if we had had cousins on my father's side, they could not have looked very different. And yet, inexplicably, the overall feeling was not pleasant.

The retinue was now filing in through the gates of the rampart that had been flung open, and a couple of security guards were hurrying towards my parents' quarters to break the news, whatever it was. It was obvious that the lady and the boys had been recognized and that they were long-lost friends of my parents. The idea that we could have relatives in such simple garb – no matter how distinguished their looks – did not enter my mind, for our kin were usually royal and dressed the part. In the meantime, half the population of the city of Hastinapura had entered the palace courtyard, and a few spirited citizens were trying to cut a path for the unexpected visitors towards the main palace. The crowd was reluctantly parting in the shape of V – like a flock of migrating geese high up in the sky.

While most of my brothers were up and about by now, we kicked and prodded the few who weren't and, completing our ablutions in record time, we rushed down pell-mell to the courtyard en mass, certain that we would have no lessons that day – by itself not an unwelcome development. As we reached the central courtyard, our parents were already approaching the visitors, their faces beaming and arms spread, presumably because they had been told about the identity of the visitors; we reached just in time to crowd behind them and get a vantage view of the spectacle which had to be made sense of.

2

I would rather have silver medals in ten skills than a gold in just one

'Kunti!' cried my parents, simultaneously extending their hands and moving in the general direction of the visitors. Ah, so this was our Aunt Kunti! In person, she looked even more majestic than what we had heard and seen from our vantage point earlier in the morning.

Questions from my parents and answers from Kunti Devi started flying thick and fast. Where is Pandu? Who are these beautiful boys? Where is Madri? Why did you not send advance word of your coming? How have you travelled all the way from the Himalayas? Isn't that where you are coming from?

Pandu and Madri were no more. The five boys were Pandu's sons, the Pandavas. Yudhisthira, Bhima and Arjuna were her sons, while Nakula and Sahadeva had been born to Madri. She and the boys had walked all the way back from the Himalayas to Hastinapura so that her sons could be brought up as princes should, came the breathless answers.

'Ah, so Pandu was able to beget sons after all!' my father interjected happily. Aunt Kunti's answer held keen interest for me. So I noted her reaction closely, without her noticing me. She seemed to be looking at my father, almost relieved he could not see her expression. But I could have sworn I saw a quick shadow move across her face, with my parents none the wiser. But she recovered and reiterated that Pandu and Madri were no more, and that she was the mother of the boys, who had been born about a year apart each.

In a muted voice, in a tone peculiar to women who can readily command past calamities to the present to inject additional fillip into their emotions, she narrated the circumstances leading to Pandu's death, concluding with how he had suffered a heart attack when Madri had been in his arms. She softened her tone as she narrated the finer details. On my part, I was listening to her intently, averting my gaze at the right moments so that I would not draw attention.

In the meantime, some of the servants brought the paraphernalia for an aarti, which my mother performed herself. Someone washed Kunti Devi's feet and anointed them and applied sandalwood tilaks on the boys' foreheads. Just before directing the servitors to take my aunt and cousins to their respective guest quarters for rest and recovery from their arduous journey, my father presented all of us to Kunti Devi and our cousins one by one:

'This is my eldest, the crown prince – Suyodhana; and this is Yuyutsu, this one is Sushasana ... this Sushaha ... Jalasandha ... Sama ... Saha ... Vinda ... Anuvinda ...

Duryodhana

Surdharsha ... Suvahu ... Sushpradharshana ... Surmarshana ... Surmukha ... Sushkarna ... Karna ... Vivinsati ... Vikarna ... Sala ... Satwa ... Sulochana ... Chitra ... Upachitra ... Chitraksha ... Charuchitra ... Sarasana ... Surmada ... Survigaha ... Vivitsu ... Vikatanana ... Urnanabha ... Sunabha ... Naka ... Upanaka ... Chitravana ... Chitravarman ... Suvarman ... Survimochana ... Ayovahu ... Mahavahu ... Chitranga ... Chitrakundala ... Bhimavega ... Bhimavala ... Balaki ... Balavardhana ... Ugrayudha ... Bhima ... Durmarshana ... Kanakaya ... Sridhayudha ... Sridhavarman ... Sridhakshatra ... Somakitri ... Anudara ... Sridhasha ... Jarasha ... Satyasha ... Sada ... Suvak ... Ugrasravas ... Ugrasena ... Senani ... Dushparajaya ... Aparajita ... Kundasayin ... Visalaksha ... Duradhara ... Dridhahasta ... Suhasta ... Vatavega ... Suvarchas ... Adityaketu ... Vahvashin ... Nagadatta ... Agrayayin ... Kavachin ... Krathana ... Kunda ... Kundadhara ... Dhanurdhara ... Ugra ... Bhimaratha ... Viravahu ... Alolupa ... Abhaya ... Raudrakarman ... Dridharatha ... Anadhrishya ... Kundabhedin ... Viravi ... Dhirghalochana ... Pramatha ... Pramathi ... Dhirgharoma ... Dirghavahu ... Mahavahu ... Vyudhoru ... Kanakadhvaja ... Kundasi and Virajas.

'And this is Sushala, our best daughter,' added my father mischievously mussing our sister's hair affectionately. Calling Sushala his *best daughter* was his favourite joke, considering she was the only one, and always managed to provoke Sushala into saying, 'No, the best child – one on top of a hundred!'

It is possible that a dozen odd of my brothers weren't quite present there and were introduced to Kunti Devi much later, but that is detail, and we needn't be too particular.

Just in case you are one who is statistically minded and fastidious and have gone ahead and taken a count of all the names above, and counted 101 names of us brothers instead of a hundred, pray desist from congratulating yourself on having caught me on the wrong foot. The odd one out there is Yuyutsu. He was our half-brother, born to my father's second wife – and so our second mother – Sauvali, who looked after us as her own brood, what with our own mother's degrees of freedom significantly curtailed thanks to the hankie around her eyes.

Beyond Yuyutsu, I stopped listening to the introductions. So did Kunti Devi, it seemed. When my father had introduced me saying, 'This is my eldest, the crown prince ...' she had turned her head towards me and thereafter it was as if her gaze had frozen upon me, and she appeared oblivious to all else. I noticed the same conspicuous shadow flit over her face as before, and stay there. And even though my father was calling out the names of the others one after the other, she kept her gaze directed at me with a bemused expression. I felt strangely unsettled and simply couldn't make out what it was in her look that was unsettling me. After all these years, I don't know if I imagine this, but I have a vague recollection that I noticed the lads who had been introduced to my parents as Yudhisthira, Bhima and Arjuna also stiffen, and take a closer look at me. At that time, I chalked it up to the usual special attention most folks reserved for a crown prince.

My father asked me to take our cousins to the youth quarters in our palace while they escorted Kunti Devi to the main palace. My brothers and I obeyed. There was a strange and ominous silence between us, like a solid wall, an invisible barrier preventing any intimacy between us cousins. Even though there was no ostensible reason for us, the Kaurava brothers to dislike the Pandavas, or vice versa, the strange aversion hung in the air like a dense fog. And then it translated into some action. Just as we were crossing the main threshold into our quarters, Bhima stumbled for no apparent reason and his heavy shoulder rammed mine with the strength of an elephant in musth, and I staggered as if on jelly legs, knocking my head against the heavy door-frame. Fortunately, the injury itself was a trifle, but when I collected myself and looked towards Bhima, he carried on, pretending he had noticed nothing of what had just transpired.

I was convinced that his stumble had not been altogether an accident and that he was merely setting the pecking order right, showing off his strength. I also noticed Yudhisthira giving Bhima a quizzical look, while the blue-black fellow, Arjuna, was trying to stifle a smile. But Yudhisthira apologized to me and said Bhima was given to such clumsiness, and that I should be a little careful when he was around. He advised me against his pranks as well.

I was beside myself with anger. Not only had Bhima just injured my head and my pride very rudely, Yudhisthira seemed to add insult to that injury by advising me to be wary of his brother – in my own palace! We royals are not taught to accept or be wary of others' authority over us, even in jest, and what had happened a moment ago had certainly not been a joke. It is considered cowardice to take such an affront lying down. It went against our DNA, because kings do have king-sized egos. Usually we were expected to return such outrage with compounded interest.

Unfortunately, however, we were also taught not to get into a fight at every opportunity. Besides, these boys were our cousins and guests, straight from the forests of the Himalayas, not used to the ways of palaces, and my parents would not take a benevolent view of a brawl between us.

And worse, Bhima had not inflicted a direct assault on me. Considering he pretended to not even have noticed his stumble and the bump he had caused me, he had created a strange situation for me, such that I would look churlish if I made much of the episode, and lily livered if I didn't. What is it you call such choices? Hobson's choice, right? Well, in the years to come, strangely, I would be subjected to many more such choices.

It may have been my imagination but, somewhere in the depth of my guts, it was evident to me that the fatso and that dark fellow knew exactly what they had done to me, and were silently relishing the fact that the episode was bound to bother me a long time. Their self-assurance, confidence that they would get away with shoving me about in my own palace on the very day of their arrival, infuriated me, but the certainty of parental disapproval prevented me from displaying any of that fury just then. Clearly, they had thrown me the gauntlet. I was determined to pick it up, but in my own time. That is another thing we royals are taught – to be patient. So I merely stored away the episode in my mind to settle the account in good time.

Insults, unlike butterflies, do not sit lightly upon royal shoulders. After all, I was the crown prince and I saw little reason to yield to the despicable tactics of a raw fat lad come fresh from the Himalayas, even if he was one and a half times my size. After all, they were just five, and we were one hundred brothers. Twenty-to-one weren't bad odds. Yes, this was going to be long-drawn-out fun. After all, we hadn't been used to another person challenging our supremacy in our own bastion so far. I would show the hulk that it does not pay to play the fool with the crown prince of Hastinapura.

But to Yudhisthira I replied, 'Worry not, Yudhisthira. My father may be blind by birth and mother by choice, but even they don't stumble across doorways; but your brother has his eyes open and will be well advised to see where he is going. There are many twists and turns around the palace that can put one in peril. If he does not keep his eyes wide open, who knows, next time it may be he who gets hurt.' I had issued my warning.

That night, when my brothers had gone to sleep and I was still smarting from the insult dealt by Bhima, I went to the palace garden to perambulate in the cool breeze and soothe the angry emotions simmering inside me. A part of me, perhaps the superficial one, wanted to believe that it had been an accident and that the hulk had merely been clumsy and ill-mannered. But then the real me mocked my superficial counterpart, 'Suyodhana, whom are you kidding? You know the jostle was anything but an accident. Such rationalization is for cowards, and whatever else you may be, you are not a coward. They have started it but it is for you to finish.'

Caught amidst such conflicting emotions, I realized that I was no longer alone. Just as I turned a corner, through the midnight mist, a hazy form – a female one – materialized from behind a bush and walked towards me. Why, it was none other than Kunti Devi! As she approached and came to rest in front of me, I bowed to her.

She said that she had been too tired to sleep and hence had chosen to take a stroll in the garden. But somehow she did not convince me. It was as if she had been waiting to intercept me when I turned the corner. But what reason could she possibly have to chat with me in the second quarter of the night? Clearly, my mind was in overdrive. But when I looked up towards the main palace windows on the second floor where the main guest quarters were, I vaguely realized that it could not have been impossible for her to have noticed me taking a walk and coming down for a chat. But what exigency could possibly urge the majestic lady to undertake such a meeting, late into the hours?

As she stopped in front of me, she held my chin in her left hand and passed the palm of the right over my head, as elders usually do affectionately with children. I involuntarily shrank from physical contact from her since, even if she was my aunt, the lady was essentially a stranger to me. From then on, our conversation went along familiar lines as can be expected between a newly found aunt and a somewhat awkward thirteen-year-old nephew. That I was a fine-looking lad; how my resemblance to her Arjuna was striking; and enquiries about how old I was; how many moons and fractions ago, and under what specific stars I was born; where I was on my learning curve; and whether I was more interested in archery, mace, wrestling or fencing.

I answered her questions without reservation, for the queries sounded innocent enough and I had no hang-ups. She then said she was tired and it would be best to catch some shut-eye and we parted. I was none the wiser as to why she should possibly have waylaid me, as I suspected she had, so late in the night. I forgot the episode, as may be expected. After all, nothing remarkable had transpired.

With Bhima in the vicinity, it was as if peace and tranquillity had sprouted wings and taken flight from my life.

You will recall my telling you that the sprawling palace held many a nook and corner for a good game of hide and seek. We may have been entering our teens, but hide and seek remained our favourite pastime during the lazy afternoons and the summer nights when we were finished with our lessons for the day.

In our version of hide and seek, as the seeker, after his count of a hundred, was preoccupied looking for those hidden, one or more of the sought would try to approach him stealthily and thump him on his back. If this was achieved successfully, that is, before the seeker had espied anyone, the seeker had to go back to the count all over again. But the seeker would be alert against this possibility and strive to espy one of the sought while guarding against such thumping. And if he managed to do so, the sought would become the seeker while the successful seeker joined the ranks of the sought.

The game held many thrilling and heart-stopping moments and presented all the trepidation, suspense and blood-rush of the chase between the predator and the prey, making me wonder if we had not inherited the hide-and-seek genes from the cavemen from the times they hunted for a living.

With as many places to hide as the number of sins man is capable of, and with time and space as free as our own spirits, we had been leading enchanted lives – until Bhima came on board.

As hosts, we were expected to include the five brothers – the Pandavas, as we were told to call them – in our games. This we were happy to do. The problem was, with the coming of Bhima, the game somehow lost its innocence. It no longer felt like a mere game, because whenever any one of us Kaurava brothers was among the seekers – and we were more often the seekers, thanks to our sheer number – Bhima, quick as greased lightning for all his bulk, would jump on our backs from the unlikeliest of places and thump us so hard that we would often injure ourselves. What is worse, I seemed to be particularly singled out for the roughest treatment. If by chance I should become the seeker, God help me. I had virtually no hope of ever espying any of the others before Bhima would jump on my back with glee and thump me so hard that I would get nasty bruises all over my body and I could be sure that I would go on being a seeker again and again, unless Sushasana, dearest of my brothers, or brave Sumukha purposely revealed themselves to me a split second before Bhima thumped me. This was most insulting because, before the arrival of Bhima, I was virtually the most difficult one to thump, thanks to my superior alertness.

The snag was, I could not pick an open fight with Bhima on this count for three reasons: First, he was playing by the rules, except that his thwack was unusually hard, and I could hardly pick issue with him on that count without appearing to be a sissy. Second, he would always apologize for his hard thumps, chalking them up to his natural strength, making me look like a weakling in the bargain. Third, he was much bigger built than me and any physical engagement with him was bound to be injurious to my health.

So if I were to wear my crown-princely dignity, I had to pretend as if there was nothing unusual about his thwacks. Of course, every now and then I would try to get even with them, when one of his brothers was the seeker, especially Yudhisthira, Nakula or Sahadeva. I would make sure that I thwacked them as hard as Bhima was thwacking me. But then, the next time around, Bhima would make it even worse for me.

Pithily put, life was no longer as pleasant as it had been before the unwelcome arrival of the Pandavas. Yes, they had indeed arrived as the rain on our parade. We were no longer drawn to playing hide and seek with the same enthusiasm as before. I found myself looking for 'genuine reasons' to play something else, and often found myself worrying if I had turned a coward. I was suffering in my own palace! It was insufferable. We all but gave up the game we enjoyed most, particularly after the snake incident.

What happened is this. We were engrossed in an

exciting session of hide and seek in a neglected corner of the palace grounds. There were the disused stables on one side, with sundry shrubs growing all around. On the other side were little hillocks meshed into walls, with cave-like apertures set at various levels, that provided fantastic hiding places. It was an evening I thought I would enjoy because, when it was my turn to seek, I had been lucky enough to espy Bhima when his fat thighs clearly showed from behind a rock. Rare luck indeed, or so I thought, and congratulated myself.

So now as Bhima set about seeking the rest of us, I could spy him from my perch from a dark cave-like niche directly above where he stood. My plan was to jump directly upon him for the thwack and thus give him a taste of his own medicine. Unfortunately, he moved away from me and sideways, till he simply disappeared from my sight. Now there was no telling what he was up to. I was doing my best to remain hidden in the dark even as I tried to get some inkling of Bhima's movements. The sun had set a good half an hour ago and it was nearly dark. Before long, I sensed him very near my hiding spot, thanks to his heavy footfalls. But I had to stay put, because if I craned my neck out, he would spot me. So I remained rooted in the dark corner, holding my breath.

Bhima seemed to stop at the mouth of the cavity in which I sat hidden. It was clear that he was daring me to sneak a peek so that he could spy me. I held my breath, my sight directed towards the mouth of the cave, where there was still some fading light, hoping he would enter the cave-like space, giving me an opportunity to thump him. My nerves were taut to breaking point.

Duryodhana

And then it happened. I saw a large hand thrust itself into the mouth of the cavity where I was standing, and fling something rope-like at me. As soon as the object landed on my neck and shoulder, it hardly called for much probing to know what it was – a snake. Now I was as brave a lad as any, but it is not every day that you have serpents flung at you in the dark. I nearly had my heart in my throat when I heard the loud hiss of a cobra, and my hands reflexively reached for the reptile's neck and found purchase an inch below its hood, so that even as it dangled in my arm, hood flared and all, it was unable to strike me. It took me a few moments to get over my first shock, and the knowledge that the serpent would more or less stay harmless as long as I kept my grip calmed my nerves. I emerged from my hiding place with the snake in my hand. Bhima yelled, 'Suyu I spy!'

'The hell you spy, you coward! Just what the hell do you mean flinging a cobra at me in the dark, you fat slob?' I roared, thrusting my fist with the snake towards Bhima, as he stood rooted to the spot, putting on a surprised dumb expression, as if he was genuinely taken aback by the dangling cobra with its hood up, its tongue flicking rapidly, probably scared that I may fling the animal back at him.

By now most of my brothers, and Bhima's, started emerging from their hiding places and began gathering around, trying to make sense of the commotion. Yudhisthira and Arjuna wanted to know why I was trying to frighten Bhima with a cobra in my hand! Indeed! I simply ignored their query and continued glaring at Bhima, the snake firmly in my hold. Bhima confessed that he had thrown the snake at me, but swore that he thought it was a harmless rat snake, because when he had picked it up, the reptile had not once opened its hood. He spoke as if it had been a genuine misunderstanding. He said he had merely wanted to scare me out of my hiding place, because he had guessed my intentions when he had seen me take note of that particular nook some time back. I noticed Arjuna trying to conceal a smile and I cursed myself for having fallen for Bhima's trick when he had presented himself to me to be spied. Yudhisthira made a big show of chiding Bhima who, in an effort to give credence to his story of innocence, took hold of the snake from my grip – a dangerous move, no doubt. Then he let the reptile slither into some adjacent bushes.

I was convinced that Bhima's actions had been deliberate. You don't go about chucking snakes like confetti upon your playmates. Clearly, he had meant me harm and I had been within an infinitesimal distance of serious harm.

Fortunately, unknown to Bhima and Arjuna, I had my own way of getting back at the brothers. Via Yudhisthira. Though we were hardly friends, I had learnt in the course of our interactions that it didn't take much to induce Yudhisthira to place a bet on virtually anything. There would be two sparrows on a branch and you could get him to bet on which of the two might take flight first. Or on whether or not the garden lizard on a branch would move one of its limbs before you could count to a hundred!

We used to play a variety of board games of chance

using kauri shells and soon graduated to placing small bets of our pocket money on the outcomes. I noticed that Yudhisthira was a very different person when he played these games. While I liked to play a game or two and move on, whatever the outcome, he was different. If he was winning, he would want to continue playing so he could go on winning. If he was losing, he would want to keep playing to recoup his losses. He was intense in his attitude towards these games. But he wasn't too keen for his brothers to find out about these bets he placed with me. This suited me fine as I wasn't fond of any of them in any case. From time to time, he would catch me alone, or even come actively looking for me with a game board tucked under his armpit, and there was many a lazy afternoon spent in such enterprise. At first I enjoyed these bets and stakes, and we won or lost more or less evenly.

I rarely enjoyed these games as much as any of the other games we played. But, before long, I spotted an opportunity to top up my pocket money. I had noticed that Yudhisthira would become extremely excitable if he was on a winning or losing streak and start betting recklessly and make obvious errors in moving his pieces. In fact, his excitement would be palpable – his hands would shake, his speech would slur a bit and one could see that he was lost to the rest of the world. His betting would soon assume a pattern, helping me plan my moves and give me an opportunity to exploit his mistakes.

One day, he brought along a new set of mottled cowrie shells that he had bought from a roving tradesman from the western coast of Bharatavarsha. The cowries had some unusually beautiful patterns on their humps and it was clear that those were extremely rare shells. Yudhisthira was raring to play with the cowries. As I inspected them closely, I noticed that some of the shells had dried mud deposits inside, making the cowries a wee bit heavier on their bulging side. I noticed before long that these shells were yielding more fours (belly-side up) than eights (back-side up). It did not take me long to realize why this was so. Obviously, the cowries that had dried mud inside were heavier on the back and were therefore falling belly-up more often as compared to clean cowries. I quickly learnt to factor this asymmetry into my play.

From then on, every time he brought those cowries to play, I found it easy to relieve Yudhisthira of some of his money. Any time I was short of cash and was looking for a teller machine, I would go looking for Yudhisthira, hoping he would bring those mottled cowries to play. Perhaps because he was so taken with them, this happened frequently. But naive Yudhisthira never figured out the behaviour of the cowries and never factored it into his assessment of the outcome when throwing them. He played as if the cowries were as likely to fall back-up as belly-up. His enjoyment of gambling was based on his emotional response to the excitement of the game. He never seemed to understand that it was necessary to *think* to improve one's odds of winning, and that planning and strategizing held a key role even in games of chance.

And I certainly did not think it was my bounden duty to make him wise to this obvious fact. This, in a manner of speaking, was my way of getting a wee bit of revenge on the brothers, who took extra pleasure in harassing me more than anyone else. Of course there were occasions

Duryodhana

when Yudhisthira did win, or rather when I let him win, because if I didn't ever let him win, his enthusiasm to play would surely wane.

Once when Yudhisthira and I were busy under the shade of a secluded tree with a board game of chance, Shakuni Mama, who loved all games of chance, happened to saunter by. He took one look at our game and halted. He sat on his haunches next to us and watched us play. On the last occasion, I had made a significant killing off Yudhisthira. So this time, I was letting him win a little.

After the game, Yudhisthira went his way with a bit of my money jingling in his fist, while Shakuni Mama and I stayed on. He thought I was cheating with the loaded cowries. I marvelled at how he had figured out that something was wrong with the cowries since he had not even touched the shells once. He had merely been observing our throws with undivided attention.

He chided me, saying that if I was playing with loaded cowries, I had to be pretty dumb to have lost nevertheless. In defence, I explained the entire situation to him – the cowries with the mud; their altered odds; my need to get back at the offensive brother; my need to lose occasionally, the works. Shakuni Mama laughed aloud and, shaking his head from side to side, said: 'I am glad you are not a cowrie-cheat; but even more, I am happy that you understand something of gambling.'

Around this time, a roving Brahmin with a flowing beard, Dronacharya by name, had entered our kingdom and, with some deft feats of erudition and toxophily (or archery if you prefer slightly less scholarly verbiage), had impressed my father and other elders to a point where they thought he would make a fine teacher to all the princes, the Pandavas included. There was little doubt that Drona was learned in practically all aspects of education – shaastras and weaponry alike – and we were enrolled under his care forthwith and our education continued under his tutelage.

It did not take me long to realize that for some reason Guru Drona had taken a special liking to Arjuna, and against all rules of teacher–pupil relationship that calls for equitable treatment of one's pupils, had started showering extra attention upon Arjuna. One would have been a fool not to notice that Arjuna was indeed superior to any of us in the art of archery. But so what? After all, battles are not won by the loudest twang of bowstrings; nor do kingdoms rest upon the sharpest points of arrows. What is more, objectively speaking, extreme proficiency in archery is not a necessary, leave alone a sufficient, criterion for bravery. Especially for royalty like us, who were being trained to rule kingdoms, it was far more important to be well-rounded generalists than sharp-shooting specialists; it was far more important to be versed in a variety of skills, shaastras and strategies rather than be focused on the eyes of feathery birds perched on trees, to the exclusion of the surrounding environment.

Yes, I am alluding to that incident, of which much has been made in the many versions of the Mahabharata. So let me put matters in perspective. I am referring to the archery test in which we were expected to shoot an arrow into the eye of a stuffed bird installed on the upper branches

Duryodhana

of a tall tree. Those were times when eyes played a big part in our lives – the bird's eye, the fish-eye (as in Panchali's swayamvara a little later, even if I am jumping the bow here), my father's blind eyes, my mother's unseeing eyes, my own eye for Panchali … At the time, I wouldn't have bet a bent paisa that it would become the most famous test in history, this side of the Indus. The overrated test was one of the many that were regularly devised by Guru Drona so that his pet Arjuna would come out shining brighter than the pole star. After the beady-eyed bird had been installed in its perch atop a tree, we were all asked one by one – Arjuna reserved for the last, if only for effect – what it was that we saw when we took aim. The truth is, based on our various answers to that question, none of us was even permitted to string the bow. Arjuna's answer, 'I see nothing but the eye of the bird', so pleased Guru Drona that before one could spell *toxophily*, he declared Arjuna the winner! I was failed, for instance, because I had said, 'I see a red-eyed bird, perched on a brown branch atop a green tree.'

Now I put it to you – imagine you are in a furious battle and so focused on your bird-brained foe's unblinking eye that you don't see a stray bow rapidly advancing towards your ear drum from either the left or the right. What then will that single-minded focus on the eye earn you, other than an arrow through your ears, end to end? So what was Guru Drona trying to teach us? What about the possible trade-offs between optimizing one's faculties over many aspects versus maximizing this or that aspect alone? And how would he know, for instance, one of us could not multitask so to speak, and focus on the eye of the bird even as one kept the second eye on the surroundings, using one's peripheral vision to make sure nothing would distract the bird to sudden flight. After all, doesn't a mother routinely keep an eye on her elder brat in a pond for instance, while still keeping an eye on the toddler behind her! How often does she make a mistake? So why couldn't we too shoot the bird's eye, even if we saw, as we should, a little more than the eye? Guru Drona may have had a point about focus, but I am convinced he was missing the forest for the trees.

As I see it, archery was Guru Drona's field of speciality and, like most teachers, he was partial to the pupil who excelled in his own field of specialization. Besides, once the Guru started singling out Arjuna for special attention to the exclusion of the rest of us, it was only natural that Arjuna grew to be better and better as an archer than us. The Guru made Arjuna work on special tricks that he did not even show his other pupils. But then that hardly makes Drona a lofty teacher, what with playing favourites and all; nor Arjuna a particularly more endowed pupil than the others, what with his preoccupation with a single instrument of war.

What is more, in playing up his pet student, Guru Drona consistently played me down. For instance, I was probably only a marginally lesser archer than Arjuna, and may be only marginally a lesser wielder of the mace than Bhima (who I concede was the best). Moreover, I was nearly as good as Bhima in wrestling, notwithstanding his much bigger physical stature, and a near-equal of Nakula in fencing or riding. In the study of shaastras and strategies I was probably as good as any, except perhaps Yudhisthira.

It was as if Arjuna, Bhima or Nakula were gold medallists in archery, wrestling and fencing respectively, while I was a silver medallist in archery, mace, wrestling, fencing, and a few other events to boot. But I certainly wasn't training to be a sportsman for medals. I was in the gurukul to develop my all-round abilities for managing a kingdom in the future. So in my mind I never conceded unquestioned supremacy to Arjuna or Bhima, which Guru Drona expected me to, and I was quite happy with how I was and never unduly suffered from any complex vis-à-vis any of my cousins. Yes, if there was one soul I deferred to in terms of overall competence, it was Karna, of whom, including Drona's treatment of him, I shall speak more later. But I was the best in the sense that I was way above average in more number of things than anybody else in the reckoning. As far as I was concerned, Arjuna and Bhima could keep their single gold medals. I was happy with my horde of silvers.

Not that my attitude did not come at a price. The most obvious price I paid was never earning a testimonial of excellence from my Guru – not that I cared about it terribly, either then or thereafter. To me, education was about putting in one's best effort, about being one's own benchmark, and being able to focus on one's all-round development rather than specializing in a narrow skill-set. Perhaps I underestimated the worldly wisdom of being overly respectful to one's teacher; perhaps I was an argumentative student given to questioning my Guru, refusing to accept his conduct unquestioningly; perhaps Guruji did not like my eyebrows meeting at the centre ... I don't know.

The net result of it all was that I do not recall my dear old father even once getting to hear from Guru Drona that whatever Arjuna or Bhima were or weren't, many of my brothers and I were at least very competent and well-rounded pupils in our own right. Had I received from my Guru even a fraction of encouragement that I consider was my due, I would perhaps have appeared a little less bitter and arrogant and a little more gracious to posterity, in whose annals I have been projected as some kind of a grand failure – a poster boy for how your child ought not to be brought up.

Guru Drona may not have liked me much, but his son, Ashwatthama, was a very dear friend of mine and would remain so forever. It is strange how the simple arithmetic rule of transitivity simply does not work when it comes to relationships between people. For instance, Ashwatthama adored his father and vice versa; I adored Ashwatthama and vice versa, but Drona and I had a healthy dislike for each other! I even suspect that Drona perhaps disliked me a little more precisely because I had taken a bit of his son away from him in having him among my best friends.

It was some time after Guru Drona had been placed in charge of our education in the royal gurukul. Our lives had set into a rhythm and we had all settled into our respective pace of learning, working as diligently as most and trying to have fun as well; at least as much as Bhima's bulk and Arjuna's arrogance would allow us.

We had a well in our premises that had gone dry. One fine morning, Drona asked one of us to chuck a wooden ball into the well. He then asked us to retrieve the ball without getting into the well. The confidence that in response we would just look at him in bewilderment as to how to achieve this impossible task was writ large on his face. Suitably happy at our confused expressions, he proceeded to pick a thin arrow with a needle-point tip. Then he tied a thin string from a spool to the stem-end of the arrow and shot the missile into the ball, while the spool unrolled, releasing a length of the string behind the arrow. The needle-sharp tip of the arrow wedged itself into the ball and Drona pulled on the string to haul up the arrow along with the ball and looked at us triumphantly. The task may appear simple, but none of us could replicate it just then, for the slightest angle in shooting the arrow could bend its tip on the hard ball, or it would not penetrate the ball sufficiently or the ball would roll.

As these proceedings were in progress, we spotted a little boy – he must have been a little younger than us – of dark complexion, standing just outside the fence of the gurukul's enclosure, watching our activities avidly. He was lithe and had unforgettably bright and intelligent eyes. As we completed our session, Guru Drona turned his head towards the boy and asked his name gruffly. The boy folded his hands in salutation and said he was Ekalavya, the son of one of our soldiers in the Magadha army.

'What are you looking for, young man?' enquired the Guru, who never seemed to have patience, except with those of royal lineage. It was as if, after having showered much of his patience and politeness on Arjuna, he didn't have much left for anyone else.

'I simply wish to learn archery under Guru Dronacharya's tutelage. I believe you are he.'

Guru Drona suppressed a condescending smile and said, 'Pick up this bow,' as he nodded towards Arjuna's bow. Now Arjuna was known to carry a bow that was heavier than usual and hence it was more difficult to control for someone unused to it. 'And here, take any number of arrows from the jumble here,' he said casually, presenting the young fellow a clutch of arrows, 'and show me what you can do with them.' Saying so, he chucked the ball back into the well.

The boy picked up the heavy bow nonchalantly, strung it, and selected a dozen or so extra-long and thin arrows, each about three hands in length. Holding the bow as if it were an extension of his left arm, he loaded an arrow on the string with his right, and then, pointing at the ball as if pointing with his finger, pulled the string to his lips and released it gracefully. With a light thwack, the arrow penetrated the ball firmly. But before we realized what he was doing or could detect any movement on his part, he had another arrow loaded on his bow, which he released so that the tip of this arrow penetrated the cross section of the previous one's stem, making it appear as if the two arrows were simply one long arrow. He kept repeating the procedure rapidly and seamlessly in a long, fluid process until he had unleashed ten arrows, one behind the other. The last of the arrows was now fairly protruding outside the rim of the well. He reached out and pulled on the string of arrows and, as the ball emerged, he plucked the orb from the tip of the first arrow and, with his head bent, presented it at Drona's feet.

Duryodhana

If we had been impressed by Drona's feat earlier, now all our lower jaws hung way below our upper ones, and our eyes fairly popped out of their sockets. Now this was a feat I doubted if even Arjuna – leave alone the rest of us – could *ever* match.

There had been no arrogance in Ekalavya's attitude, none of the exhibitionism that had been evident in Drona's own countenance when he was trying to impress us. This little boy had simply done what came to his mind naturally. Evidently, he did not see why a pure archer should contaminate his skill with the use of a string, the only purpose of which in archery is to provide tension to the bow. He viewed his test as whether or not an archer could do the task with arrows alone. Perhaps this was the logical lesson which very likely Drona himself would have demonstrated in his next session.

Little did the Little Master realize that the Guru had not taken kindly to his being undermined in front of his royal students. By now you should not be surprised at my ability to spot shadows on faces. Impressed at the young lad's feat, I was looking at the Guru to see his reaction. I could see the initial and spontaneous admiration reflect on his face, then fade as a thoughtful expression came over it like a patch of cloud overshadowing the moon, and then sink into a blank expression – all in a flash. I was reminded of how once, during a picnic, I had seen milk rise on the boil, halt when just over the top of the vessel, as if momentarily pondering whether or not to boil over, and then settle down abruptly as the cook sprinkled some cold water over it before taking the vessel off the fire.

With a stony expression, the Guru patted the boy's

head and said, 'Young man, whatever you said your name was, this is a school for princes. You say your father is a mere soldier in the Magadha army. How did you imagine that you could be accepted in the royal school and be taught by me?'

The little fellow held his head high and said, 'Gurudev, if so, I too am a prince, the prince of Nishadha. My father, Vyatraj Harinyadhanu, is the chief of a tribal principality in the Magadha forests. His tribal army is always at the disposal of King Jarasandha of Magadha. My mother tells me that I am the son of a soldier who leads from the front. I told you that my father is a soldier because I think that is where my need to learn archery from a mighty Guru like you mainly stems from. It just so happens that he is also a humble king.'

The Guru, momentarily flummoxed, made a quick recovery by pulling the caste card, stating that since the boy was a tribal, and hence low-born, it was not for him to receive education of, and with, the royal Kshatriyas.

My heart went out to the boy. I am sure that, had the Guru sought my father's intercession, the boy would have been admitted. We were always taught that a person is defined by his deeds or karma, and not by his birth or janma. So why was Ekalavya rejected? Given the boy's unusual talents, had I gone to my father and narrated the incident, he would have accepted Ekalavya in the royal gurukul, even if Magadha was not on the friendliest of terms with Hastinapura. Unfortunately, I was a mere lad myself, barely into my teens, and didn't have the courage to thwart the Guru's plans by interceding with my father. I had to choose my battles. Besides, if the Guru was forced to accept the boy by my father's decree, both Ekalavya and I were certain to get a raw deal from him – an idea that hardly appealed to me because as it is I sensed that he was not giving me or my brothers a fair deal in education. I looked towards Arjuna to see his reaction to the injustice that had just been meted out and found him busily foraging for something in his bag.

From that day onwards, the Guru started spending even more time with Arjuna, leaving none of us in doubt as to why Ekalavya was given short shrift.

It had been nearly two years since Aunt Kunti and my cousins had come into our lives. I was still young, about fourteen, but I wasn't being groomed to be the future king for nothing. Over and above my own eyes and ears and 200 more of my brothers, I had cultivated hundreds of other eyeballs and eardrums among the many courtiers, charioteers, servants and stable boys, with whom I was always generous with tips and eye contact. It was therefore not surprising that, before long, all sorts of information began to float into my ears.

For example, starting as hushed whispers, it soon became common knowledge that Yudhisthira, Bhima and Arjuna were Aunt Kunti's sons, but they were not born of Pandu, who was known to be infertile. Little birds would chirp into our ears in confidence – quoting authentic sources as can be expected in such cases – naming Yamaraja, Vayudeva and Indraraja as the boys' respective fathers. But exactly how the three venerated idols ended up fathering Kunti Devi's sons was largely left for the world to speculate. Kunti Devi herself would maintain a stoic silence at all times. According to reliable gossip, Nakula and Sahadeva – born to Madri – were also not sired by Pandu but by the renowned twins and physicians, the Ashwini Kumaras.

Such was Kunti Devi's standing – both social and moral – that no one ever dared question her directly about these things. And to any gentle prodding on this subject, Kunti Devi was always most diplomatic and coy, and would say, 'Wasn't Pandu's very purpose of going to the Himalayas to carry out rigorous meditation to atone for his childless state? Why should anyone doubt that his penance had borne fruit?' Clever! Everyone thought it decent to leave it at that.

I could never learn exactly what my parents thought about it, for the subject was taboo in their presence. However, we were growing boys who were rapidly learning a lot about procreation through the right and the forbidden means alike. My knowledge on the subject may not have stood up to scratch in terms of the finer details, but I knew that Uncle Pandu was incapable of begetting children, and also that there was no such thing as immaculate conception. In the darkness of my nocturnal cogitations, I began to develop a pretty clear picture of how my cousins may have been fathered. But I kept it secreted in my head.

About the same time, I couldn't help noticing how my father frequently stared into space with his sightless eyes, with a perennial crinkle on his brows. All my questioning as to the reasons for his pensive cogitations had been to no avail. But as usually happens, the reason for his moodiness didn't remain hidden for long.

Duryodhana

It unfolded in due course (though I did not get to learn of it until much later) that the quiet world of my parents had been unhinged after a dialogue that Kunti Devi had with them. And now, after so many millennia, as I try to recount my tale, I am afraid the version I have is not necessarily crisp and in perfect chronological order as it should be in a good soap opera.

At some stage, Kunti Devi had – in a carefully planned off-hand manner, no doubt – mentioned Yudhisthira's date of birth to my father. And with the same ease added that if Suyodhana was the eldest of the Kauravas and the Pandavas put together, by the rule of primogeniture it was only right that he be the crown prince, and some day rule the combined might of the Kauravas and the Pandavas.

My trusting father took this as Kunti Devi's affectionate endorsement of the crown prince, namely me. Thanks to his advancing age and inability to hyper-connect information at the best of times, he failed to realize that the date mentioned by Kunti Devi made Yudhisthira marginally older to me! This realization came upon him only much later, as his elderly mind processed the different bits of information at leisure. Ah, then the coin fell – so to speak – with a click. When I heard about this conversation, the reason for my father's sullen distractedness became manifest.

I knew Father loved me, and that all these years he had wanted very passionately for me to be the future king, as if to make up for the years he had lost by not being the hands-on king in the earlier years. Obviously, he had been in deep conflict thanks to the revelation by Aunt Kunti and the realization of its consequences, and hadn't been sure how to broach the subject with me.

Apparently, my poor blind father's natural affection for his half-brother Pandu – to whom he also felt somewhat beholden for having managed the kingdom in his earlier years – prevented him from seeing through Kunti Devi's delicate move. And by the time he had been able to really appreciate the import of what Kunti Devi had conveyed, the situation had turned tricky. My father had been overheard saying, 'After all, Kunti Devi had been graciously willing to accept Suyodhana as the crown prince and his subsequent rule of the mighty kingdom, *should* he be the eldest. But now that it transpires that it is Yudhisthira and not Suyu who is the eldest, should we not accept Yudhisthira as the crown prince with equal grace and let him rule the kingdom?'

Though I knew that my father's muddled thoughts were distressing him as much for my sake as for the sake of his own ambitions for me, I was furious that he should even *entertain* any conflict in his head about who should succeed him. For the life of me, I couldn't figure out how my father could be so naive. Where was the question of Aunt Kunti's graceful acceptance of my status as the crown prince *should* I be the eldest, when the truth was that I was – as the eldest legitimate son of my father, the legitimate ruling king – the *only* legitimate crown prince of Hastinapura?

In my head, Aunt Kunti's motivations were as transparent as mountain dew. The weak monarch that he was, my father had not been able to tell off Kunti Devi directly that by virtue of his being the eldest son of his father and the living king of Hastinapura, and by all accepted norms of primogeniture, it had to be his own eldest son who had to succeed him to the throne, and not somebody else's, so that Yudhisthira being younger or older to me was completely irrelevant.

By the time these murmurs reached my ears, I clearly heard the clang of the pieces of a huge jigsaw puzzle falling into place: The morning of her arrival with her sons in tow two years ago; the prophetic voice inside my head; the shadow that passed over Kunti Devi's countenance when my father asked her if Pandu had been able to beget sons after all; the same shadow when I was introduced to her as the crown prince; Kunti Devi's waylaying me at an odd hour; her sly question about the date of my birth, planted amidst a horde of other innocent questions, like a crafty seductress planting a poison pill in the folds of a multi-layered betel leaf ... The events of the day of Kunti Devi's arrival with the Pandavas in tow played themselves before my eyes, scene by scene, in slow motion.

And now the first assault upon my status as crown prince had been made!

Kunti Devi had played her cards with consummate skill. Having gleaned the information about my date of birth, she had not foolishly rushed to my father the very second day of her arrival with the story of Yudhisthira being the eldest. She had adroitly waited two years and even then, she never referred to my age or date of birth. Nor did she ever directly link my age with that of Yudhisthira's.

She took her time, and slowly and cunningly first planted the idea into my father's head (knowing his affection for his half-brother Pandu) that the Pandavas and the Kauravas were birds of the same flock and, so, the eldest of the two taken together should be the crown prince. With subtle manipulation, she managed to make my father believe that he had acquiesced with her argument because he had not expressly countered it. Father probably never countered her explicitly because there was no reason to believe that I wasn't the eldest – Kauravas and Pandavas put together. After all, Yudhisthira, for all appearances was much smaller built than me and looked younger, so that I appeared, and probably was (not that it mattered), older to Yudhisthira.

However, in due course, she had shrewdly let my father know of Yudhisthira's date of birth, which she had placed a day ahead of mine. With the cunning of a vixen, she left it to my father to discover in his own time that this made Yudhisthira older to me by a whisker. And by the time Father had worked out the arithmetic of calendars, Kunti Devi had him wriggling in the dead centre of her carefully woven web.

If she had made one mistake, it was to underestimate my memory and my ability to connect dots. She probably thought a mere fifteen-year-old would have forgotten that 'innocent' chatter of the first night two years ago. Well, Guru Drona was not the only one to misjudge my abilities. Welcome on board, Kunti Devi.

I was equally alive to Kunti Devi's hand behind the excessive fondness Guru Drona had for Arjuna. Clearly, she had positioned her sons as future claimants to the Hastinapura throne and had carefully cultivated a rivalry between her sons and us to a point where Bhima had thrown a poisonous cobra at me. She had slowly but surely set the ball rolling among the courtiers to start taking sides with 'either' of the two crown princes when in reality there was only one.

As reports of Kunti Devi's machinations trickled in, my blood began to simmer and then boil. Not a practitioner of subtlety at the best of times, one night I marched into my father's private chambers in long strides, to find out the truth first-hand. My mother was with him as well. I must mention something rather interesting about human nature here. One would imagine that a blind couple (even when one of the pair is blind by choice) would have rather plain and functional quarters, considering the need for minimal clutter and the irrelevance of pomp and show. But these rules of average folks do not apply to royalty. My parents' quarters were not merely regal, but were a good deal more imperial than any monarch's, east of the Indus. I think there were two reasons for this. One, a blind king is usually more insecure than your standard variety, because he suffers more intrigues in his court. It takes a mere whisper into such a king's ear about the relative grandeur of another monarch for the blind king to burst a vein or two. Two, there is the danger that the king would take lesser grandeur as a personal affront, a disagreeable acknowledgement of his handicap by whoever may be in charge of arranging his quarters. Since no one wants to take such risks, everyone feels it safer to go a tad overboard.

And so my parents' quarters were an exercise in extreme opulence, complete with precious-stone–studded, colourfully painted walls; beautifully carved doors with ivory inlays; tastefully lit lanterns causing an intriguing display of light and shade; fragrant water ponds; pulsating water fountains; a variety of rubber plants and fruiting trees planted in large pots; and even peacocks, cockatoos and finches from distant lands populating the palace veranda and courtyard. Of course there was a battery of staff to clean up after the birds. If you ask me, the peacocks, thanks to their sheer size, were the worst offenders in this regard, but let's not go there.

I walked through it all up to my parents, touched their feet and, looking towards my father, without preamble or notice, asked point blank, watching his face intently: 'Father, am I or am I not the crown prince of Hastinapura?'

His blind eyes blinked more rapidly than ever – a sure sign of anxiety and nervousness. I saw his ever-ready tears, not unusual in the blind, welling up quickly, as my mother reached out to hold his hands. My father's lips quivered. His voice crackled, sounding hoarse, and he whispered: 'You will always be *my* crown prince, my son.'

I retorted tetchily, 'I wasn't asking about being *your* crown prince; I was inquiring about whether or not *I* continue to be *the* crown prince of Hastinapura.'

To this, he replied in his halting way: 'Suyu, I was meaning to speak with you. There have been some developments, and things are no longer as straightforward as they were earlier. You are my eldest son, an able, brave and a model one at that, and I love you with all my heart. I have never had any doubt that one day you *may* have made a fine king.'

At this point, I felt a lump rise in my throat. '*May* have made a fine king?' What was he trying to say?

Duryodhana

Oblivious of the effect his words had just had on me, he continued, his speech becoming more unsure by the minute: 'But now we need to consider other factors. As you well know, your cousins are here as well, and they are my brother's sons. What is more, it turns out Yudhisthira is not only the eldest son of Pandu, but also the eldest of all you cousins put together – eldest of the Kurus. He is older to you and that makes him the eldest prince of Hastinapura. Surely you don't mind letting Yudhisthira run the kingdom just as I let Pandu run it? Shouldn't the eldest of the princes be the natural choice for the crown prince? How can I disagree with Kunti who was gracious enough to accept you as the crown prince when she did not know Yudhisthira was older to you?' (Aha! So my intelligence reports had been accurate!) 'After all, had Pandu not left for the Himalayas, he would still be in charge of Hastinapura, wouldn't he?'

'Had Pandu not left for the Himalayas!' Listening to my father, I did not know whether to laugh or cry. I had always known him to be a little weak, both as a person and as a ruler, but this was as if he had plumbed new depths of weakness. Also, he could never shrug off the burden of Uncle Pandu, even though it was really my father who had bestowed the honour of regency upon his half-brother. But that he should even suggest that I was not the crown prince was the limit. His statement came upon me as a cloudburst. I felt blinded. I did not know where to start. I was known to be short tempered and given to flying off the handle at the least provocation. And the provocation here was the question of my future; my life; my being turned into a subject rather than a ruler; my own father putting a question mark on my moral, legal, regal, natural and ethical claim to the throne of Hastinapura. I was not only being told that I *may* no longer be the crown prince, but was being counselled to hand over the privilege to another *willingly* – as if we were talking about giving away an extra puppy from a fresh litter.

Uncertain which of his observations I should counter first, I let words spew forth from the depths of my soul: '*Had Pandu not left for the Himalayas?*' I mocked, repeating his words. 'Then he would still be unsuccessfully trying to make a son!'

I saw the shock on the face of my parents, but I was beyond caring. However, I immediately changed tack, shifted down a gear and continued, 'Father, you repeatedly refer to your brother having run the kingdom in the past, as if *he* did you a great favour. First, isn't it true that he was only a regent? And not your brother, but a half-brother? And even so, considering you always had the option of choosing from among Pandu, Bhishma and Vidhura, why can't you see that you did Uncle Pandu a favour by trusting him as your regent? Also, is it not true that Uncle Pandu tested the waters by referring to himself as the ruler from time to time – even in your august presence – to see how far he could stretch himself, and you were too weak to correct him? Tell me, is that not true? If Yudhisthira gets to be the crown prince being the eldest, weren't you always the king, being the eldest? Isn't it a king's eldest son who succeeds him? If Uncle Pandu ever ruled, whether as a king or a regent, it was because of your blindness. But I am not blind! So on what basis do you even equate your handing over the running of the kingdom to Pandu with my handing it over to Yudhisthira?

Please swear upon my head that you truly want me to move aside in favour of Yudhisthira ...' Here I bowed my head before him and took his right hand with my left and dragged it towards my head, whereupon he pulled his hand back with a jerk.

'So there, Father, there, you have spoken at last, even if your diffidence prevents you from saying so openly. But why, why this duplicity? You know you love me. You know I am the only legitimate heir to the throne. You know I deserve to rule Hastinapura. You know I am capable of it. And yet you are willing to consider divesting me of my crown on such pathetic grounds?

'And that begs another question. You tell me that Yudhisthira is older to me by a day. How do you know? Just because Kunti Devi told you so in all innocence. As for her innocence ...' I blathered on, beside myself with rage, and recounted the conversation we had two years ago, on the very first night of her arrival, word for word.

My head reeling, I was barely cogent as I choked and spoke at the same time, but as I came up for air, I continued my verbal assault with vigour: 'In any case, let us not make a big deal about Yudhisthira being a wee bit older to me. What difference would it make even if he were older to me by ten years? The truth is, you are the king and I am your eldest son. Or am I not your son, like Yudhisthira and his brothers, who are not Pandu's offspring?' I spat out, but was immediately somewhat contrite, especially as my mother was also present.

That I should be aware of such things seemed to surprise him no end, as was evident from the expression on his face. Repentant or not, I continued my harangue relentlessly. 'Father, you refer to Yudhisthira as

Panduputra. You also refer to the five brothers as my cousins, when you know well that not a single one of those five is a Panduputra, though Kuntiputras and Madriputras they may be. Nor is any one of them my cousin. You may lack sight, but must you also lack foresight to realize the repercussions of your accepting Yudhisthira as the crown prince? In any case, you surely do have a keen sense of hearing, thanks to which you are known to shoot arrows unerringly at targets. Surely the words that have reached my ears haven't escaped yours. Or are you innocent of the knowledge that the fathers of the five brothers are certainly not my uncles? Not one of them. Is Yama your brother? Or Vayu? Or Indra? Or the Ashwini Kumaras? Surely you are aware that your half-brother could never beget offspring? So how are they Panduputras or my cousins? And what right does the eldest of such a bunch have upon the throne of Hastinapura?

'Talking of Uncle Pandu's foresight or your lack of it, he started calling himself the ruler to your face when he was only a regent, and since you indulged him by not challenging him, or were too delicate to do so, we now have his wife and her sons claiming a right to our kingdom, even though Uncle Pandu is dead. I don't see why I should play along with that absurdity. We have let them call themselves Pandavas long enough, and even you, leave alone the rest of the world, are referring to them as Panduputras even today, when you know well they are as much Panduputras as I am Goddess Parvati. So, Father, how do you even tolerate five strangers staking a claim to even an inch of our kingdom, more specifically, *my* kingdom of the future, under the strict laws that govern royal lineage?'

Duryodhana

I ranted on and on, just as my father had earlier. Soon, we were rambling alternately and simultaneously. We rambled on for days, maybe even weeks and months. But, after all the millennia that have passed since then, the gist of the conversation is all I can relate now. Father said something to the effect: 'It does not behove you, my son, to speak thus of your aunt, uncle and your first cousins. As far as I am concerned, they are my brother's sons, because they are his wife's sons. What is more, no one, *but no one*, may question the chastity of Kunti Devi. She is beyond reproach and I will not have a chit of a boy casting aspersions on the character of a lady like her even obliquely. It is not beyond the pale of possibility that her conversation with you was perfectly innocent and that Yudhisthira is indeed the eldest of the Kuru children, and that, by sheer coincidence, he is marginally older to you.'

Personally, I was never one to believe in coincidences with beautiful patterns in them. What else could I call Kunti Devi's 'coincidental' meeting with me on the first day of her arrival, asking for my date of birth, casually proclaiming Yudhisthira as being marginally older to me, offhandedly bringing up the matter of primogeniture and hence claiming the crown for her son, but a beautiful pattern of coincidences? In any case, I knew my tirade had hit home, because I could sense that Father was rapidly losing conviction.

In due course, my little exposé of Kunti Devi's designs slowly but surely seeped into my father's psyche. But at the same time it was evident even to me, young though I was, that we could not quite challenge Kunti Devi openly about her claim to the Hastinapura throne based on her sons not being Panduputras, or call her bluff (or at least what I seriously suspected to be a bluff) regarding Yudhisthira's age. On my part, I was clear that I was not going to give up my legitimate claim in favour of any interlopers, even if they came calling themselves my aunt and cousins. I had also made it plain to my father that I had no intentions of letting Yudhisthira rob me of my status of crown prince. Ever.

My father and I fell into a quiet acceptance of this status, and followed a tacit 'don't ask, don't tell' policy. Soon, I brought my brothers up to speed as well, on how things were unfolding and how the Kuntiputras (even if two of them were really Madriputras) had an eye on our kingdom.

From here on, I, and occasionally even my father, missed no opportunity to refer to me as the crown prince – my father as if reinforcing his confidence and I meaning to rub it in the face of the brothers. Kunti Devi, Yudhisthira and his brothers soon realized that they weren't about to get Hastinapura on a platter. Nor in a hurry either. This increased the tension between us cousins, and skirmishes between us Kauravas, and Bhima and Arjuna became more persistent and frequent. Yudhisthira, Nakula and Sahadeva, as you may have guessed, didn't count for much in our scheme of things. I realized that Guru Drona wasn't all that wrong about focus in his archery test after all. If I wanted to keep my crown and kingdom, I had to remain focused on these two, to the exclusion of all else. Yes, very focused indeed.

3

*Kingdoms aren't for giving away –
No rajadharma endorses it*

The trouble in dealing with Arjuna, or even Bhima, was that neither ever came across as boorish. If you approached them as underdogs, tail tucked between your legs, so to speak, they were agreeable enough. They were also tolerably pleasant if you met them after a sufficiently long time. It was during one such interlude – when Bhima and his four brothers were sitting atop a wall, their legs dangling – that I happened to pass by on my favourite young horse which had barely crossed the colt stage. This was a destrier I had trained personally, with great effort.

Bhima, who sported the girth of your average American today, seemed to be in a particularly jovial mood and made some agreeable remarks about how grand my stallion looked. Now this steed was a fine specimen indeed, a gift from a friend from the western hills and one particularly close to my heart. You could say this horse was among horses what a Ferrari or Lamborghini is among cars. Besides, I loved the animal as much as one can ever love one's horse.

Bhima generously praised the horse and sought my permission to ride it. And the way he asked, it was as if he were asking me for a special favour which, if granted, would gratify him no end. Now it is human to feel flattered when one's nemesis applauds one's favourite asset. I suddenly felt overwhelmed with generosity and any ill will I may have harboured against Bhima seemed to vaporize in a trice. So I brought the charger near the wall where he was sitting.

I obligingly got off my horse with a flourish and gestured with my hand towards it, sort of saying, 'Come, be my guest!' The horse was right under where Bhima was perched on the wall, some five feet above the back of the animal. Hardly had my invitation been concluded, when Bhima simply slid off the wall and landed on the back of my colt, one leg on each side of the saddle, with such mighty force that the young horse emitted a tortured whinny and its legs buckled with a cracking sound as if they were made of matchsticks. The horse could never get up again.

Bhima who with surprising agility had jumped off the falling beast, stood transfixed, as if genuinely surprised and contrite at the turn of events, fussing over the poor creature, as did his brothers, all of them sombre, looking like poker-faced porcupines. The horse had ceased neighing and was lying on its side, body twitching, the whites of its eyes showing, nostrils dilated, mouth half open, full of froth, showing pink gums and whitish yellow teeth.

It seemed as if all the blood had rushed to my head, and I had suffered a severe physical blow myself. I was blinded with rage and, had I been armed at that moment, I swear I would have dispatched Bhima's head from his body in one swing. Unfortunately, I wasn't, and Bhima, even a seemingly flummoxed one, couldn't simply be taken unarmed.

The animal seemed to be screaming, except that the screams were silent. Nakula, the expert on horses, even pretended to try to bring the horse around, but soon gave up. He turned to me with an expression that clearly conveyed that the horse would trot no more. He took out a little dagger from his belt and, with his eyes, sought my permission to end the young horse's agony, which I gave with a curt nod. Though rather young, he knew exactly which vein in the neck to nip lightly and the blood gushed forth from the thick vein and the shuddering body relaxed and the animal's thrashing legs stilled gradually.

It was as if the wind stood still for a few seconds, and the birds had stopped mid-flight, to mourn the unnecessary and untimely death of the young and noble animal. While the Pandavas put up a great show of concern at the loss of the horse, I had little doubt that Bhima had killed my favourite horse on purpose.

It became increasingly evident that my cousins were unhappy that I seemed in no mood to gift-wrap my crown and hand it over to them with my compliments. Bhima had tuned up his belligerent bullying of me and my brothers a turn or two. And this wasn't the only manifestation of his pique.

One lazy afternoon, some fifteen of my brothers and I were sitting happily on a fat and safe branch overhanging a particularly deep segment of a nearby river. There was a gentle breeze and we were biting into some raw mangoes plucked off the tree. Sushasana was exhorting eight of our brothers who could not swim to take at least basic lessons in swimming: 'You never know when it may save your lives. Every Kshatriya must learn this life skill.' At least three of them – I think Sushaha, Sama and Anuvinda, who were virtually aquaphobic – nearly shrieked in protest, saying it was better to avoid water altogether than learn a bit of swimming and gain false confidence, which was sure to drown you some time or the other. We were all engrossed in this ping-pong of exchanges about the relative merits and demerits of learning 'at least a little swimming', when suddenly the world around us exploded!

Our perch gave way, a million leaves and twigs raining all around us; a zillion parakeets that had taken refuge in the tree took off in a cacophony of shrill squawks; there was an ear-splitting banshee hoot of devil-knows-what, and all of us, to the last brother, plummeted some thirty hands down in an assortment of limbs and heads into the shimmering river.

Sushasana, Survimochana, Chitranga and I swam pell-mell to save the eight who could not swim, as the others scrambled to the shore on their own. We emerged from the river onto the bank, our wet hair plastered upon our heads and foreheads like inverted baskets, dripping water like the backs of ostriches in monsoon, and there stood Bhima chuckling, holding his big belly, while the other four stood around, bent double with laughter, with not one having moved a muscle to help us.

Duryodhana

The trigger for the cataclysmic explosion we had just survived soon became evident. Bhima had stealthily crept up above us on the tree, and had sat on a higher perch, quietly listening to our conversation. When he heard that some of us couldn't swim, he thought it a good idea to jump upon the branch we were sitting on with such fierce force, accompanied by an ear-splitting hoot, that if we weren't to die of drowning, we were certain to die of heart attacks. Well, I must confess he had managed to give our lives a good shake, figuratively and literally.

As we tried to eject the excess water swallowed by some of our brothers, Bhima pretended extreme contriteness at the knowledge that these guys had nearly been drowned. He swore he was not aware that some of our brothers could not swim and that he had just arrived at the spot, and had climbed the tree only moments ago to just give us a harmless scare. Harmless indeed!

Yudhisthira, as if suddenly remembering that if they wanted the kingdom or even a share in it in the future, treating us thus was not the best way to go about it, controlled himself quickly, pulled up Bhima for his whacky sense of humour, shushed the other three, and patted me on the back patronizingly with a put-on sympathetic expression. Once again, he had added insult to injury. I gave him a mighty shove, telling him to keep his paws off me. No sooner had I done so, Bhima set upon me with all the advantage of his superior size.

And now we had a proper pandemonium on hand with several of my brothers bunching up to rough up Nakula and Sahadeva – the easier ones – while three of my brothers engaged with Arjuna. Yudhisthira was pretending to restrain everybody. To my satisfaction, he was getting a fair share of random kicks and blows from my brothers whom he was trying to disentangle from his siblings. Bhima was all over us like a raging elephant and Arjuna had managed to maul Sushasana and Jalasandha impressively, and they sported a black eye apiece. As for myself, I was so infuriated with Bhima at the time, I did not realize until we all reached our quarters that my face was a collage of black and blue discs, and my knuckles very bruised and bloody – evidence that they had been well deployed. There were also some consolation prizes, like a deep cut on Bhima's left temple and a swollen cheek upon Arjuna. The rest didn't matter. But the fact that eight of my brothers could well have drowned that day stayed with me. I always suffered from long memory.

These skirmishes between us 'cousins' heightened the tension in our already uneasy coexistence. It was clear to me – and to everybody else, if one went by the whispers in the palace – that Kunti Devi had led the Pandavas to Hastinapura with the express purpose of staking a serious claim upon our kingdom. What was all along a dull and unspecified ache in the midriff had become an open and bleeding appendix.

The Pandavas had arrived as our guests only a couple of years ago. As usurpers trying to wangle something which wasn't theirs, they had to be all smiles and politeness to all and sundry. Maybe they were also endowed with the natural humility of seekers. But we, as you will well appreciate, had every reason to bristle at their unwarranted and objectionable challenge to what was legitimately ours.

Besides, we were on home ground where you often take your authority for granted, and dispense with undue formalities. I could also concede that perhaps we, the Kauravas, did to an extent suffer from the natural haughtiness of blue-blooded royals, which could have made us look almost arrogant. But then we were not guests enjoying a host's sanctuary where you have to be at your best behaviour all the time. So I would hardly have been surprised if, in a popularity poll, the Pandavas had scored higher than us. In that sense, I do confess that the Pandavas may well have been the fragrant and popular roses, while we were the royal lotuses – all grandeur; no fragrance.

And why not? After all, royals do not please; they are pleased.

Now all this disequilibrium was most challenging on the one hand but disheartening and disturbing on the other. It was becoming clear that the Pandavas were trying to bolster their case from several angles, by weaving a web of arguments so subtly that, before we knew it, it would be difficult for us to honourably wiggle our way out. The various threads of their web went something like this:

a) Since both Pandu and Dhritarashtra had been kings of Hastinapura, the former's sons had as much right over the kingdom as those of the latter.

b) By the previous argument, the eldest of all the princes put together ought to be the crown prince.

c) As Yudhisthira (as claimed by Kunti) was the eldest of us cousins, he should ascend the throne.

d) Not accepting the above strand of logic amounts to denial of legitimate rights to the Pandavas.

Let me begin at the beginning. I question the pari-passu status implied to Pandu and Dhritarashtra in thread (a) for which, I forward the following counter argument:

There are only two possibilities – either Pandu was a regent in my father's initial years, or he was duly anointed king.

If he was only a regent, could his first born have any claim to the throne?

No.

And if he was a duly anointed king, could his first born be entitled to succeed him?

Yes. But only if my father had given up the throne of his own volition. But history points to the contrary, so that he was more likely guided by the elders, when he was still far too young, to give up the throne because of his blindness. But the rules of primogeniture should support us nevertheless, since we were the children of the king who was forced to step down because of a handicap that never actually proscribed his right to ascend the throne.

But aside from that, even if we accept the argument that Pandu's first born should succeed him, where exactly was 'King Pandu's' first-born son? Yudhisthira was certainly not Pandu's son, first born or not.

And then, of course, there are several ancillary questions that needed answering, namely:

Didn't Pandu abdicate his responsibility when he left for the Himalayas with his two wives in tow to meditate upon his childless state?

Do the offspring of kings who abdicate their throne have a claim to the throne?

No.

And there is yet another point of principle. Assuming Pandu was indeed king before my father, he was no longer alive. And so, when a former king is dead and the current king is legitimate, alive and ruling, whose eldest son should ascend the throne after the ruling king's term?

The son of the ruling king.

Are kingdoms like inherited property, to be distributed among many sons or claimants?

No.

In (b) and (c) much is made of Yudhisthira's claim to the title of the crown prince, because he was supposedly the eldest.

But before I respond to these two threads of arguments, let me ask a simple question:

Was my father a lesser king because he was congenitally blind?

That question is easily answered. In our times, primogeniture was the supreme rule for inheritance of the kingdom. That is why the royal constitution of Hastinapura, or of any kingdom for that matter, did not forbid a blind man from ascending the throne if he was the eldest son of the legitimate king. Even my grandfather Vyasa's original edition of the epic must stand testimony to that. Had the constitution prohibited a blind man from being king, my father could not have ruled after Pandu's abdication. Yes, birth is indeed an ovarian lottery which can make you a monarch or mar your sight. Well, my father drew both the lots. Indeed he was blind, but that did not make him any less of a monarch. As long as Pandu was around and available, it may have been my father's pleasure to let him manage the kingdom on his behalf as his regent; but after Pandu's abdication, it was his pleasure to rule directly, and he did a good job of it too.

On the other hand, let us assume that I am mistaken and Pandu was indeed installed king after Vichitravirya died, by some puerile ministers on the misguided premise that, though older to Pandu, my father, being visually challenged, was less capable of governing the kingdom. In such a scenario, had Pandu had sons when he *was* the king, a case could be made for the eldest of his sons to succeed him. But having abdicated the throne of his own volition, he was no more the king. As a matter of fact, he was *no more* at the time Aunt Kunti staked a claim on Hastinapura. And also as a matter of fact, Pandu never had a son. And what's more, Dhritarashtra was the reigning legitimate king. And I his eldest son. So where was the case for the so-called Pandavas staking a claim on Hastinapura, in full or in part?

Kunti Devi's claims seep lies like a sieve does water and I assert that her claims are mala fide in intent and constructed with the sole objective of claiming Hastinapura for herself and her and Madri's sons.

Now don't get me wrong. I am not one to pass judgement on the activities of consenting adults. Royals had lovers all the time and sired or carried many an offspring outside of wedlock. It is unlike me to make a fuss about a queen's personal affairs. The issue of *legitimacy* I refer to has to do simply with offspring born to a queen outside wedlock staking a claim to the throne. For instance, it may happen that the first born of a king is not born of one of his queens; however, by laws of primogeniture he may well be a legitimate contender for succession to the throne. But there is no law or tradition that entitles the first born of a queen (who is queen of a kingdom by virtue of marrying the king) from a man who is not her wedded husband (the king) to stake a claim to the king's throne or a share in his kingdom; more so when the legitimate heir is alive! And in this case, Aunt Kunti was not even the queen, as Pandu was never a king; and certainly not the reigning or even a living king.

No inheritance law entitles a share of paternal wealth to an offspring when that child was had by the mother of a man who was not her husband. And in our case what was at stake was not just some property but a kingdom – that of Hastinapura, no less.

In making that last statement, I mean no disrespect to Kunti Devi. Or Madri. Why, even my father wasn't seeded from his mother's wedded husband Vichitravirya but from Vyasa, who in turn was born to an unwed Satyavati. God help our family here. But that was a decision Satyavati, King Shantanu's queen, took when the very continuance of the race was at stake since both Chitrangada and Vichitravirya had passed away prematurely. In our case, there was no such exigency. As my father's son, I was a Kuru and there was no threat to the race. Nobody could question that I was a legitimate son of the ruling king.

I do not wish to insult anyone, least of all my aunts Kunti and Madri or for that matter the five brothers – not after all these millennia for God's sake – who could not have helped whom they were seeded from. Whatever Kunti and Madri may have done to procreate is their private concern – a matter strictly between them and their husband Pandu. They had obviously devised some ingenious means to get around Pandu's sterility so that they could enjoy parental bliss.

However, it was one thing for Pandu to have been a party to the arrangement, but quite another for the Kuntiputras to expect any share of the kingdom of which their mother's husband may at best have been a caretaker for an interregnum; and not even that at the time of his sudden postcoital death in the Himalayas.

Also, Kunti Devi was only married into the Hastinapura royalty. If her sons were not sired by Pandu, none of them had the Kuru bloodline and therefore had no right to stake a claim to Hastinapura, or even to a share in it, or to be called Kurus, or Pandavas.

It is an irony of fate that I should even have to justify my rights to the Kuru kingdom vis-à-vis Yudhisthira, when he and his brothers were not even Kurus.

I mentioned earlier in my narration that there could be other reasons why Vyasa may have been partial to the Pandavas. I do not wish to put too strong a point on it, but could one of the reasons be that irresponsible parentage provided a strong binding factor between Vyasa and the Pandavas, given that one was the son of an unwed mother and the others born of a mother whose husband wasn't their father?

So now you know why I was in no mood to hand over my kingdom or split it in favour of my half cousins who, in reality, were not even that.

Had the Kuntiputras approached the matter without any element of intrigue, and with the humility of supplicants, petitioning to our goodwill, we would probably have considered granting them generous estates for the sake of their adoptive father. But they staked their claim as a matter of right and privilege, and this was absolutely not acceptable to me, for I had a far greater right to reject their claim than they ever had to make that claim in the first place.

Much has been made of my refusal to 'part with enough land to fit on a pinpoint' in favour of the Pandavas. But this statement from me came much later, when much water had flown under the bridge, to use the cliché, and the positions had hardened significantly on both sides.

Any true royal has a good nose for intrigues. And in this case, one didn't even need a particularly sensitive nose. It was patently obvious that Kunti Devi had no illusions about Father or me ever agreeing to let Yudhisthira replace me as the crown prince. She had already toned down her demand and had gone from asking for the kingdom itself to just a share in it. She was merely being a great practitioner of human psychology. How?

Today, your society has it on the authority of research that those who ask for more, on average, end up getting more; the reverse being equally true, that is, those who do not ask for enough get much less. Perhaps this is the reason why astute Kunti Devi staked a claim for the entire kingdom by positioning Yudhisthira as a trifle older to me and hence sought to replace me as the crown prince. In contrast to this huge claim, when she diminished her demand to a mere share in the kingdom, she appeared very reasonable and it was that much more difficult for my father to refuse her *reasonable demand*.

She was also playing on another aspect of human

psychology, namely the psychology of persuasion. For one, she intuitively understood that people feel strongly obliged to reciprocate any act of kindness or munificence shown to them. Her stroke of brilliance was that she understood, long before your behavioural scientists today, that even when a supplicant reduces her demand, psychologically it amounts to an act of generosity on her part! For instance, we had experienced that from time to time we would have a mendicant approach our court and ask for a dozen cows to help him earn a living. This appeal would obviously be turned down as being excessive. He would then climb down from his demand and say, 'Alright, My Lord, can you at least spare two puny milch cows for a penniless Brahmin?' We would often find ourselves tricked by the clever panhandler thus. He had shown us great 'generosity' by slashing down his petition steeply. Now this large-heartedness had to be reciprocated by our agreeing to his diminished plea! Now imagine if the mendicant had started with a demand of only two cows. He would have been lucky to be given even one!

This is what crafty Kunti Devi had done. By asking for the entire kingdom, she had set the stage beautifully so that when she diminished her demand to just a share in it for her sons, even if they weren't Pandu's offspring, her petition would appear so reasonable that we would appear petty if we did not reciprocate the 'generosity' of her 'concession'. And boy did she succeed! She didn't merely manage to make us look small before our contemporaries; she managed to make us look positively villainous before posterity.

And it is precisely this scheming and careful strategizing

that I had seen through long before my father and uncles did, which drove me to take a position that appeared much more uncompromising than that of the elders in the family. As a matter of fact, my elders had already been trapped in Kunti Devi's silken web of persuasive skills. They were gently, and in very reasonable tones, beginning to persuade me to spare a part of the kingdom in favour of the 'Pandavas'.

Can you see another Hobson's choice staring me in the face? If I gave in, I was diminishing my future kingdom; and if I didn't, I was in the running for the Champion Villain.

I could clearly see through the game being played by Aunt Kunti and her putras. That the suave Kunti & Sons should succeed in their game plan to a point where my own near and dear were taken in and making earnest entreaties to me to accommodate their *reasonably* reduced demand made my resolve stronger! The 'reasonableness' being preached to me by my father was the very vector that had been deftly deployed by Kunti Devi to carve out a kingdom for her sons out of what was legitimately mine. The truth was that Kunti Devi was playing my blind father like a fiddle; and like a virtuoso fiddler at that! My father was getting old and was understandably given to pacifist ways, a tendency that age usually brings in its wake. But I was a young man and my kingdom – or at least a hefty chunk of it – was being hacked away from me, and it would be up to me, and me alone, to try and prevent it.

Arjuna may have been a better archer than me, or Bhima a better wrestler or wielder of the mace – not that with his size it really mattered, he would steamroll you anyway, mace or no mace – but when it came to understanding strategy, I considered myself second to none. As a matter of fact, I could see plainly how this whole convoluted charade involving the claim of the Kuntiputras was going to play out. Even as we were all growing into adulthood together, it was clear to me that the Kuntiputras in general, but particularly Bhima and Arjuna, were increasingly taking a rather belligerent stance on their so-called claim on the kingdom. The aggression would never show itself openly for others to notice, for the Kuntiputras always wore the guise of gentility and polite behaviour before the world at large, allowing their raw true self to be flashed only to me and my brothers. It was clear as daylight to me, and through me to my brothers, that even if we promised them a share in the kingdom, things would hardly stop there. They were bound to grow in their ambitions and pose a threat even to Hastinapura and its supremacy one day. This would be borne out in due course as you shall see.

PART II

4

Royalty is a full-time job, starting rather early in life

I hinted earlier how in their day-to-day conduct the Kuntiputras were probably more charming and winning in their ways than us Kauravas, who behaved with the haughtiness intrinsic to royals. But this image of amiability and likeability, especially when powerful elders were around, was probably also a consciously cultivated one. As a consequence of the steady upkeep of the façade on their part and utter abandon and foolishness on ours, the gap between how people perceived the Kuntiputras and us steadily increased over time. In fact, the put-on politeness of the Kuntiputras would often make our blood boil and, as hot-headed youngsters, we would react with visible anger and belligerence more and more often. Our growing-up years were forever caught in this vicious circle which kept making the usurpers appear better than they were, and us, the legitimate heirs to the throne, worse. In this regard, I must confess that the Kuntiputras handled their public relations rather well; certainly better than we did.

It was evident that Bhima and Arjuna were ambitious lads. With the spark of a share in the Hastinapura crown set alight by their mother, they now had a small flame of ambition going, which they were keen to fan into a fiery blaze at my cost. It was therefore increasingly clear that if we did not address the issue speedily, a major and expensive war would become inevitable. This, it took little imagination to foresee, would be a war in which cousins, friends, uncles, grandfathers and gurus would all be forced to fight and kill each other. I could see that even if we gave them a part of the kingdom, Bhima and Arjuna would exhort Yudhisthira to expand their kingdom to establish their suzerainty over neighbouring kingdoms – a conflagration that would also subsume and consume us. It was clearly for me, and no one else, to try and prevent such an eventuality.

While my father and his venerable advisors were taken in by the fake graciousness of the Kuntiputras and the goddess-like visage of their mother, I knew better. They were threatening the very future of Hastinapura, wanting it divided – like one of the harlots in King Solomon's court, a couple of millennia after our time, who would claim to be the real mother of the child she wanted possession of, and wasn't averse to the idea of the baby being cut into two and divided equally between her and the real mother! And nor were Bhima and Arjuna likely to stop at the division. Expansion would be their next logical step.

It was evident to me that the very unity of my rajya, my kingdom, was at stake. It was at the verge of being lost or at the very least hacked. From all that I had learnt about rajadharma at the gurukul, I understood that for a king and a royal, there was no dharma higher than rajadharma. Being the crown prince, was it not my foremost dharma, then, to protect my kingdom first, given that my elders did not see the danger that I saw plainly? Which was the higher dharma? Listening to one's father and elders, or protecting one's kingdom? I had nothing but my instincts to guide me.

Years later, Krishna would lecture Arjuna about one's dharma, as the armies of the Kauravas and Kuntiputras waited. He would preach that, when faced with conflicting dharmas, the higher one prevails; and how rajadharma was the highest dharma for a royal. And thus would he exhort Arjuna to go to war with his near and dear. He would render a mighty sermon to Arjuna, the long and short of which will be that it was perfectly all right to kill your family and friends, teachers and well-wishers, young and old, in defence of your kingdom, which was integral to rajadharma.

Arjuna, to be fair to him, standing at the brink of war, would show some hesitation in killing his kin and kith; but Krishna would urge him on, telling him it was cowardice not to kill those on the opposite side when it was rajadharma at stake. It would also be at Krishna's behest that Bhima would kill Jarasandha in an unfair fight; Karna would be prevailed upon by Lord Indra in the garb of a Brahmin to give up his armour; and Bhishma, Drona and Karna would be killed by flouting all norms of fair warfare. Krishna's sorry little justification was that 'little adharmas' were justified at the altar of the highest dharma.

Well, to be sure, we indulged in our share of unfairness too, both before and during the Kurukshetra war, like my assassination attempts, first on Bhima and later on Kunti & Sons; or when several of us ganged up and fought young Abhimanyu, Arjuna's brave young son; or when Ashwatthama, overcome with grief and momentarily losing his head, slaughtered the residual Pandava clan towards the end of the war when they slept ... But then, we were fighting for our rajadharma as well.

As I said, unlike Arjuna, I didn't have the benefit of Krishna's advice when I was going through my difficult teenage years. Such was the overbearing influence of Aunt Kunti and her sons that I cannot recall my childhood without an accompanying sense of insecurity that always hung in the air about me, like some lingering bad smell. As the crown prince, I was lonelier than the king, my father, who at least had his advisors advising him. Worse, I was in a situation where my father and his advisors – though my well-wishers – did not or could not see plainly what I could, and considered me more than somewhat uncharitably disposed towards the Kuntiputras.

Well, even without help from Krishna, it was clear to me that it was my highest dharma to save my kingdom. *At any cost.*

It may be that my thoughts are not articulated as well as the glib Krishna's, but I had arrived at more or less the same conclusion – that no price was too high to save my kingdom. If you have the maturity to separate the message from the messenger, you will see that the conclusion that I instinctively came to – of which I shall speak presently – was the best and the 'lowest cost' option when compared to the war of Mahabharata.

Now the question was, as a mere teenager, how could I ensure the safety of my kingdom from the usurpers when my own father seemed to be veering towards the idea that the Kuntiputras could be given a chunk of the kingdom? Clearly I could not count upon his support to thwart Aunt Kunti's ambitions. This meant, whatever I had to do, I had to do on my own, or at best take a few of my brothers and close and trustworthy aides into confidence. Worse, I had to settle the issue before it set me up against my father. That meant I had very little time – and resources.

So then what was the best way to eliminate the entire set of Kuntiputras? Openly fighting them was out of the question, given their favourable image in public and among the elders, and the ferocity of Bhima and Arjuna, as the backlash would be brutal. Also both Arjuna and Bhima, one on one, would prove too much for me, apart from the fact that our elders would almost certainly stop any such adventure before it even started.

How about stealth? Eliminating all the five brothers without arousing all-round suspicion was out of the question. I had no doubt that every single finger of suspicion would be raised against me like so many sign posts. In sum, I had very few resources available and very little time to do something, and also very little profit if all suspicion pointed in my direction. These considerations also meant ruling out any major adventure. And yet, rajadharma was the highest dharma and doing nothing was hardly an option. So thwart the nefarious designs of K & S I had to.

Night after night, I would go to bed only to lie awake, eyes wide open, with every night-sound beating to the rhythm of 'rajadharma is the highest dharma; rajadharma is the highest dharma; rajadharma is the highest dharma'.

So who was the most dangerous of the Kuntiputras? Only Bhima and Arjuna seemed to pose problems. Arjuna was indeed a master archer even at his young age and the more calculating of the two, and Drona's pet to boot. And hence the more formidable. Bhima, though a relative simpleton, inspired awe in anyone, me included, with his sheer bulk, ferocity and temper. Though my own preferred forms of fighting were the mace and wrestling, it didn't help that Bhima was in the extra-super-heavy-weight class of both, while I was probably more in the middle-weight category, so to speak.

So, given the limitations, the best strategy for me was to neutralize just Bhima and/or Arjuna on the quiet. I was tempted to consider taking off both of them at the same time, but soon ruled that out as it was a near impossibility. Killing them one after the other had its challenges too. The moment I took one out, even by stealth, the other would be on guard and, from that moment on, could not be taken away quietly. Neither could that course of action be passed off as 'accident'. So I had to pick only one of the two; the question was who it would be.

An enemy with weaknesses means chinks in the armour to exploit. What were Arjuna's and Bhima's weaknesses? Trying to find an answer to this question became my full-time preoccupation. And a few more sleepless nights yielded the answer.

Arjuna had no obvious weaknesses one could put one's finger on. But Bhima had one foible: good food. He could eat gargantuan amounts of food and would almost never say no to what you fed him! Surely this could be exploited to fulfil my rajadharma?

And then one sleepless night, the solution fairly jumped before my eyes. And it was absurd in its simplicity, as brilliant schemes usually are, and hardly original!

It gave me the advantage I wanted and required virtually no resources. It could be carried out at short notice. There would be no finger of suspicion in any direction, leave alone in mine. And best of all, it involved least loss of life. Sadly, Bhima alone would have to pay that price. But then he had thought nothing of trying to drown eight of my brothers, and had killed my favourite horse needlessly. And if his loss safeguarded my kingdom, was it not a worthwhile trade? Was it not consistent with rajadharma?

I did not even have to take any of my brothers into confidence; just a couple of aides. A picnic hunt and lunch would be arranged post haste, with a royal shamiana spread in full splendour on the wooded banks of the large river some three hours' ride from our palace. After the hunt would follow the full spread of a royal lunch. During the hunt, I would be most polite and goody-goody to Bhima, pointing out as many prey for his benefit as I could, thus winning his confidence. He was sharp as a butter-knife and not terribly suspicious by nature. I would ply him with course after course of good food and, in due course, escort him a little out of the way from the rest of the crowd and his brothers, and top him up with some venom-mixed dessert, which would shortly put him into a sound sleep. And then to tie up his hands and legs and tip him into the river when all the others had left would be a matter of mere detail.

In statecraft, killing is neither unknown nor unusual. As a matter of fact, it is considered a good bargain if by assassinating an individual you can save a kingdom or avert a war or some other calamity. True, I was not yet a king. *Yet*. But I was the prince who would be king. I was the crown prince manoeuvring to save my future kingdom. I was studying strategy and statecraft with keen interest, and that's how I was able to follow Kunti Devi's wicked moves aimed at carving away a chunk of our kingdom. From my viewpoint, she had launched a nuanced attack on our kingdom and it was my highest dharma to deflect it. That is what I had been taught and that is what I had learnt. My father and his advisors had not caught on to Kunti Devi's designs fully, but I had. As far as I could see, Bhima and Arjuna were the biggest threats that stood between me and my kingdom. My rajadharma told me that if I could minimize that threat, it was best done sooner rather than later.

I had very little attachment to the Kuntiputras as 'cousins', especially since we had not shared our early childhood breaking bread together. Their late arrival in our lives, Kunti Devi's shenanigans and direct manipulation involving me personally, Bhima's bullying, Arjuna's arrogance and being the teacher's pet, the brothers' façade of extreme gentility – the list of off-putting grounds was endless, and had created within me a sense of healthy revulsion towards the whole bunch. I knew that, born to five different men, none of whom was my father's brother, Yudhisthira and gang were hardly our cousins. But even if they had really been my first cousins, I doubt if I would have wavered in my scheme, unless they had a legitimate claim to the kingdom. As I see it, I was doing no worse than what Krishna later urged Arjuna to do. The only difference was that the kingdom legitimately belonged to the Kauravas; no one else. I may not have the erudition of a slick Krishna, but my strategy still involved the loss of only one life, unlike Krishna's plan that snuffed out hundreds of thousands.

As for my use of stealth – or chhala in Sanskrit – it had always been a weapon in statecraft we royals routinely deployed in practice, even if theory only spoke of saama, daama, danda and bheda. After all, didn't Lord Rama kill Bali by stealth? For that matter, the means employed by our adversaries to kill some of us during the war were no less stealthy. Using direct force against an adversary who is one-and-a-half times one's size is foolhardy and a recipe for suicide. So stealth it had to be. Unfortunately, my ploy failed, for which I assume full responsibility. A pity it didn't pan out the way I had hoped. But whoever said life is fair?

Well, you may have heard of how my plan to eliminate Bhima finally played out and how Bhima escaped from the depths of the river which, if you believe some accounts, involved some snake-ladies sucking the venom out of his system, thus resuscitating him and such rubbish. The problem with the world is, when it wants to make a hero of someone, it concocts all sorts of absurd stories.

If you are interested in the first-hand account of what transpired that day, let me give you a 'ball by ball' account of the morning.

My plan had been working like a charm. The day of the picnic had arrived. We had all been camping overnight in the deep and thick forest of the Himalayan foothills. The idea was to commence our big-game hunting in the early hours of the morning. Early dawn, well before sunrise, is when the big predators such as tigers and their smaller cousins, the leopards, are most active. This is also the kind of light in which they enjoy a superior vision over their prey, like the bison, neelgai and other assorted antelope. After a night of rest, the animals of prey are usually at their sluggish best, with their limbs still stiff from their overnight folds. As they rise to stretch their limbs and forage in the grass, they offer a perfect opportunity for the predators to stalk them, aided amply by the thick foliage. And for the hunter who understands the unspoken language of the jungle – the chattering langur, the screaming peacock, the fluttering jungle fowl and the slinking fox on the trot – they present a vast book to read and decipher.

It had been a long night of drinking and eating jungle meat. Roasted jungle fowl, bison meat grilled on neem branches which inject a gentle bitter-sweet taste into the meat, venison, peacock eggs poached in white butter, and just for novelty, black bear broth had all been washed down in equally impressive quantities of somarasa, a wine-beer hybrid of our times, made from ingeniously mixed fermented grains and wild berries. There had been much music and rowdy dancing. There was a stand-up comedian who did a great take impersonating my father the king, Bhishma, Vidhura, Drona, me, Arjuna, Bhima and many others, and kept us in splits. We slept fitfully, as the jungle seemed alive with a roar here, or a bark there, and barely managed to snatch a two-hour wink before some of us had to be up for the first part of the hunt, while a few others could catch another couple of hours of sleep, because they would participate in the second part of the morning's hunt.

Let me explain this bit about the first and second part of the hunt. Some of us, who fancied ourselves more brave or skilled than others, had decided, unknown to our parents, on a ground-level hunt. This, we called part one of the hunt. This is a dangerous hunting method, for it involves hunting big game at ground-level on foot – the hunter's back supposedly watched by some select men at a distance with torches, while the hunter stalks the big predator as it is stalking its own prey. This part of the hunt involves waiting patiently for a predator to make a kill and then taking its kill away, either by killing the predator itself or driving it away – both equally risky. The hunter may also trail a large herbivore, like a pachyderm or a bison, or an omnivore like the bear, the encounters with all of which are every bit as hazardous as confronting a raging tiger, or worse.

This window of hunting lasts a maximum of an hour and a half, by which time the sun is well above the horizon and the asymmetry of sight between the prey and the predators begins to lessen. As the sun rises, the predators begin to retire to their resting places, while the prey animals begin to stir for grazing. Now the strategy of human hunters changes. A gang of beaters – a seasoned crowd of young men – using drums, foghorns and the power of vocal chords, create enough ruckus to drive the devil out of hell. Hunting an animal, be it even the king of the jungle, driven out of its hideout along well-appointed pathways dotted with marksmen poses much less challenge. As the game runs through these pathways, the marksmen covering the path take aim from the safety of elephant backs or treetops.

Bhima and I were in one group of part one, while Sushasana and Arjuna were in another, with the rest of our brothers and others assigned their roles only in part two. Of course those of us from part one would join part two as well, just for some additional excitement.

Bhima and I took to one direction with our team of back-watchers, while Arjuna and Sushasana took the other. I tried to remain a step ahead of Bhima – it didn't pay to bring up the fellow's rear, for he blocked out much of your view. We were marching excitedly and fast and soon lost our rear guard. Before long, we came upon a clearing where we spotted a herd of chital. We concealed ourselves behind a tree and observed the herd carefully for a quarter of an hour. We noticed a large stag with majestic antlers, still covered by its velvet sheathing, two or three younger bucks whose antlers hadn't had time to grow beyond a palm span, about six or seven does, and three or four calves. The calves were jumping as if they had springs under their feet. The white spots on the pinkish coats of the fawn were quite visible. We were some fifty hands away. Fortunately, there was virtually no breeze; so there was little danger of our whiff being carried to the herd. The big stag was grazing with rapt attention on some figs on the ground, probably thrown down by some rowdy monkeys in the course of their treetop feast. One buck was standing with two front legs high up on a tree trunk, yanking some leaves off a low branch of a tree with its hard lips.

Another buck was clearly on guard duty. It stood erect and was looking to its left with a flick of its ears and a twitch of its short stump of a tail, and from time to time stroking the ground gently with one of its front legs. The does continued grazing without a care, knowing the guard on duty would give them ample notice of any approaching danger. The calves just kept jumping around, close to their mothers. Just as we were about to move on, we noticed the guard buck look in a particular direction raptly. It lifted its tail, showing its white underside, and farted; and we saw a few pellets eject from its hindquarters, even as it emanated a low-pitched bellow. Clearly the young stag was looking at something that it was afraid of, but not so afraid as to give a clear warning of danger. The rest of the herd noticed the sentry's reaction and went on with its grazing, secure in the knowledge that whatever it was that was drawing the guard's attention was not yet a real danger. However, they lifted their heads from grazing every now and then, looking in the direction of the guard a little more frequently. In a while, the sentry's guard relaxed a little.

And then a peacock called harshly at a distance.

Bhima and I glanced at each other. At that moment, there was no animosity between us. We were just two young hunters on a common mission. Without speaking, we read the signals to mean that there was a predator approaching from the direction the buck was looking towards, but that whatever animal it was, it was still some distance away. Had the predator been close, the buck would have given the alarm call. So we backed up a little, lest we disturb the herd, and confabulated briefly and decided to take a little detour so as to intercept the predator that was undoubtedly moving towards the herd, even if taking its time.

It took us about half an hour to go around to the other side of the herd, as we had to make a wary progress through thick undergrowth. No sooner had we reached about a hundred steps from the herd on the other side, a peacock called again in urgent tones, even as we heard a few monkeys chatter in panic. When a tiger is spotted, you have an unusual mix of alarm calls and silence. Except for the jungle fowl or the monkeys or the deer that keep up their intermittent alarm calls, chatter or barks, there is absolute silence around the predator. Even the day-time cicadas fall silent. It is as if no beast, bug or bird, except those on safe perches or those who trust the speed in their legs or wings, want to give themselves away by so much as breathing.

We knew that a large predator was close by, but it wasn't clear if it was on the move. However, it had to be a tiger or a leopard. We were between the chital herd and the predator, but much closer to the latter, whatever it was. Bhima and I quietly agreed to branch out a little so that we could go around the predator a little bit from either side, and stalk it. We were now entirely on our own as the men on our rear-guard duty had been left behind long ago. We had our bows loaded and our naked daggers ready for a quick draw.

We had barely walked some fifty paces when I heard some blood-curdling caterwauling. I froze, trying to focus my gaze in the early-morning twilight to pinpoint the source of the devilish wailing. This was my first solo hunt on the ground. I felt an unfamiliar sense of fear run down my spine. Even at that early hour, I was beginning to sweat profusely, and yet I felt unusually excited, with each and every part of my body on high alert.

Before I could take stock of the situation, I heard the heart-stopping roar of a humongous angry male tiger bounding towards where Bhima had been headed, while from a corner of my eye I simultaneously saw a tigress leap at me from the right. I was glad I had not internalized Guru Drona's lesson on focusing on one target to the exclusion of the peripheral vision.

From here on, things unfolded with lightning speed.

I had my thickest arrow already loaded on my powerful bow, the string stretched to my ears, and even as the tigress attacking me was mid-air, I spontaneously swung to my right and released the shaft, which met the tigress mid-leap in the centre of her chest. It was an unusually lucky strike, as the arrow apparently penetrated the heart of the beast and it fell four hands from me like a sack of potatoes. It had happened in less than the blink of an eye.

Clearly, we had disturbed a pair of tigers during their

mating ritual, when they are famously at their irritable worst. Without waiting to celebrate my kill, I rushed towards where I thought Bhima should have been and, as I rounded a large bush, found the huge growling tiger and a fearless Bhima facing each other, about fifteen paces from each other. Tigers in the lower Himalayas usually attempt to get their prey in a single bound, as the forests are so thick that they rarely have the space to chase their prey. Nor do tigers like to make frontal attacks for they prefer to attack from behind, just as they would while chasing a prey. However, alerted by the loud roar, Bhima had clearly turned to face the charging tiger fearlessly, with his back pressed to a large tree trunk. Faced with this strange vertical animal, not showing its behind but a pair of eyes, a tad above its own eye level, the infuriated tiger stopped mid-stride, and stood snarling, looking a trifle confused, unaware of the fate of its mate at my hands, and even unaware of me.

It was clear that as long as Bhima remained motionless, pinned against the tree, the brute would not charge. But the slightest move on his part would lead to an immediate reaction. And if the tiger charged, Bhima stood no chance. He did not have the elbow room to manipulate his bow and arrow or even draw his dagger, assuming it could do any good, drawn or otherwise. True, Bhima was a six-foot-six giant of a youth and weighed some 100 sers and was carrying a nine-inch dagger at his waist. But what we had here was a veritable sabretooth, eleven feet from nose to tail-tip, and not a ser less than 300, give or take. Add two pairs of four-inch canines and twenty switch-blade claws each three inches long, pitched against Bhima's

Duryodhana 121

solitary dagger (the bow being useless at that proximity), Bhima was in serious trouble. I stood absolutely still, lest an inadvertent movement from me provoke the beast to attack Bhima.

I am not sure if it was five seconds, five minutes or five hours, but time stood still, as did every life form in the deathly silence which pervaded the little clearing. The tiger, now crouching, was no longer growling. But it continued to inch closer and closer to Bhima on its haunches, in rapt attention and silence, as if compensating for the lost sexual pleasure with some cat-and-mouse play with Bhima, who remained absolutely still, waiting for the tiger to make the first move. I was still numb at the drama that had unfolded in the last few moments and my heart was still going like a blacksmith's hammer. Looking at Bhima, I detected not a trace of fear on his face. He seemed perfectly calm. How dumb can you be, was my fleeting thought.

Ten paces from Bhima, the tiger stopped its advance, and then, as Bhima deliberately and slowly pulled on his dagger as if challenging the tiger to attack, the animal sensed the movement and leapt at him with a roar which would ordinarily and justifiably have the effect of its prey emptying its bowels there and then, making it easier to flee. Though the roar nearly had the same effect on me, it was all I could do to resist the natural temptation.

At the same time, I must have been loading my bow with another thick arrow unconsciously, making my own minuscule moves every time the crouching tiger made a movement. Let me explain this. In our well-taught theory of hunting, we had learnt that when a crouching tiger moves, its attention is so focused on its own noiseless movement that it is the best time for one to make a small movement unobserved. I was mighty glad that the lesson had stayed with me. The tiger focused single-mindedly on Bhima to the exclusion of my presence, which may have gladdened Drona's heart, if the bird-on-the-tree test can be recalled, but it was about to cost it its life. I had the full flank of the tiger available to me – a large target at that range.

Bhima had his sight on the tiger and, just as it pounced, he moved aside like greased lightning. As the big cat was in the air, it presented me a large, if fast-moving and rising target, so that I spontaneously aimed my arrow at the armpit of the tiger. Today was my day. I had been lucky with the tigress and now I was hugely lucky with another prize. The arrow entered the soft skin near the elbow and, moving upwards, found the heart once again, making short work of the big tiger. The animal slumped on to the ground. As for Bhima, he was looking nonchalantly at my handiwork.

Two glorious kills within half an hour of a single morning! End of part one. But if I expected Bhima to feel any gratitude for my saving his life, well, there was no evidence of that. He acted as if what had happened was no big deal, though I can say in all honesty, had the situation been reversed, he would have done no less. He was an honourable fellow that way. Anyway, secretly I was happy that he did not express any gratitude. Had he done so, it would have been a little more difficult for me to carry out my plan reserved for the latter part of the day.

Duryodhana

I know the big question raging inside your head which you are itching to ask me. After all I had chosen this day to terminate Bhima through somewhat un-glorious means. And here I had a god-sent tiger all set to do the deed that I had taken upon myself to accomplish. So wasn't I an idiot to save Bhima's life, only to try and end it myself later in the day, with all the attendant risks?

Well, let me answer that question by asking you another:

'Why does your present-day justice system provide health care to a prisoner on death row?'

Whatever your answer, mine was simple. To begin with, I do not even think I had considered this question consciously in the frozen time that I had spent watching Bhima and the tiger. We were on a hunt together. There is a dharma of hunting. And this dharma dictated that I protect Bhima from the predator the two of us had set out to hunt together. So I did what I did, and what I did was a spontaneous, unthinking action.

The possibility of letting the tiger do what I in any case was set to do later in the day did not even enter my thoughts.

And even if I consciously thought about it, would I have acted any differently? I don't think so. I had put Bhima on the death row in my scheme of things, to safeguard my crown and kingdom, which I regarded as my rajadharma. Letting the tiger kill Bhima would have violated the dharma of the hunt as well as somehow contaminated the purity of my rajadharma, by making killing him more devious than it already was. Besides, not coming to Bhima's rescue would have forever branded me a coward – an epithet a future king can ill afford. What is more, by rescuing Bhima in the morning, any suspicion of my killing Bhima later in the day would be naturally dissipated.

Now I am not saying that I thought through all this consciously. I had merely acted by my intuition. A good king or a crown prince must, above all, have excellent intuition. There are any number of occasions when intuition serves one better than logical thinking. However, knowing which one to trust when is what wisdom is all about.

Pardon me if I got carried away giving you a rather elaborate account of that morning of the hunt. Perhaps it is because tigers have always fascinated me. Our narrow escape generated much chatter that day, inducing some of the others to recount their own moments of danger and acts of valour while hunting big game. Every dead tiger or leopard had grown at least two feet in the recounting; the bison had gone heavier by a few hundred kilograms; six-foot bears towered ten feet tall; dead wild boars had grown nearly as big as a mid-sized water buffalo; a sixteen-hand python (I know because I was there when it was measured) was being elevated to a twenty-two hander. All in all, everybody was having a good time.

But let me proceed faster from here on and bring you up to speed on the developments of the rest of the day. With part one of the day's hunts concluded, the proceedings of the morning moved to the second part. From here on, the rules, the tempo and the nature of excitement changed. It was a big melee. As the morning progressed, I ensured that Bhima was seen with a number of others, and not just me. Then it was lunch time, the lunch consisting mostly of game meat.

Post-lunch, making good use of the general chaos that prevailed, I casually led Bhima away from the rest. After I had plied him with the venom-laced dessert and he had gone to sleep as expected, I joined the rest, and soon it was time for everyone to head home. When everyone was packed up and the pack horses had been loaded and it was time to head home, the rest of the Kuntiputras started looking for Bhima. But no one had a clue as to where he was. I joined a lot of other voices saying he had perhaps left ahead of us, or must have decided to play some prank on us which we would presently discover en route home when the prank unravelled. Then, as everyone left the spot and the sun had nearly set, a couple of my paid aides tied Bhima's hands and feet and shoved him into the river, as decided.

What probably happened thereafter is more or less this: as the aides were struggling to tie up Bhima's heavy limbs, he probably came half awake in a reflex action and the duo, in a panic, made a rather shoddy job of the trussing, and didn't or couldn't carry and shove the heavy and drowsy Bhima into deep enough waters.

As for the rest of our party, it took us nearly four hours to reach the palace, since part of the return journey was after sunset and hence in near total darkness. Back home, once Bhima's absence was discovered, there was consternation for about two or three hours when servants went all around the various palaces and Bhima's usual haunts, just in case he had arrived early and had gone goofing off. At last, search parties were sent in all directions, with a larger contingent going in the direction of our morning outing. By now it was late into the night. The search parties were slow in their progress, what with all the shouting and dawdling that search parties are wont to indulge in. It must have taken them nearly five hours to reach the picnic spot, by which time it was morning. In the meantime, I had a difficult time carrying a detached but concerned expression on my face, with no one into the secret except the two aides, who had already been sent away on a longish furlough with goodly reparation. All was well. Or so I thought.

The palace was a crucible of activity all night as it stayed awake waiting for some news of Bhima. For me, this was the longest night of my life so far. The next day, it wasn't before the sun was fairly near the zenith that the first of the contingents was seen on the horizon, returning. And then another from another direction. They would invariably signal their lack of success from a great distance so that we did not have to wait till they reached us to know the outcome. At last, the contingent that had gone in the direction of our previous day's picnic was spotted, and soon it was signalled that they had found Bhima, alive and kicking. I let out a quiet sigh of disappointment, but managed a deadpan expression. Kunti Devi rushed halfway to meet and fuss over her lost-and-found son. As the crowd approached the palace, Kunti kept hugging Bhima again and again. To me, their approach seemed to be taking forever.

At last the contingent entered the palace ramparts with

a Bhima who did not at all look any the worse for all the wear and tear of the previous night. Mercifully, but strangely, he made light of the night out and said to all and sundry in his characteristic carefree manner that he had merely fallen asleep and had no clue when, how or where; but that when he came to, it was with water sloshing all over him, with his limbs bound. He sought out eye contact with me in the front row of the crowd and winked before continuing, 'I had some help from some very pretty snake girls, who unbound my knots and escorted me to the surface, all safe and sound, after giving me some mouth-to-mouth resuscitation.'

I nearly panicked at his wink, imagining in my guilt that he had seen through my game. But I needn't have worried. The next moment, he guffawed at the open-mouthed naiveté of the gathering, saying, 'Oh for the love of snake girls! Can't you see the obvious? Whoever heard of snake girls undoing naughty knots in the depths of a river, or for that matter outside of it? True, I was in water, but not far from the shore; and if I had been bound by ropes – my wrists do feel funny – they had probably come loose of their own accord, and all I had to do was to wade out of the water, none the worse for my experience, except for a succession of half a dozen mighty sneezes.' And he winked in my direction again.

Only then did I realize that his wink was nothing more than what we all did with each other all the time – winking at one another when we were pulling a fast one. There was no way he could have suspected me of trying to kill him. He had probably looked towards me only because I was the last one with whom he had had a good time gorging on his favourite food. But I nearly had my heart in my mouth for those few fleeting moments.

He still sported a red bulbous nose, as if in testimony to his sneezes. But yes, he announced he was mad. Mad as a March hare. Because he was ravenously hungry and needed to tuck into a sumptuous breakfast speedily.

When he passed me in the general melee of his prodigious return, he gave me a strange look – or was it my imagination, I would never know – but neither he nor any of his brothers ever said anything about the episode later.

It dawned on me quickly that Kunti Devi had once again played her master stroke – if that's the word for a lady's stroke – when she rushed out to meet her son. Those repeated hugs may have looked like a demonstration of maternal love sloshing forth, but they had not been without their deeper significance. I had little doubt in my mind what she had conveyed to Bhima in the course of those hugs, and subsequently to the other four sons: She had asked them to strategically play down the episode. Her quick-silver brain had grasped that by trying to point a finger at me or any one of us, without concrete evidence, they were unlikely to gain favourable currency with my father and our other well-wishers. And this would not suit her long-term plans. This carefully cultivated popularity would forever be as much a part of their arsenal as Arjuna's bow or Bhima's mace. That is also why, though just one beautiful widowed mother and five boys, they made a very formidable adversary. Even my own father and his advisors could never really see their true colours, so that I would almost always be without their wholehearted support in thwarting the creeping takeover of our kingdom by the Kuntiputras. My carefully laid-out plans to save our kingdom had been thus dashed, and my next attempt, if any, had been made twice as difficult, for Kunti and the Kuntiputras were bound to be on high alert from now on.

In the days and months to come, there were always some whispers, insinuations and allusions here and there that my courtiers brought me, from which it did appear that in some quarters it was indeed suspected that I might have been behind Bhima's unsuccessful drowning, but it was clear that nobody had any concrete evidence. As a matter of fact, the very failure of the attempt turned out to be my redemption, for the general relief at Bhima's survival took away the eager-beavers from probing too deep into the conspiracy theory.

Besides, I had ensured that the two aides on furlough were given a generous pension for not returning.

5

You may be the best, but you may not be good enough

A few more months went by. Under Guru Dronacharya's tutelage, we continued our lessons in various forms of weaponry and the shaastras. Arjuna seemed permanently ensconced as the Guru's pet and had grown ever more obnoxious, preening perennially before the Guru's fawning eyes.

It is about this time that I made a significant friend, who would remain my friend for life. I had known Karna, the son of Adhiratha, my father's charioteer, ever since we were all knee high to a grasshopper. Now and then, young Karna would accompany his father to the court. Bright and spunky as he was, I made friends with him even before I realized that he had become my friend. My father was also rather fond of him. Even as a kid, Karna would insist that he be dressed as a soldier, complete with golden body armour and prominently matching earrings. In his growing-up years, poor Adhiratha had a full-time job on hand, apart from his charioteering that is, trying to fit new armours on little Karna's ever-growing body every few months. Such was Karna's fondness for his body armour and earrings that he could never be found without them, night or day, and we would often say in jest that he was born with them. Little did we know then that our light-hearted remarks on the dual fetish of Karna would be taken literally by posterity! It is said that, repeated often enough, a lie grows into a truth. It seems to me, this is probably how even myths come to acquire a reality of their own. Why else would you believe that Karna was actually born with built-in armour and earrings or that Bhima was saved by snake girls?

Karna's fine body structure, which held the promise of an unusually tall and well-built man, and his near-golden complexion gave him the appearance of royal birth. As a matter of fact, it was impossible to believe that he was the son of an ordinary charioteer like Adhiratha, who was dark of complexion, and much smaller built. Adhiratha was supposed to belong to the Suta or Shudra caste, and Karna did not fit the stereotype. Moreover, he also showed unusual promise in skills such as archery and was well ahead of most of us in his knowledge of virtually everything.

Not long after Ekalavya had been spurned by Drona, things got awkward once again. This must have been a year or two after the five brothers had entered Hastinapura that fateful morning. This was an evening, when father and I had decided to take one of our impromptu tours of the city streets. While we did go on various official tours around the city and the state, we were aware that such visits were not quite the same as impromptu ones. This is because, during our official tours, local officials would ensure that every street we passed through was perfectly clean, sprinkled thoroughly with water to keep the dust level low, roads cleared of cattle and stray animals, and so forth, so that the conditions we encountered were never quite normal. By undertaking occasional impromptu excursions, we aimed to learn whether the city streets were kept clean and dust-free at all times and for all citizens. In fact, such tours would yield treasure troves of information about the state of our kingdom. I would invariably accompany my father on such visits, giving him a running commentary as we sped along on our light, simple and unostentatious chariot, meant for such a purpose.

Adhiratha was taking us through the city thoroughfares. We randomly passed through a vegetable market where all the shops were well laden with produce. While the street was alive with the aromas of farm produce, there was much garbage littering the street. Some cattle was grazing for discarded vegetables in the lane and I passed on the information to my father. We passed through a whole street of spices and condiments, and my father nearly went into a spasm of sneezes, even as I desperately tried to cover my nose and mouth with a kerchief. To our relief, we were soon upon the textile lane that had rolls upon rolls of silk, cotton and linen in various hues displayed beautifully in the shop fronts. The street was lit on both sides with high oil lamps. We passed through the street of wood works and furniture, wooden toys, utensils for the kitchen, jewellery, a whole street dedicated to headgear, and so on. And the last lane was one of eateries. Again I noticed many stray dogs and cattle dotting the path. I mentioned this once again to my father, knowing he would call the local official responsible to address the issue.

By the time we returned home, it was dark. When we were dropped off at the palace portico, instead of taking leave promptly as he usually did, Adhiratha stood shuffling his feet, his head bowed, indicating that he wanted a word with my father. I drew Father's attention to him and he, having a deep affection for Adhiratha, immediately stretched his hands out for him. Once he was within reach, father placed his right hand upon Adhiratha's shoulder and asked him what it was that he wanted to speak about. Adhiratha responded in his soft voice that he wanted his son Karna, who was doing exceedingly well in all aspects of his education, to join the royal gurukul.

My kind and large-hearted father, aware of Karna's abilities, readily agreed to this, and called one of his aides, dictated a brief edict for Karna's admission to the royal school, placed his seal on it and handed over the slip to Adhiratha, asking him to contact Guru Drona at the earliest.

The world thinks that a king's wishes are his commands. This is largely true, but only in fiction. True, in matters such as which country to attack or not, which crimes to make punishable by death, or whom to appoint as ministers and such, a king's commands may have the ultimate weight. But in matters of everyday details, it is usually the humble officials who usually prevail.

So when Adhiratha took the royal edict to Guru Drona next morning, seeking admittance for Karna into the gurukul, the Guru at first raised his eyebrows and then, with a sigh, summoned Karna for a test. Soon, the test reached levels that were nearly a couple of years ahead of most of us, and maybe a year ahead of even Arjuna. The targets for archery were impossibly narrow and moving – not just horizontally or vertically, but rapidly oscillating. And yet there was no let-up in Karna's performance. The Guru rapidly cut the test short and told Adhiratha that his son had been admitted to the school, but not before adding, 'Usually royal schools are only for Kshatriyas and not for Sutaputras; however, since you have wangled the king's recommendation, I am making an exception. But if you ask me, stick to your station. Why, with a seasoned chariot-hand like you as a teacher, this son of yours would make an even better charioteer than an archer. Do think about it.'

Adhiratha was a humble man, not given to challenging higher authorities. He merely shrunk further into himself and retreated quietly. And young Karna had no option but to accept the insult without demur.

One would think the royal edict had served its purpose, even if not graciously. But that's not how it turned out. The next morning, when Karna came to join the session that Guru Drona was about to commence with us princes, Drona raised his eyebrows and asked Karna harshly, 'Sutaputra! What do you think you are doing here with the princes? Your session has been arranged in another group that we run especially for other Sutaputras and non-Kshatriyas like you.'

For several moments, young Karna stood rigid and tall, nearly as tall as the Guru, eyes like two piercing arrows, but without any expression. The world seemed to stand still and silent for what seemed like an age. It was as if an entire epic – one that would befit the Mrityunjay, as Karna would come to be heralded as – had been written in those few moments. An epic that would silently tell the saga of a destiny which, despite all its raw deals to Karna, would accord him a place in mythological history that Drona would never be granted. This would be Karna's first brush – of many – with the pitiless world of a castiest society.

Karna turned abruptly and walked out with dignity. I, who was nearest to Karna as he was leaving, turned my head towards the Guru with all the hatred I dared muster in my eyes, and also looked towards Arjuna and Yudhisthira to see if they had perceived the gross wrong that had been done. But once again, they chose just that moment to rummage through their bags, searching for nothing in particular.

I turned and followed my friend, if only to stand by him and offer him some solace in his time of distress. Though I was young, it wasn't lost on me that the Guru, neither rude by nature nor having any reason to nurse personal animosity against Karna, had chosen to break the spirit of the young boy for some reason of his own. I had a good idea of that reason who, along with Yudhisthira, was looking for nothing in particular in his bag right at that moment!

For reasons best known to him, very early in his days, impressed with Arjuna's uncommon potential with the bow and arrow, the Guru had resolved to make Arjuna the greatest archer the world would ever know. He was probably also determined to live his own glory through Arjuna, who was a 'Pandu' prince. Perhaps he saw greater potential for his ambitions as a king-maker on the Pandavas' side than merely as a Rajguru on the Kauravas'. I had always suspected that teachers are not above thinking small. And Drona was proving my hypothesis.

Little wonder then that, as evidence after evidence – in the shape of Ekalavya and Karna – came his way to cast doubt on the supremacy of Arjuna, the influential Guru began unleashing his power to ensure that he would not be thwarted in his resolve by mere providence.

One reason why the Guru resented me was because it was evident that I was in no mood to cede my kingdom, or even a tiny fraction of it, to the Kuntiputras, especially if they continued to insist on the share as a matter of their right. And this hindered the Guru's ambition of king-making. It was also not lost on the Guru that I never held him in the same reverence that Arjuna and his brothers did. On my part, I had always resented his special treatment of Arjuna. The turning away of Ekalavya had not raised his stature a great deal in my eyes either. And his treatment of Karna brought it down several more notches. My walking out in support of Karna certainly did not endear me greatly to the Guru; nor was I about to shed any tears on that count.

Karna and I walked towards the gardens within the gurukul premises to a secluded spot. Karna was contemplative. I tried to comfort him saying that I intended to take up the matter with my father. Drona had no business disregarding the king's edict. However, Karna told me to exercise restraint. Though despondent at his experience of that morning, always ahead of his age in wisdom, he told me: 'Suyu, I know you mean well. But there is no point in your doing so, except that you may end up embarrassing your father and annoying the Guru. And this is something that neither I nor my father would want at any cost. Besides, Drona has been shrewd enough not to contravene the king's orders technically, because I have indeed been admitted into the royal school. Who teaches whom in the gurukul is entirely Drona's domain and, even if the king takes up the matter with Drona, he would defend his territory with ease. The only consequence of your pains would be that Drona would single me out for more insults and harsher treatment, even if he doesn't dare do that to you openly. After all, as long as I study in this gurukul, I would always be under his overall supervision, won't I? There is no point living in the river and making an enemy of the crocodile.

'I don't intend to give much credence to his deliberate insult; by doing so, I would only be walking into his trap. He wants the satisfaction of seeing me react to his insults. I shall deny him that. He wants to break my spirit, for reasons he knows best. I shall deny him that gratification too. This will be the best response to his insults. In any case, I am no longer enthused about learning from a Guru who may be knowledgeable but whose conceit and ego do not speak of one who is truly learned. The learned are unfailingly fair and civil, and my interactions with the Guru do not show him to be so. Nevertheless, I intend to show him that Sutaputra I may be, but I will be the greatest archer ever to graduate from the gurukul; and that, without his blessings.'

From then on, Karna would be in and out of the gurukul all the time. There would be occasions when for long periods one would hardly be able to find him. His movements would be mysterious, like a jungle cat's, and we never could find out exactly who taught him what, even though he was outstanding at virtually every aspect of education at the gurukul, and way ahead. It was as if he was gathering knowledge both inside and outside the gurukul. In the gurukul system, attendance was not compulsory as the students were expected to be self-motivated, and so his periodic disappearances would cause no raised eyebrows as long as he was doing well in his schooling. Any question from me on his disappearance would elicit no more than a laugh and evasive replies. At all times, however, Drona steadfastly pretended to be unaware of his existence, leave alone performance.

Our newly shared antagonism towards Drona and my bold show of solidarity to Karna made us bond more than ever before. In the days and years to come, we would spend more and more time together in play and mischief. Before long, I started confiding in him the machinations of Aunt Kunti, and the Guru's obvious plans for Arjuna, setting in this context Ekalavya being turned away from the gurukul. I also maintained that his own shabby treatment at the Guru's hands was linked to the Guru's larger plans for Arjuna and the Kuntiputras. I of course did not share with him what I had tried to do to Bhima. I probably wanted to protect him, the commoner that he was, from the sins of palace intrigues as much as I wanted to hide my own less-than-chivalrous conduct, par for the course though it may have been in royal circles. Karna simply didn't look the kind who would have approved of such strategies.

Days, months and years went by rapidly. I was nearly seventeen now and in another year or so, we would be graduating. One new-moon night, Guru Drona took a bunch of us, Arjuna and me included (but not Karna, for obvious reasons), for an overnight hunt in the deep forests, where we were to practise shooting in the dark, basing our aim only on our auditory senses — a method called shabda bhed. After we had practised for several hours in the dark, we were all tired and decided to pitch our tents under a tree to catch some sleep. Hardly had we assumed a horizontal position than a dog started barking, as strays usually do — a staccato yowl ending in a long, continuous howl — the sheer repeated rhythm of which is enough to wake the dead. For some reason, this seemed to cause considerable mirth amongst us, as such things usually do among teenagers, and we worked hard at stifling our giggles in the darkness, lest we disturb Guru Drona in the adjoining tent. But soon we were aware of the Guru twisting and turning in his marquee at this rude interruption to an otherwise peaceful night. Nor could we catch any sleep, though our sleep-ridden eyelids seemed to weigh a tonne each.

Finally, in sheer desperation, Arjuna and I came out of the tent and thought we might as well practise our shabda bhedi skills by trying to silence the irritating cur in the dark. The night was filled with all sorts of sounds, from cicadas to howling foxes to the occasional grunts and coughs of larger predators. But the howl of the dog drowned out every other sound, like the voice of the soprano singer dominates the accompanying music. What is more, unless stopped soon, the yowls could attract a passing leopard – an avoidable situation when we were still rookies at shabda bhed.

So both of us tried shooting several arrows, but the wily mongrel seemed to be all over the place, only howling louder than ever before. At one stage, the mutt howled even louder, as if in some sudden pain, but did not let up on its barking. At last we retired defeated, back to our camp. The Guru was sitting on the camp-bed with the flaps of his tent turned up and a lamp lit beside him. We could see the dyspeptic look on his face – framed in a halo of white hair – in the lamp-light. His eyebrows and beard, also white, reflected light, as if made of silver. We stifled our giggles and our breath, lest we draw his attention needlessly.

Just then, we heard the crisp twang of an arrow leaving a bow, followed by a loud howl, which rapidly petered out into a low yelp, and then gradually grew silent altogether. We could almost see Guru Drona raise an eyebrow, as if surprised, muttering something under his breath. With the silence restored, he promptly went back to sleep, and so did we.

First thing in the morning, the Guru led us in the direction we had heard the dog howling the previous night.

Unmindful of the gentle morning breeze and the variety of birds chirping low and high on the trees and the bushes, and the warm rays of the sun filtering in through the trees, we tried to locate the animal. Before long, we found the wretched cur sitting on its haunches with a woebegone look, its chin resting sideways on its front paws which were stretched straight ahead. But what was remarkable was that there was a thin arrow that had pierced its mouth at an angle such that it had entered the upper jaw and just penetrated the lower jaw, sealing the mouth shut. The wound around the arrow appeared clean and the animal did not look in as much pain as might have been expected. There was another arrow, much thicker, on the butt of the mutt, hanging limply, which had caused a superficial wound. This arrow was clearly Arjuna's.

To seal a barking dog's mouth shut on a new-moon night with such dexterity was the finest example of a shabda-bhedi arrow. Guru Drona had all of us stand around him in a semicircle and held a tutorial on the spot, explaining the lessons inherent in the shooting of such an arrow. The archer had used a lean arrow with a thin head to ensure a clean and narrow wound; the wound was not intended to be life-threatening; the control exercised was just sufficient for the limited purpose of silencing the dog – no more, no less; the angle at which the arrow entered the mouth ensured that the shaft would seal the jaws shut with minimum pain; and all this in total darkness upon a moving target, and hit with such extraordinary precision that the dog would not be in excessive pain, as long as it adopted a comfortable posture, which it had. Arjuna was spared a lecture on his aft-shot on the poor animal just then, and no sooner had he removed the two arrows than the dog trotted away, largely unharmed, except for the slight limp upon one of the hind legs and a slightly exaggerated jiggle of its hindquarters, as if taunting Arjuna.

We were all speechless. Surely the archer must be a great master of the craft! Who could it be? There was only one way to find out. With Guru Drona directing us, we followed the trajectory of the arrow and were soon upon a little clearing where a tall, dark and handsome young teenager, about our age, wrapped in a loincloth but naked otherwise, save a quiver on his back, was practising archery. He had with him a bunch of assorted arrows of various shapes, and a variety of belled targets hung all around him. His eyes were tied with a strip of black cloth, clearly to simulate the darkness of the night to extend his training hours. Near him was a life-sized likeness of a sitting human form with flowing beard in terracotta which bore a striking resemblance to Guru Drona. The youth had his bow in his left arm, which was stretched straight ahead, rigid as marble, his right hand pulling the bowstring with a loaded arrow stretched to his ears. He was on the verge of releasing the arrow at one of the targets.

Upon our approach, his keen senses alert, he swung around in our direction as if on a pivot, his loaded arrow pointed directly at us. The knowledge that with his eyes tied, he couldn't be looking where his arrow was pointed – that of course being the very purpose of his practice – had our hearts momentarily pounding like so many hammers. Guru Drona, with great presence of mind, immediately greeted the youth, introduced us and himself, and explained the curious purpose that had drawn us to the spot, upon which the youth immediately slackened the tension on the bowstring as well as the ambience by unloading the arrow and transferring the bow to his naked left shoulder. Within a fraction of a moment, the youth walked the few steps between him and the Guru, the black cloth around his eyes still in place, and kneeled right in front of the Guru, his head bowed.

The Guru blessed the youth for his prodigious talent and bade him rise by holding him by his shoulders to a standing position, and asked who he was. With his head still bowed in natural humility, the youth replied that he was the very Nishadha who was not blessed enough to be schooled in Guru Drona's gurukul. Since I had been witness to the episode a few years ago, it all came back to me suddenly! Ah, Ekalavya!

'Then who is your Guru?' enquired Drona. His head still bowed, 'You, Gurudev,' replied Ekalavya, taking all of us by surprise. But he pre-empted our questions by pointing to the life-sized terracotta statue of Guru Drona and said, 'Gurudev, as you could not have me in your gurukul, I decided to keep you in my heart, adopting you as my Guru, and have ever since been practising before your likeness here. To me, there is no difference between the real you and that figure, both of whom are my inspiration to learn in equal measure. I am blessed that today you have appeared in person to bless me, as if to consecrate my graduation. I salute you.' Saying so, Ekalavya once again kneeled, bending to touch his head to the Guru's feet.

The Guru bent once again to symbolically help Ekalavya rise, and lifted his head with a crooked forefinger, even as

Ekalavya's eyes were focused towards the Guru's feet in humility and gratitude. The Guru asked, 'Well, if I have been your Guru, where is my guru dakshina?'

'I am truly blessed, Gurudev, that you have at last acknowledged yourself as my Guru. My life is now actualized. Ask, Gurudev. What can I offer at your feet? There is nothing, absolutely nothing that I will not place before you in guru dakshina. Please tell me what it is that you demand of me.'

The Guru sneered, and said, 'Young man, for a Nishadha, you are making rather tall claims. You strike a humble posture, but your words are arrogant. Measure your words before you utter them.'

Frankly, I was taken aback by the Guru's uncalled-for pugnacity. But the remark did not change the expression on Ekalavya's face, which remained calm like the surface of a mountain lake.

'I seek your forgiveness, Gurudev, if I have given you such an impression, for my intent has been nothing more than doing your bidding. Pray, ask for your dakshina. You shall not find this pupil wanting.'

'Well then, young man, since you are so cocky, are you willing to give me the thumb of your right hand in dakshina?'

Stunned, and my mouth agape, I involuntarily turned to look at Guru Drona, unable to believe what was pouring forth down my ear canals. But even in that split second, I did not fail to notice the Guru's eyes dart towards Arjuna momentarily, though his head remained turned towards Ekalavya.

'But of course, Gurudev.' The youth did not flinch for

an instant – and I should know, expert as I was at reading facial expressions. He simply took out a sharp arrow from his quiver with his left hand and cut his right thumb in a single jerk as if he were cutting a small cucumber. He picked up the thumb with his left hand, un-selfconsciously blew the dust off it, placed it on the palm of his right, which now had only four fingers, and stretched the bleeding palm towards the Guru, kneeling and head bowed.

I opened my mouth involuntarily to express my dismay, looking towards Yudhisthira and Arjuna for moral support. But the two were finding a squirrel nibbling at a nut up in a tree of grave interest. And Drona gave me such a stare that I considered silence the better part of valour. He abruptly turned and walked away with long steps, and we had no choice but to follow. For the rest of the journey back to Hastinapura, the Guru was resolutely silent and kept Arjuna close to him, as if to draw some solace from his proximity for what he had done that morning.

Over the years, we would hear about Ekalavya's great feats of archery off and on, but they would never be what they could have been, thanks to our Little Drona. Drona's private mill for projecting Arjuna as the *greatest* archer continued to grind.

Pardon me if, from here on, I use the smaller 'g' for my guru, because from that day, my teacher stood permanently diminished before my eyes.

We were in the final stages of our scholarship under Drona. Always fond of showmanship, especially if the show could highlight Arjuna's prowess, the guru had arranged for a competition in various combat techniques. Since archery was to our weaponry what cricket is to your sports, it was understandably the climactic event of the tournament.

There were several reasons why archery was considered the king of weaponry in our times. In my early years, I always felt that Drona placed a disproportionate weight upon archery simply because he was himself a master of the weapon. It was only much later that I realized the true significance of archery in warfare. An archer's weapon had a reach much greater than any other. An arrow can maim a target with far greater accuracy than, say, a spear or a disc. In battle conditions, the archer would always trump over a mace wielder or a swordsman, as a mace or a sword would prove effective only in close combat, while an arrow would pre-empt the need for close combat. An arrow could be discharged from the ground, from a chariot, from atop an elephant or horse, or a housetop. It could be deployed as much as an offensive weapon as a defensive one. An archer could set off a fire at a distance, say in an enemy camp, by throwing a flame-tipped arrow. Even inaccurate arrows could kill if the tips were poisoned. Curved arrows could be made to return, like boomerangs. A master archer didn't even have to see his target; he could direct the arrow by sound (as in shabd bhed). Even a woman could wield a bow and an arrow and hold her own against a male enemy. For hunting, especially, there was no weapon superior to an arrow. A suitably selected arrow could bring down a dainty bird as swiftly as a leaping leopard. Simply put, an arrow was a versatile weapon.

Unfortunately for me, being an individual fond of direct action, I took to the mace as my preferred weapon rather than the bow and arrow; not that I wasn't competent in other forms of combat, including archery. The mace is a weapon with which you hit your opponent directly from close proximity and you win if you are better and lose if you aren't. I was probably among the best wielders of the mace, but I always fell short of Bhima, given his sheer bulk. While he was always a head taller than me, as we grew up, the overall difference in our bulk became even starker, because as you will know, our heights vary linearly, while body frames vary by squares and body bulk by cubes. The fellow was humongous – and probably still growing at eighteen – nearly double my size in overall body mass.

However, in my free time, I tried to make up for my smaller bulk vis-à-vis Bhima by training with Balarama – crown prince of the Yadavas – my close friend, and Krishna's elder brother. Balarama, though largely a pacifist, was considered unparalleled in the art of mace fighting. I had trained hard and trained well. The upshot of my efforts was that I was certainly more nimble than Bhima; but he could any day take more blows from me than I could from him; and if and when his blow did fall right, the adversary remained felled. But being a combat sport, unlike the entertainment sports in your Kaliyuga, there were no weight categories in wrestling or fighting with the mace, so that I always suffered a serious handicap with respect to super-heavyweight Bhima.

That I would come out alive and un-maimed itself was testimony to and a reward for my superior speed and skill; there were no other awards; not from Drona and certainly not for me. But yes, this entire charade of a graduation-day ceremony was primarily to present Arjuna and Bhima as ace archer and mace-man respectively before my father, his advisors and the city at large, probably to strengthen their case for a share in the kingdom. Portraying the Kuntiputras as being mightier than they were, and my brothers and me as weaker than we were would create a gap of perception between us, which Drona probably hoped to drive his chariot through, certain that it would help his protégés carve out a share in the Hastinapura kingdom.

As far as my brothers and I were concerned, there was nothing to it but to go through the motions. As expected, I was bound to be second best at most events. And there were no awards for being an outstanding all-rounder.

6

Excellence needs no introduction

Our graduation-day ceremony is branded in my memory. It was a fine and clear morning. The ever well-tended grounds were being pruned some more. Workers and volunteers with goat-skin pouches slung over their shoulders, with a rhythmic twist of their hips, were sprinkling water on the grounds to keep the dust down. The oval-shaped ground was being lined white with lime, marking the spaces reserved for different events. A raised pavilion with an awning to seat the king and the rest of the royalty was being readied with rows upon rows of thick cushions on low couches, so as to provide a clear view of every event. The common spectators would be seated all around the stadium on coir mattresses spread on levelled ground.

Preparations for hot refreshments were under way at numerous stalls. We were told there would even be a special stall for bhang for adults (adults or not, in the last one year, we had relished the light-headed floating sensation of the narcotic sufficiently to be excited about it!

We would still have to be careful of our elders and there was no question of touching the stuff before the competition and closing ceremony of our graduation). Youngsters would have the option of partaking of a variety of fruit juices.

Volunteers were being briefed on picking up litter in and around the ground. Torans made of leaves folded in the shape of little parakeets interwoven with flowers had been hung in sagging curves along the perimeter of the ground on bamboo poles. Near the royal pandal, a low platform was being prepared for the musicians. Men were lounging about or moving busily. Some would pretend to become busy as they espied me in the vicinity.

At the main entry to the ground and in front of the royal pavilion, young lasses in colourful silks were bent, busy completing some hypnotic patterns of rangolis on the ground with their dainty hands, which were themselves beautifully patterned in red henna. Several young men, dressed in their best, were loitering around the bent women, making clever comments. Most women were pretending not to notice the attention they were drawing. One belle was pretending to be completely unconscious of all the attention she was drawing from a swarm of young men. I took good advantage of my vantage position to ogle at some pretty faces, pretending to be supervising the overall preparations, hoping to catch their eye, and succeeding in some cases. Some of the girls were darting surreptitious glances at me, pretending not to have noticed me, which I pretended not to notice.

All in all, the atmosphere promised a good time to everyone, even if I wasn't feeling on top of the world, knowing who the real heroes of the day were going to be. The event was to begin in another couple of hours and would last until sundown. I was aware that the royals and non-royals would be competing separately. The forenoon was reserved for the non-royals, while the afternoon belonged to the royal competitors.

I was looking for Karna, who was to compete among the non-royals. So long had been his recent disappearance that I had not laid eyes on him for a few weeks. Usually, there would be no question that the royal winners would perform way beyond the best of the non-royal competitors. So, even without a direct competition between the royals and non-royals, the superiority of the royal winner as the overall champion of the day in each event would be self-evident. But today, maybe it would not be all that obvious. No prizes for guessing that Karna would win the non-royal segment hands down, in virtually all events. As a matter of fact, given his demigod-like appearance and talent, it seemed incongruous that he should compete among non-royals. Nor would such a win console Karna, whose abilities, I was convinced, were way beyond Arjuna's. I had been looking for him for the last few days to discuss his plans for the graduation celebrations, but he had proved elusive. Surely he should be here shortly, as the event would be commencing soon?

Vidhura was presiding over the morning event. As soon as three girls in silken finery had sung the invocation, he had lit the auspicious lamp and announced the event open. Opening speeches were made. The stadium was rapidly filling with courtiers and commoners. However, the real crowd would build up only by afternoon, for that is when most royals would turn up to watch their respective wards and favourites perform. And the arrival of the royals was an added attraction for the crowds.

There was no sign of Karna yet.

The various events absorbed all our attention. Every now and then we would spot an unusually talented youth showing off his skill and a collective roar of approbation would build up to a small crescendo. Senior officials from our royal militia from different divisions were on hand, keeping an eye out for good talent to recruit, as also to keep rowdy elements in check. Now and then, I too would draw the attention of some of the officials to some gifted youth.

It is surprising how time flies or crawls depending on whether you are on your feet outdoors or in your seat indoors. Before long, it was time for the climax of the morning session – the archery competition. I desperately looked for Karna. Surely he couldn't be missing the one event where he could showcase his talent? But no, Karna was nowhere to be seen. The competition ended with a fairly talented fellow we had taken note of occasionally winning the archery event.

Now it was time for lunch. Crowds suddenly seemed to swell like boiled milk. The food stalls offered sumptuous options for every palate. There was the vegetarian counter, to which every Brahmin in the assembly was headed. But a large majority preferred the counters that were serving delicacies that included deer and lamb meat, quail egg soup, grilled fowl, a whole range of fish, and much else besides. These stands were teeming with people all of a sudden, each person trying to claim the attention of their respective vendor simultaneously, without any semblance of order. The vendors, as if endowed with multiple hands like Ma Kali, were simultaneously catering to two or even three customers at the same time. The bhang stall buzzed like a beehive. Little urchins were guzzling two, three or even four tumblers of juices.

The non-royal competitors had a stall of their own where the winners, surrounded by their fawning well-wishers, were narrating the thrills of their victories. And soon, as lunch time approached its end, the royals started arriving, with my parents being the last to arrive, accompanied Kunti Devi. Soon, with my parents taking their seats, calm was restored in the rest of the field and it was time for the royal competition to begin.

The events of the second half of the competition began to unfold. I will spare you the details, for there is not much to tell, except that in event after event, the expected were winning. Nakula excelled on horseback. His climactic act was to ride an unbridled horse standing on its bare back, with his hands folded in salutation as the horse ran a full round of the ground at full gallop to a huge applause. Bhima and I expectedly fought for the top honours in the wrestling and mace events, with the results – surprise, surprise – going Bhima's way. Finally it was time for archery, and Drona ensured that Arjuna was reserved for the very end.

After Arjuna had won the standard competition, the

guru arranged for Arjuna to show off his special skills. A single broomstick was shredded by Arjuna with his arrow at twenty-five paces; a mango tossed high into the sky was picked clean by him before it reached the ground; a bamboo arrow shot by the guru at Arjuna from fifty paces was bisected mid-journey by him into two; a clay pigeon was knocked to smithereens by an arrow shot backward, as he looked at its reflection in a copper disc.

Needless to say, with each feat, the crowd, including the royals, was on its feet, feting Arjuna. An aide was constantly rendering running commentary on the proceedings for the benefit of my parents who, essentially good and simple folk, were truly happy for Arjuna. Their happiness was evident. I could see my father repeatedly wiping away happy tears from his eyes. Kunti Devi looked radiant in her pride.

To be fair to Arjuna, such skill had never before been witnessed on those grounds – or any ground – in our memory. Even I had been unaware of the lofty level Arjuna had attained in archery. I could not but admire his skill. What the likes of me could at best do once in three attempts – and even then may be not all the tricks – he had done effortlessly. He had obviously worked hard. After all, the guru had spent hours and hours with him to the exclusion of most of us. And it was now evident that the guru had not entirely wasted his time.

The judges, seated atop a podium, had been unanimous on who the Champion of the Day was going to be.

Soon it was time for the concluding events. We, the contestants, were seated just under the royal pavilion, the royals to the front and the others to the back. Drona stood up and, after a perfunctory speech, presented the non-royal winners of the morning in various events to the king. Each winner, starting with the Champion of the Morning, who was also the winner of the overall archery event, walked up to the pavilion where my father stood, and received his award at his hands. My father made it a point to stretch his hand, and when the candidate came within his reach, Father exchanged some words with the youth, patted his head and handed over the designated trophy before the next one arrived and the process repeated itself several times. The few moments each youth spent receiving his honour were enough for the court artists seated close by to sketch the scene swiftly, which would be handed over to the prize winners later.

It was now the turn of the winners of the royal events. Once again, Drona made a short speech and was about to announce Arjuna Champion of the Day.

And then, suddenly, there was pandemonium. A tall youth – why, it was none other than Karna! – sprang forth from among the spectators straight on to the royal pavilion and, standing at a respectful distance from my father, with his hands folded and head deferentially bent, hailed the king in salutation and said, 'O compassionate king! I am Karna, son of your proud charioteer, Adhiratha.' Before he could utter another word, two of Father's bodyguards leapt forth and held Karna from both sides, while a third one jumped to Karna's back, with the point of his spear pressing against his spine. But Karna stood calm, showing no signs of agitation. Nor did he resist the soldiers in any manner.

From where I sat, I could only see Karna's back, but I could see every single detail that the angle offered: the rippling muscles, sinewy limbs, the knots along his spine and the curls of his golden hair. I could also hear every word he spoke. He was in a spotless white dhoti, worn cross-style, as we all did, with a simple black half-sleeved cotton vest, waist-length. His biceps were bulging, straining to escape from his sleeves. I could spot the black string of an amulet playing hide and seek on his right bicep. His back, forearms and calves were clad in a sparkling armour of gold; so must be his chest. Large golden earrings dangled prominently from his large ears. He wore his shoulder-length hair loose and it spread around his head like a golden halo. A silk cummerbund woven in golden strands was tied to his slender waist, and the two ends dangled under a half knot to his left. I could see his massive bow, and a large quiver full of assorted arrows to the left and right of his substantial shoulders respectively. Why, even from behind, he looked formidable and majestic. Maybe because I was sitting, he seemed unusually enormous, even though he stood with his arms folded and head bent. I shuffled some of my brothers around so I had a good profile view of him.

From the gap between Karna and my father, I could spot the beautiful Kunti Devi, whose face seemed aglow at this handsome specimen of youth that had materialized in front of her. My mother merely stood clutching my father's right shoulder, her expression unreadable.

The aides were whispering in my parents' ears. My father raised his hand, as if to calm them. Suddenly, a hushed silence fell upon the ground. The guards relaxed their grip over Karna and my father extended both his arms towards him, beckoning him to come closer. And when Karna did so, Father patted his shoulders affectionately and said, 'Speak, son. Though I used to see more of you when you were really young than I have in recent years, I would recognize your voice anywhere. While this is most unexpected, do say what you are here to say. And how is it that I haven't heard of your feats today? Surely you should have been participating in the events? I hope no injustice has been done to you in the competition? Oh, but let me hear you out first. Speak.' At the same time, after another momentary exchange with his aides, he loudly asked his guards to step away from Karna, and they briskly obeyed.

Karna expressed his gratitude to my father and continued his interrupted address. 'O king, no injustice has been done to me under your benevolent regime. At the outset, I would like to thank you in person for having given me the opportunity to study in the royal gurukul. Not being a royal, I may not have had the good fortune of studying directly under guru Drona, but I have received tutelage in weaponry and shaastras in the royal gurukul and am thus under your direct obligation. I have worked hard, very hard indeed, even outside the gurukul scheme, if only to be worthy of your munificence in granting me the scholarship in the gurukul. I believe my abilities to be second to none.

'With due modesty, My Lord, I seek glory as much as the shaastras consider it a worthy man's duty to seek it. I seek glory not incommensurate with the hard work I have put in and the prowess I believe I have achieved. I seek glory as much to quench my personal ambition as to be able to serve my kingdom in a capacity that may be my legitimate place. I believe – and I am sure, so do all present here – that the Champion of the Day must, beyond question, be the best all-rounder and archer of the day. The city has witnessed the feats of Arjuna as the climax of the day. I only seek your leave to display my skills before the entire city present here this evening. If I fall short of Arjuna's skills, I will only embarrass myself before the whole of Hastinapura, but in any case would have provided at least some entertainment to those present here. But if my skills do surpass Arjuna's, I am sure even he would have no objection to my being called Champion of the Day. I seek but an opportunity to compete for the only glory a graduating student can aspire to.'

With these words, Karna once again assumed his humble but dignified posture and awaited the king's response. For a moment, there was hushed silence. And then there was a spontaneous explosion of voices from all around the ground in support of Karna's prayer. Drona listened to Karna's speech with a sneer on his face and whispered to Arjuna, who had been standing right next to him in readiness for his being anointed Champion of the Day. Arjuna soon assumed a smug expression.

The king briefly consulted his aides, one or two of whom looked towards Drona, who rolled his eyes to convey that he had no objection to the young man's wishes being granted, and the aides whispered back into the king's ears. And then the king gave his consent to Karna.

Karna thanked the king, saluted Drona and stepped down from the pavilion. He looked to his left and right, and did something strange. He curved his two palms and joined them together such that his thumbs were together, making a good imitation of a conch-shell, and blew loudly into the hollow, making a loud bellowing sound. Within moments, a magnificent white horse, its mane flying, head thrown high, mouth open in a grin, came galloping in from the direction of the main gate of the ground, and as it was about twenty paces from him, Karna started running in the same direction as the horse, parallel to the tracks that ran all round the ground in front of the royal pavilion. For a moment, it appeared as if the horse was chasing Karna. But soon the horse was running alongside Karna and, in the flicker of an eye, Karna had jumped smoothly and was standing on top of the galloping horse, one foot slightly ahead of the other on the animal's bare back as it continued running between the two white lines marking the track.

Even as the horse continued to gallop, Karna produced a plum that had been tied to the knot of his cummerbund, and threw it really high up in the air towards the middle of the ground. The horse was now turning the first bend on the track. Thanks to the already considerable height of the horse, the plum was thrown really high into the sky. It rose and rose in the air, till it reached the zenith, stopped for an instant, as if in indecision, and then started its journey downward. By now the horse was running on the opposite side of the pavilion, on the marked tracks, just crossing the halfway mark. At that instant, Karna took off his bow and pulled a slender arrow from his quiver, loaded the arrow, aimed at the plum and released it – all in one fluid motion. The arrow took a trajectory well below the plum in a low arc. But as the fruit hurtled downwards, the arrow advanced and, as if in a pre-decided rendezvous, connected with the falling fruit, going right through its middle. Then the arrow continued on its trajectory, and plonked on the ground, tip first, exactly in front of the royal pavilion.

There was hushed silence in the stadium – even the birds seemed to hold their chatter in deference – except for the thuds of the hooves as the galloping horse completed its circle and was just in front of the seated royalty again. Karna jumped off its back smoothly and waited as the horse came to a stop within a few paces and then turned and trotted till it stood right next to Karna, prancing daintily, head thrown back.

Karna retrieved a bag near the steps of the pavilion, which he must have left when he had gone up earlier. From it, he retrieved a short brass pole the length of a hand, to one end of which was attached a mirror. He affixed the pole between the horse's ears, into a hollow tube attached to a leather strap that went around the horse's head, so that the short rod jutted vertically above the horse's head, with the polished mirror shining bright at the top. Karna mumbled into the horse's ears, as if talking to it, and the horse began trotting, as Karna started jogging alongside, now in the opposite direction to the earlier round. Soon the horse started cantering and Karna once again jumped, as if weightlessly, on to the horse's back in one mighty leap. Now the horse was galloping again around the course.

Within moments, Karna retrieved a clay pigeon, half the size of the one that had been used by Arjuna. He threw it high behind his back and, in one fluid moment, lifted his bow overhead, and pulling an arrow once again, he aimed at the tossed pigeon, looking at the reflection in the slanted polished mirror that was now projecting a hand above the horse's head, and shot the arrow backwards. Even as the populace gawked, open-mouthed, the little clay pigeon exploded into a million little pieces!

In one demonstration, Karna had surpassed Nakula and Arjuna combined! He was now exactly on the opposite end of the ground from the royal pavilion and from the horseback, even as the horse was galloping, he called me, 'O Prince Suyodhana! Will you be so kind as to shoot a bamboo arrow at full force at me, when my horse is about twenty-five human paces from you? Kindly do not delay, and do aim at my chest.' Even as he was saying these words, he was pulling four lithe arrows from his quiver and loading all four simultaneously in a single grip. I got up, confused, for I had no time to think. I had just seen the astonishing display of his archery skills and I was still open-mouthed. I had no time to think. I knew that close shots to the body were more difficult to avoid or counter as the opponent had much less time to react. But I had no time to waste. I stood up hastily, took hold of my bow and nocked an arrow, pulling the bowstring all the way to my ear, and waited a couple of instants for Karna to clear his last turn. And then, just as Karna was coming towards me, and when I thought he was about twenty-five paces away, I released my arrow. Karna nonchalantly released all four arrows at once. Three of those arrows made four equal pieces of my arrow and his fourth cut my bowstring, just where it was tied to my bow. As the horse reached me, slowing down a little, Karna jumped down lightly, and his horse, as if it had been told precisely what to do, continued running and exited the grounds.

Karna immediately came to me, sincerely apologized for snapping my bowstring and pressed his own bow into my hands, saying I could use his, until my own bow had been fixed. It was evident to all there that what Arjuna had done on the ground, Karna had done riding his horse, standing on its bare back, adding additional layers of complexities to the task, thus making Arjuna's feats look rather ordinary. I realized for the first time in life that excellence needs no introduction.

Once again, the grounds had exploded in spontaneous cries of *Jai Karna ... Jai Karna! ... Karna, Champion of the Day! Can Arjuna better that? Arjuna, you were good; but Karna, you were awesome!* The din was unbelievable for a while, as if the skies were falling upon all of us gathered there.

The aides were breathlessly trying to explain what Karna had done to my parents. I was feeling a strange sense of satisfaction, happiness and even pride, for I considered Karna my friend. My father's facial expressions were changing like a kaleidoscope (though we didn't have kaleidoscopes those days) as each feat of Karna was being compared with Arjuna's. I was intrigued by the look on Kunti Devi's face. While there was consternation, there was also happiness somewhere. It was as if the two emotions were vying with each other for dominance. I found this a bit confusing. Drona looked momentarily clueless and lost, and had aged about ten years in the span of a few minutes. Arjuna was still trying to collect himself and didn't look half as cocky as he had done moments ago and had found something near his feet to investigate. The other four Pandava brothers kept deadpan faces. My brothers were clapping and whistling for Karna. None of us had been aware that he had come this far in his skills. If Arjuna was a mile ahead of us, well, Karna seemed ten!

And that's when it struck me that if Karna was this good, and if he was my friend, and remained so, he could well be my antidote against Arjuna. The truth is, Arjuna and Bhima had been causing me not a little disquiet.

Karna ascended the royal podium once more and touched my father's feet and thanked him again for giving him the opportunity of displaying his skills before the assembly. He stood up, walked to the side and stood, with his feet at ease and arms crossed, and threw a dignified and questioning look towards the judges. Without uttering a word, he was asking the judges – there were three of them – who the Champion of the Day was. The judges did not seem to have to strain their brains to decide who it was. They stood up as one, walked up to Drona and confabulated in low voices. It seemed clear that there was some disagreement between Drona and the judges. Judges they may have been, but Drona as the rajguru towered over them in stature, and it would not be easy for the judges to disregard the royal teacher's views. Besides, this ceremony was entirely Drona's show.

Soon, the judges assumed their seats and Drona came forward to announce the champion.

'Your Royal Highnesses and gentle folks of

Hastinapura, there can be no doubt that we have had a very fulsome and entertaining day. Nor can anyone say reasonably that this lad here, Karna, is not without some talent. It is not as if Arjuna here cannot better these feats. If he kept his display low-profile, he was merely being modest. As the judges had unanimously adjudged him champion before this young fellow disrupted the proceedings, Arjuna did not have to show off his higher skills.

'Be that as it may, we cannot but deplore the high-handedness of this Sutaputra – who enjoys education in the royal gurukul thanks to the benevolence, magnanimity and charity of our king, in whose employ this ambitious young man's father works as a charioteer – in interrupting the august proceedings of this important day of the royal gurukul.

'Why, everyone is aware of the rules of the competition. The morning belongs to the non-royals and the afternoon to the royals. This young man, if he desired glory, should have competed in the morning session, which is where he legitimately belongs, rather than interrupt the proceedings of the royals. But the young man did not participate in the morning and the Champion of the Morning has already been declared. Arjuna, as the best of the royals, as per our standard rules, has already been adjudged Champion of the Day by the judges. This is how we have always conducted the proceedings and we are not about to change our traditions because some upstart nurses fancy ambitions.

'O King, and gentle folks, I do sincerely apologize for the inconvenience caused to everyone present here by this rude disruption delaying the proceedings, even if the interruption was in the manner of cheap entertainment. Mind you, what we hold here is a solemn competition of talents, and not a display of street tricks. So, to get on with the proceedings ...' Drona held Arjuna by his arm as the Kuntiputra seemed to espy an insect crawling near his toes, and continued, 'I hereby declare Prince Arjuna the Cham ...' The rest of Drona's speech was drowned in a collective groan, which gathered momentum in a matter of seconds, to become a torrential roar of disapproval at what had just transpired.

PART III

7

A man is what he makes of himself by his karma; not what he is born into by ovarian lottery

Karna looked serene. Neither anger, nor righteous indignation or even grave provocation had brought any colour to his face. When he stepped forward, his composure was like that of a still pool of refreshing water. His arms still crossed, he stood right next to Drona, towering a good hand above his head, and turning half towards him and half towards the spectators, spoke loudly and clearly in a crisp baritone.

'O esteemed gurus of the gurukul (he did not refer to them as 'my gurus'), my dear fellow students, respected members of the royalty, parents, and citizens present. Let the setting sun attest that it was never my intent to disrupt the proceedings of this august day, nor to display a spirit of one-upmanship, as guru Drona would have you believe. To nurse ambitions of glory, I suppose, is neither a crime nor undesirable in a man, young or old; nor the preserve of a special few. After all, what is this championship but an opportunity to prove one's competence before one and all? True, I could have competed among the non-royals and, for certain, could have won the championship of the morning, and reined in my ambition to compete for the Champion of the Day. The tradition of championship the guru spoke of is true indeed. But I ask him, is it equally not true that this tradition was never challenged in the past because, in the past, there never was a non-royal champion good enough to challenge the royal winner? Is that not the reason that led to the winner of the afternoon session being labelled the Champion of the Day? Would Arjuna himself want the dubious title of Champion of the Day when he has not won it convincingly? Would it not then be fairer to have the tradition of three titles, namely Champion of the Morning, of the Afternoon and of the Day? Yes, Arjuna is the champion of this afternoon, but let him compete fairly for the Champion of the Day.

'I understand from the shaastras that undue arrogance is immoral. But by symmetry, I would like to believe that undue humility is no less so. I state before you all, in neither arrogance nor humility, that I consider myself second to none in my graduating class, royals and non-royals included. Guru Drona has stated that Arjuna kept his display low-profile, only out of humility. If so, Arjuna, I ask you directly,' and Karna turned towards Arjuna, 'would it not be truly exciting for the two of us to compete for Champion of the Day? Wouldn't the contest thus won be more worthy of a true champion and more entertaining to all those who have assembled here to witness the best of the royal school?'

And with these words, Karna looked expectantly towards Arjuna, whose eyes had suddenly turned shifty,

Duryodhana

looking alternately at Drona and Karna, not quite sure what he ought to say or do. My father, hardly an exemplar for the quick-witted, was just about grasping what was happening and collecting his wits for a safe answer when, as if inspiration had suddenly hit him, Drona intervened in a voice that was carefully modulated for the benefit of the entire assembly.

'Sutaputra, do you even know whom you are talking to? Lest you did not pay heed in the gurukul, this is Arjuna, the *Pandu prince*, who rides the chariots which the likes of you will be proud to steer in time, just as your father steers our noble king's today. O son of Adhiratha, have you not even learnt that royals compete only among their equals? Hailing from the family of the lowest born, you sought and were granted state benevolence to study in the royal gurukul. Hailing from the family of the lowest born, you sought and were granted by the generous king the permission to showcase your cheap skills this evening. And now, shedding all humility, emboldened by repeated royal generosity, you, who ought to be minding horses and chariots alongside your humble father in the royal stables, dare challenge the Pandu prince? You expect us to be impressed because you are comfortable *atop* a horse when being *behind* horses is the vocation of the family you are born in? You charge in here looking for glory, hoping to challenge royalty, just because you think you have learnt well under my tutelage? Go back, O Sutaputra! Go back to where you belong and spend your time more profitably, training your horse to steer a chariot. And it is not as if there is no glory in being a charioteer. Your father is a glorious charioteer. Go train under him and wield a switch and reins instead of bow and arrow, and let us get on with this interrupted evening.'

I was stunned at this outburst by guru Drona. I looked at Father, desperately hoping he would intervene. Karna's fair face had turned red, though whether from the exertion of trying to keep a calm countenance in the face of the insults heaped upon by Drona, or because of the insults themselves, it was difficult to tell. And yet, he seemed somehow detached and dignified, as if he knew exactly what Drona was up to. It was difficult to read from his face whether he was more angry or more pained by the insults. And once again, before my befuddled father could respond, Karna himself spoke in a clear and firm voice, addressing himself as much to Drona as to the assembly, just as Drona himself had done.

'O rajguru Drona, I shall be guilty of insincerity if I said I am not saddened by your words. I am. But I am not dismayed because you were offensive in referring to me repeatedly as a Sutaputra, though it is not lost upon me that your objective was to dispirit me with that word. Nor am I disappointed that you endeavoured to insult the vocation of my father and forefathers. Or that you underplayed my skill and talent. I have far too much respect for your scholarship, judgement and temperament to know that it is not in your nature to be offensive to someone when a gentler demeanour would do, least of all towards someone much younger to you, who has committed no offence. Nor are you one to lose control of your intellect and track of your reason to the point where you become unaware that your words may not be worthy of someone of your stature. I don't dare disrespect your knowledge of the shaastras by imagining for a moment that you do not know what we were taught in the royal gurukul itself: that one's destiny and hence one's varna is determined by one's karma and not by one's janma. I consider it disrespectful to you to think that you would not be discerning enough to know that one is a Sutaputra only if one has done nothing ever to lift oneself above the fate dealt one by the lottery of fate, over which no man, beast or god has any control. And even if this were not so, and assuming that Sutaputra is indeed a title acquired by birth, you, rajguru, are bound to know that a child does not choose the womb it is born out of and hence it is hardly becoming of the wise to insult someone for something upon which he has no control.

'So, rajguru Drona, it is as evident as a tuft on a Brahmin's scalp that your piercing words were chosen for a purpose. So while I am not saddened by your insults, I am disappointed nevertheless that the entire city should have witnessed a learned elder employ language unworthy of his stature, and that too against a mere student who meant nobody any harm, least of all him. What could have been the reasons for your outburst? I can divine three:

'One,' Karna closed his right fist with only the index finger extended, symbolizing one, 'you never quite wanted me at the top of the heap in the gurukul and now you are unhappy that I undoubtedly am. On the very first day at the gurukul, when hair hadn't yet sprouted on my chin, your words were as carefully crafted to insult and demoralize me as they have been this evening. You could not have forgotten, surely, that you had asked me never to come near your sessions since, in your words, Sutaputras and such were not to be educated in your proximity. Though today, whether it is a fleeting testimony to my talents after all or a momentary lapse of memory of an aging man, I cannot say, but you referred to me as *having learnt well under your tutelage*. It may be true that I have learnt well while enrolled at the royal gurukul, rajguru, but with due respect, not under *your tutelage* – not by a long shot – because you banished me from your tutelage.

'Two', he indicated the number two with his fingers, 'you hope to break my spirit like the back of a serpent. Yes, my father is a charioteer by profession. You have done what you can to make it sound like a dirty word, as if I ought to be ashamed of the fact. Any son who loves his father must know that as long as it involves no adharma, one's father's vocation can never be shameful; and it is what has given me my bread, blood and breath. The truth is, I am perfectly comfortable with who I am, and have never longed to be a royal. I have never heard the king himself speak with disrespect to my father or discredit his profession. When a king wins battles and wars, I hardly need state that a significant credit accrues to the skill of the charioteer. Tall men, I have been taught, seldom belittle honourable vocations of other men, especially when those professions involve high skills. But O rajguru, you think by calling me a Sutaputra repeatedly, you will succeed in breaking my spirit. You did not succeed when I was fifteen. And you have not succeeded today.

'I do not say this to cause you any hurt, and if I do, I earnestly apologize. But I do want you to know in all sincerity that while I am rather proud of being Adhiratha's son and a Sutaputra; with what I have witnessed of you today, I wonder if I would have felt the same way being your son – a Brahminputra.'

Ashwatthama, Drona's only son, and a fine fellow, in all fairness, who was standing not far away, seemed to be sinking into the ground, trying to look as inconspicuous and diminutive as possible.

'No, rajguru, I have no reason at all to be saddened by your words, for your insults have the same effect upon me that raindrops have over ducks' backs.

'And lastly,' Karna added his ring finger to the other two, 'you wish me ill on account of Arjuna. I hold no grudge against the prince. He has done me no harm. What is more, he is indeed an accomplished archer, and better than *most*. The truth is, you want him to be the best of *all*, as being better than most is not nearly good enough. I can quite relate to that need. I am not a child any more. But even as a youngster, I recall being told about your treatment of Ekalavya who had visited you, seeking your tutelage not long before I first came into your gurukul. And soon thereafter, when you meted out the same treatment to me, your motives came up in clearer relief. The idea got sculpted into belief last year when you sought the right thumb of Ekalavya – whose only fault was that he was way ahead of Arjuna in archery – as compensation for him *considering* you his teacher. I am glad that after you turned me away, I did not think of you as my guru, for I am sure you would have sought no less of me this day. I am glad to have my thumbs intact. And now your treatment of me to ensure unchallenged supremacy for Arjuna appears more comic to me than tragic.

'So, rajguru, though you chose your words deliberately,

in the presence of the entire city, to break my spirit, I hardly find myself dispirited by your words. It is as clear to me as the mountain dew that you have systematically hacked away at Ekalavya and me, only so that you can showcase Arjuna as the greatest living archer. If both you and Arjuna are happy calling him the champion by carving away the thumb of one fantastic archer and refusing to compete with the other, hiding behind caste considerations, I don't know who should be more sad – you, Arjuna or I.

'Perhaps it should be Arjuna,' said Karna and nodded in the direction of Arjuna before addressing the royal teacher again. 'Your tactics to anoint him the champion will ensure that his status shall forever remain tainted, unless Arjuna is willing to better me. As a matter of fact, you have already tainted his greatness, because the missing thumb of Ekalavya, far from going missing, will forever cock a snook at Arjuna's great skill and remind posterity how the absence of a thumb on Ekalavya's hand rather than the presence of all the fingers on Arjuna's, made him the greater archer of the two. I had hoped that you would not want to taint your favourite any further.

'I have sensed your single-minded devotion to establishing Arjuna as the best warrior and archer of all yugas. But if you persist in your methods, he may never acquire the authority of a champion. You may make him the *best known*, but never the *best* warrior and archer. And this I promise you, O rajguru. I shall with diligence ensure that I thwart your ambition, so that when history speaks of great archers, Arjuna's greatness, such as it may be, will always be qualified with an exception or two, one of which shall be me. Every time Arjuna scores a point on the charts of fame, the discerning will know exactly how that point accrued to Arjuna. With studious industry shall I ensure that Arjuna's greatness will always be viewed through the tint of my own skills. He shall never achieve what you wish for him, for true and lasting greatness can never be achieved through scheming and machination. And this alone shall be my revenge for your exertions of today.

'But enough words,' Karna continued holding his right palm up, turning towards Arjuna, 'O Arjuna, from what I saw of your prowess, you are a very able archer, and undoubtedly better than most. But I am sure being better than most hardly satisfies you. It certainly does not satisfy me. I challenge you to the title of Champion of the Day one last time. It is entirely up to you to prove your undoubted superiority, O Arjuna, by competing with me, in any format of your choosing. I know you as a brave man. Let the best of us get the title of the championship. Are you willing?'

I was listening to Karna intently. Not once had he raised his voice. Not once had his pitch changed as he delivered his impromptu lines evenly. Not once did he reflect any animosity, anger or emotion through any inflexion in his voice or visage. He merely carried a hint of a slightly lopsided, haughty smile, even as his eyes refused to smile even once. Not once did he address Drona as 'gurudev', for that would amount to according him the place of *his* guru, and consistently addressed him only by his official title of rajguru. He stood tall and shining, his hair spread around his head like golden halo, under the setting sun, as if he were the sun personified on earth, his face a large question mark in the direction of Arjuna.

The hush in the stadium following Karna's oration was like the tinnitus that follows a heavy hammer blow on steel. For nearly three minutes, the only sound in the stadium was that of birds trying to find their perch on nearby trees. I used the time to study Drona. His visage was difficult to decipher. Was it anger? Rage? Indignity? Mortification? Embarrassment? An admixture, maybe, of all of these? After all, Karna had in most respectful tones called his bluff, and equally respectfully, and in perfectly calm and collected cadence, called him partisan, a pigmy, boorish, bigoted, unworthy of respect and greatness, while maintaining every visible symbolism of respect in words and tone, making his words a thousand-fold more hurtful to Drona than the latter's insults could ever have been to Karna.

Arjuna's eyes were working hard to avoid Karna's gaze, as if desperately trying to find a perch somewhere near Drona's eyes. Drona's eyes had problems of their own, gazing anywhere but at Karna, as if searching for their own parking spot. Just as their pupils finally found anchor in each other's gaze, the crowd's trance broke and indistinct cries involving exhortations to Karna and Arjuna began to penetrate the air. Arjuna looked provoked and took a step forward in a clear sign of readiness to accept the challenge.

At this point, Drona's voice boomed, 'Partha!' and with his eyes, he signalled Arjuna to step back. The disciple looked distinctly unhappy but did as bid. The two held a quick, whispered conversation. Father's aides were busy whispering into his ears, and he himself was nodding or shaking his head every now and then. As for me, I had never felt the kind of joy I felt that day, when I could see conclusively that my friend Karna was more than a match for Arjuna. I was keen to see where it was heading. Nothing would give me greater satisfaction than to see the arrogant Arjuna humbled.

When I call Arjuna arrogant, in all fairness I need to qualify the adjective. I have nothing against arrogance per se. To be honest, I was arrogant myself. After all, what kind of a crown prince of Hastinapura would I be if I didn't carry some royal arrogance about me? So I would have happily put up with some arrogance on Arjuna's part. Unlike Bhima, Arjuna had never tried one-upmanship over me openly. So then what was it in his arrogance that I disliked? Perhaps it was the suggestion of a swagger in his walk that irritated me. I found his swagger quite misplaced, uncalled for, and even unbecoming, given his (and his brothers') humble beginnings in the forests and the circumstances that had led them to seek permanent lodgings in our palace. His haughtiness seemed to stem from his belief that he had a *right* to *my kingdom*, with no trace in his demeanour of the favour of shelter we had bestowed on them.

His confabulations with guru Drona complete, Arjuna shuffled a step forward and the crowd immediately shushed itself to silence, as if aware that something momentous was about to happen.

'O Sutaputra,' addressed Arjuna, 'for one who was merely seen around the periphery of the gurukul, but never heard, you have spoken enough in the presence of royals for a lifetime. Now listen to me. As I may not be in conversation with you very often, listen to me carefully,

O Sutaputra. And don't go about spreading a spiel that I am trying to insult you. I am calling you Sutaputra because that is what you are, just as I am a Pandu prince (whom are you kidding, O Partha, was my thought) and therefore to be addressed as one. So let us call each other what we are and don't you dare get on first-name terms with me, as you did while addressing me.

'That said, I do not deny that you performed some good tricks on horseback with your bow and arrow. The antics were calculated to better my display, while mine were spontaneous. Nevertheless, you are a competent archer. But do not waste your energies challenging those not of your social class. If you are looking for a challenge, go look for another Sutaputra, and if you can't find one ... why, that would make you the best archer and warrior among the Sutas! That should be good enough for you. Challenges look good only when exchanged among equals. So I am afraid I cannot accept yours. What if every citizen in our kingdom was to challenge me? Do I go about fighting every individual to prove my superiority? That's why challenges are always exchanged among equals. And a final word of advice. You carry a swagger disproportionate to a Sutaputra. Go, first learn some modesty from your father at the stables. I wish you well!'

It wasn't lost on me or anyone else watching him carefully that Arjuna had delivered his little speech from his tongue and not from his heart. The expression on his face didn't quite match his words. It was clear that he had been tutored by his brand manager Drona to deliver those words and desist from competing with Karna.

Once again, there was a total hush in the stadium,

broken by the tweet of a single silly bird. I had goose pimples on my arms. I had seen enough and heard enough. They had done everything in the book to insult, humiliate and break the spirit of my friend.

Before I could even think clearly, I was on my feet and, in three bounds, upon the royal pavilion. The bird stopped chirping. I stood between Karna and Arjuna and addressed the entire stadium though I turned my head towards my father.

'King Dhritarashtra, my father, you have heard all that has gone on here. You have been given an eyewitness account by your aides of what the entire city has witnessed. So, Father, you, who hardly need eyes to see what goes on around you – surely you must have seen what is going on? So let me not dwell long on issues which Karna has substantially addressed in any case. For a student, what can be a greater glory than being at the top of his peers? So what is wrong if Karna aims for the greatest position in his batch? After all, isn't Drona trying to protect exactly the same glory for Arjuna? Talking about challenges to be bandied about only among equals, aren't Karna and Arjuna both graduating students in the royal gurukul? Doesn't that make them equals? Isn't this competition about graduating students of the gurukul? So when there is a competition for the Champion of the Day among them, where is the question of royals and non-royals? Isn't a man what he makes of himself through his karma rather than what he is by the accident of birth, as unequivocally stated in our shaastras and ably pointed out by Karna? Who can question the wisdom of his words?

'In the past, the Champion of the Morning and the Day

may never have clashed for the obvious reason that the latter champion was undoubtedly the superior one. Today, that superiority has been challenged by Karna. So why is Arjuna hiding behind the lame excuse of social inequality? After what has been witnessed here today, is there a single sorry soul in this gathering who doubts who the real champion is? Truth be told, it does not matter any more whether or not Arjuna wishes to compete with Karna, for the truth has been witnessed by one and all. It is patently obvious that Arjuna, already stripped of his coveted glory in the minds of all those present here, is trying to hide behind the fig leaf of caste considerations.'

At this point, I was tempted to lay bare some home truths about Arjuna and his brothers, who were hardly *Pandu* princes. So didn't that make them a somewhat dubious bunch of royals? But I let it pass, for all this was family dirty linen, and not to be washed in a public assembly.

So I continued, 'But, Arjuna, I am willing to go some length in humouring your sense of propriety in social status. It also pleases me to remove that fig leaf. Since you say you are a royal and are loath to competing with non-royals, I, Suyodhana, the crown prince of Hastinapura with several principalities under my charge, can remedy that situation immediately. I hereby award the principality of Anga to Karna and declare him Angaraj.'

Saying so, I took off my blue–green necklace of emeralds and lapis lazuli stones embedded in gold and put it around Karna's neck. In the next breath, I beckoned Sushasana who was nearest to me of all my brothers, and knowing that he would understand, I took his ceremonial crown that we had all donned for the graduation ceremony, and placed it upon Karna's head, saying, 'I hereby declare you Angaraj, the king of Anga. You shall rule the state of Anga as its independent ruler, as an ally of king Dhritarashtra. This, by the virtue of powers vested in me as the crown prince, I am fully competent and empowered to do, given that it has been a few months since I came of age. My announcement has the force of full royal decree and let nobody, but nobody have a speck of doubt on that score.' At this point, I gestured to one of my aides who had materialized as soon as I had taken to the pavilion, to formalize the arrangement with a royal writ.

Only a few days ago, as I had turned sixteen, I had been given independent charge of a segment of the kingdom, which included the principality of Anga. This was standard practice to prepare a crown prince for statecraft. Once I had revealed my intentions to my father in no uncertain terms, he had understood once and for all that there was no way I would ever acquiesce to Yudhisthira replacing me as the crown prince of Hastinapura. Consequently, the Kuntiputras had automatically pared down their demand for the kingdom to a share in it, so that my status as the crown prince was certainly not in question (not that I had ever doubted it for an instant). The only question was whether I would come to rule the full kingdom or a shrunken one. And once again I had no doubt that I was the crown prince of the former.

While my father, true to his diffident nature, may not have spoken up for Karna, I was confident that he would not object to my action. After all, I was doing the right thing by Karna. Besides, by binding Karna, who was an ideal counterbalance to the Arjuna–Bhima axis, into a closer bond of friendship, I was making him my formal ally and strengthening Hastinapura.

With this confidence, I continued, 'So now, O Arjuna, Angaraj is your equal at least in social status, though I suspect he is your superior as an archer. But it is up to you to prove me wrong. You said much about Karna's parentage. Well, at least we seem to know for certain that he has a legitimate father in the good old brave Adhiratha.'

I hadn't meant to insert this snide observation in public but it had been uttered almost unwittingly in the heat of the moment. Not that I was terribly sorry, since Arjuna's insult of Karna had been no less public.

It immediately became clear from the many drawn breaths that what I had left unsaid had been heard loud and clear in the assembly. I had openly aligned with Karna and had forever put myself in opposition to Arjuna. Arjuna took a threatening step towards me. I just smiled at him sweetly. The mixture of anger and helplessness on his face was easily worth half my kingdom, or more. It was quite clear that even without any direct reference to his own procreation out of matrimony, I had extracted a good deal of revenge for the words he had uttered against Karna.

There was a commotion behind me. I turned to see that Kunti Devi had passed out. Someone was sprinkling water on her face. I was so beside myself at the shenanigans of Drona and Arjuna that afternoon that if I felt any guilt at her plight, I have little recollection of it today.

At this point, Adhiratha rose humbly from a section of

the crowd where he was apparently seated, unseen by us all. He stood up and, with a measured gait, walked up to the pavilion and climbed the steps. Standing in front of me, his arms folded in humble submissiveness, he sought permission to say a few words. I was surprised by the request, but nodded in assent. He coughed a couple of times, as if to muster his strength – as much physical as psychological – for unlike us, it was not often that he found himself speaking before a large gathering.

'I am a humble man and a mere servant of the good king. As a Sutaputra, it is not my place to speak in such an august gathering and at such an occasion. And yet, what I wish to say must be said. I am certainly not in favour of Karna challenging Prince Arjuna, especially if the prince does not wish to engage in such a competition. And yet, I am saddened beyond words for young Karna, who has had to endure some very harsh and hurtful words today on account of me. I am pained too that I have kept this secret from Karna until this day. But if I continue to keep my lips sealed after all I have heard today, I will be the most selfish soul upon this earth. I only pray to the gods that I will not lose my son today.'

There was the usual unintelligible murmuring from the crowd at this strange address from Adhiratha. My father leaned closer. Aunt Kunti had come around and seemed all ears. Arjuna stood there with a bland expression. Karna stood as if struck dumb. I placed my hand around the old man's shoulders, since he seemed to be overcome with emotion, and waited for his next words.

'The truth, O citizens of Hastinapura, is that Karna is my legitimate son, but not my biological son. But I swear upon Karna himself, for no one is dearer to me than him, that had he been my own, I could not have loved him more. The truth is that, over eighteen summers ago, one morning when I was at the river Ashwa for my morning dip, I found a wicker basket floating down the river a little distance from the bank. I swam in and retrieved the basket, only to find a child, golden of complexion, clad in large golden earrings, sleeping peacefully with his soft golden hair spread out like rays issuing from the sun. Someone had indulgently fitted the baby with tiny gilded armour plates. The child was wrapped in the most expensive silk, though the wrapping carried no royal insignia. It was clear that the child was of royal origin and some unfortunate circumstances must have led him to be left adrift. There was nothing for me to do except to report the matter to the chief of the palace guards and take the child home. In the early days, the chief sent messages to the upstream states about the discovery of a royal baby, but could get no news of a child gone missing. In the meantime, my wife and I fell head-over-heels in love with the adorable baby and wanted it brought up as our own. In due course, we were allowed to bring up the child as our own by a palace decree. The elders back in my village know about the episode ...'

Adhiratha could not continue and broke down. Karna was with Adhiratha in a flash. He hugged his father tight, saying, 'But, Father, why do you cry? What do I care about the man who sired me and the woman who gave me birth, only to abandon me? As far as I am concerned, you are my father and Radha my mother. I am perfectly happy being your son. If I was unhappy about being a

Sutaputra, it was only because it was preventing me from being the Champion of the Day. But my friend Suyodhana has set that right. God knows that being a royal or not makes not a jot of a difference to me, except in so far as now Arjuna must accept my challenge.' Saying so, Karna turned towards Arjuna.

I loved Karna's resolve to settle scores with Drona, through Arjuna.

Suddenly there was commotion behind us. Kunti Devi had passed out once again. The Kuntiputras rushed to her side. Surprisingly, even Karna moved closer to where Aunt Kunti was lying, with her head on the lap of one of her maids. Fistfuls of cold water were being sprinkled on her face now. Soon, she came around once more and when she opened her eyes, she fixed her gaze on Karna. There was a strange mix of sentiments upon her face – surprise, shame, sorrow, shock, angst, alarm, regret, release, relief, pain, pleasure, dismay, horror, and whatnot. Karna gazed at her uncomprehendingly. As their eyes made contact, Kunti Devi uttered incoherently, 'Consider Arjuna your own brother, son ...' and she passed out once again, as if making a habit of it.

Adhiratha took this moment to remonstrate with Karna to give up his challenge. Of course, he agreed with Kunti. How could he challenge Prince Arjuna, whom Karna indeed ought to treat as his younger brother, now that Kunti Devi had addressed him as *son*.

Karna was suddenly silent, and seemed spent. He simply folded his hands in general salutation to all around him and exited the assembly, his arms firmly around his father, holding him as close to himself as he could.

8

No king can run away from the possibility of war; when he is not waging one, it may be waged upon him

We were all adults now. I had a court of my own. Karna, along with others like Uncle Shakuni, Sushasana, Yuyutsu and others, was now a part of my inner circle. We would meet often and address issues of state administration. The Kuntiputras had graduated from being a low-grade headache to a full-fledged migraine. There wasn't a day they would not be making an appeal to my father and lobbying with other senior advisors like Bhishma or Vidhura for a slice of the kingdom. On occasion, they would also have a word put in through their friend Krishna. Nor would they miss any opportunity to milk some public sympathy for themselves, if only to give their illegitimate claim upon our kingdom more traction.

If I had one reason to lose sleep, it was this: my father was a weak man. He had the dangerous combination of a mushy heart and a malleable mind and was not the most difficult of subjects to manipulate for a deft Svengali. This was bad news for a king and worse for the kingdom and, I was afraid, Aunt Kunti was a very deft manipulator. It was clear that Kunti & Sons had set their sight unwaveringly on our kingdom. If I did not do something about it, sooner or later Hastinapura would be shrunk or truncated. We would lose a part of it because clever Kunti Devi would worm her way and that of her sons into the minds of my father and his advisors as some kind of legitimate claimants to a share in our kingdom; my kingdom-to-be. If Hastinapura was to be saved from these usurpers, it was only up to me.

Beyond all convoluted verbiage, what I had understood of the duties and responsibilities of kings in statecraft was simple and straight. A king had two sets of responsibilities: those towards the subjects and those towards the kingdom itself.

The ruler's duties towards the subjects were well known. He had to be liberal, generous, charitable, honest, just and of high moral integrity; he had to be gentle, kind and empathetic, with ears to the ground. He had an obligation to use the riches of the state exclusively for the betterment of his subjects.

At the same time, he had certain duties towards the state itself which, at a meta-level, in my considered understanding of the shaastras, took precedence even over his duties to his subjects. The duties towards the state are what vest in a king the right to rule. Thus, the right to rule and the duties towards the state were flip sides of a king's coin.

For a king, the right to rule is an absolute, the highest

and the most sublime of rights. It is intrinsic to his sovereignty. A king is expected to strengthen his kingdom by adding territory, wealth and subjects to his state; not by subtracting them from it. This is fundamental to statecraft. More often than not, peace is merely another name for detente, which is invariably among equals where neither can be certain of winning over the other, while wars have always been waged, since time immemorial, by the stronger states upon the weaker ones. No king can run away from the possibility of war. If you do not wage it, it may be waged upon you. That is the law of statecraft. That is why a competent king ought not to be weak – in mind, muscle or means – for then he is ripe for the picking. This is why a proud and brave king does not readily abdicate in favour of a rival, or even gift away territory in armistice. States are serious responsibilities of the kings; not inheritances, possessions or chattel to be gifted away. This is also why a far-sighted and powerful king will do his best, without compromising the fundamental principles of statecraft, to avert the possibility of war. A war kills hundreds of thousands of men and renders women widows prematurely. It makes orphans of babies. It maims large swathes of the population. It destroys crops and commerce. It bankrupts kingdoms. That is why, if an otherwise inevitable war can be averted in exchange for a few key lives, a wise king takes the opportunity. This is strategic statecraft.

This is also why powerful kings go all out to make imperial claims. They do not relinquish their kingdom in favour of a rival, simply because the rival claims to have superior skills in state administration. Their royal duties demand that they learn the best methods of statecraft from everywhere, and administer their subjects to the best of their ability. When they falter in this regard, their hold over their kingdom weakens, making them good targets for annexation by more powerful rivals – just like underperforming corporate houses; only more so.

On matters of fundamental ideologies, like the right to rule, a king gives in to neither threat, nor sycophancy; neither blandishment, nor bribe; neither emotion, nor adulation. He gives in only to reason and principles. To safeguard these principles, a king is allowed acts and actions that are not allowed an ordinary man. That is why killing in a state-sponsored war is considered a noble act, while killing without such sanction, common murder. That is also why a king may make, amend or annul laws. He may, exceptionally, when the very sovereignty of the state is at stake, even be a law unto himself, though such a role can be a double-edged sword in the hands of a ruler who lacks the discretion to know when and how to wield such a blade, and such a king comes to grief sooner rather than later.

But these privileges or burdens – call them what you will – are seldom enjoyed or suffered by lesser mortals. Actions that may be called unfair, cowardly and deceptive in day-to-day life may be perfectly acceptable and commonplace in statecraft. What to a common man is a sneaky snitch may be a sly spy in statecraft. What may be treacherous murder to an ordinary citizen man may be the assassination of a traitor in statecraft. Subterfuge is elegant strategy in statecraft. That is why a wise king goes to sleep at peace every night knowing what he committed that day was not murder but a call of duty to protect his state against treason and sedition. In short, the rules of common men do not apply to kings and kingdoms.

A king has a million detractors, who may come in the garb of friends or foes. Often they have a common objective – to peck away at the state, like a sapsucker, at the king's expense. That is why he cannot have friends, at least not many, in the same sense as a common man does. That is also why history is replete with instances of the closest relatives of kings involved in the most sordid of court intrigues in which many a king has come to grief because he momentarily forgot that a king does not have a family in the same sense as a common man does. The stakes in a kingdom are too high for a king not to be wary of friends and family in equal measure. The fact is, friendship can only be among equals; and a king has no equal in his realm. And with those outside the realm, there can only be friendship treaties.

Take me, for instance. I had always been somewhat fond of Karna. But I had made him my 'friend' formally, as Angaraj, only because I had witnessed enough evidence that he offered a handsome counterbalance to Arjuna. By announcing him the king of Anga, I had merely formalized a friendship treaty. My feelings for him were genuine, but they had to be carefully measured and evaluated from time to time, though I wish it could have been different.

I was only a crown prince. But I had come of age, and had been given significant charge of a part of the kingdom, for I was ordained to succeed my father. Father was known to be a weak king and the consolidation of the kingdom in the past had been achieved by the likes of Bhishma and

Duryodhana

Pandu. Pandu was dead, Bhishma was aging, and it was entirely up to me to ensure the health of the kingdom from there on. And that is how my father saw it too. So I was de facto king and had been trained to think like one.

I had a piquant situation on hand. Hastinapura had a king who was more than somewhat irresolute, ineffectual and suggestible, and was constantly being worked upon by Aunt Kunti and her sons. And that was not all either. In the course of time, the courtiers and advisors of a king come to mimic him in attitude and character, so that some part of my father's naiveté in affairs of state had long since been slowly but steadily rubbing off on his advisors as well. As a consequence, charismatic Kunti Devi was steadily beginning to gain the mind-space of many of my father's advisors like Bhishma, Vidhura and others. As a princess herself, Kunti Devi was fundamentally political in her attitude, and quite adept at playing the cards dealt to her by providence to her best advantage.

She had a variety of cards at her disposal – the helpless-woman card, the former-queen card, the mother-of-five-fatherless-sons card, the sister-in-law card, the sympathy card, the emotional card, the Pandu-was-the-king's-brother card (never saying half-brother), the Pandu-was-the-erstwhile-king card (ignoring that he was actually only a regent), the pleasant-but-poor-relatives card, the Yudhisthira-is-the-eldest-brother card, the subtle-threat card ('We must avoid brothers having to fight among themselves at any cost') – and used each of these and many more cards to ensure that she secured a slice of the kingdom for her sons. The one card that would upset her game was the 'none-of-the-"Pandavas"-were-fathered-by-

Pandu card' which, out of politeness, neither my father nor I played against her. But to me, this was the most important card to hold Aunt Kunti from succeeding in her plans.

Maybe as a mother she was doing what was best for her sons – a mother's dharma. But as a king, I had to do what was best for my kingdom and my subjects. Given their transparent imperial ambitions, I could see plainly that the Kuntiputras would go all out to stake their non-existent claim on our kingdom and would wage war if I did not give in. And since I had absolutely no intention of giving in, a major war was inevitable. And if it could be averted, it was my duty to avert it.

I was occupied with these thoughts night and day, insomniac by night and restless by day. My eyes would sometimes shut out of sheer fatigue, and suddenly Arjuna and Bhima would be standing over me, as tall as the clouds and then melt into the horizon, only to be replaced by Yudhisthira sitting smugly on a throne, smiling ear to ear, even as Kunti Devi stood at the foot of the throne asking me how old I was, and I would open my eyes with a start. I would be disturbed by the dreams, though in reality, with a hundred brave brothers, Karna, Shakuni and many other allies, I had no reason to be afraid of the Kuntiputras. But why was I getting these nightmares? This irritation would keep me sleepless, increasing my fatigue even more, and this cycle of insomnia, fatigue and nightmares would take turns to torment me, night after night.

Then suddenly came an inspiration. It is funny how simple solutions look when they finally come to you, and then you wonder why they did not occur to you sooner! With the answer at hand, the nightmares stopped. I knew exactly how I was going to keep the kingdom intact and avert a war that would be disastrous to my subjects. True, the solution was not terribly honourable to us Kauravas, but I reasoned that it was our *kingdom* at stake, and where kingdoms are involved, secrecy and intrigues are legitimate weapons. I just had to work in such secrecy that our honour would not be compromised.

I had to eliminate Aunt Kunti and the Kuntiputras. As long as they lived, they would continue to pose real danger to Hastinapura. If they got a slice of Hastinapura, they would make a grab for the rest.

If a large number of lives could be potentially saved by eliminating just six, it was an acceptable bargain – an excellent one, in fact. Killing such people on the quiet was necessary statecraft and not treachery. I simply had to make the pre-emptive strike.

A year-long festivity was being planned in the forest resort of Varanavata in honour of Lord Shiva. What if we could induce Aunt Kunti and her sons to fall for the charms of the place and get them to spend a year-long vacation in Varanavata, in a specially built palace? I could always ensure that the palace was built of combustible material. Such a building could always catch fire *accidentally*, so that Kunti & Sons would meet their maker, leaving Hastinapura safe, strong and undivided. True, it was not necessary for Nakula and Sahadeva to be thus sacrificed, but sadly they had to be the collateral damage.

The trick was to carry out the plot with not a soul the wiser. But this was easier said than done. The plan had two significant challenges. For one, it would take a whole year from concept to commissioning, during which period, a lot could go wrong. And the plan could leak. Secondly, it required several souls to be in on the secret.

I had to ensure that none of my brothers (except Sushasana) or even Karna was aware of the plot. Not that I did not trust them. It is just that I did not fancy burdening them with the weight of what were essentially my duty and my baggage to carry as the crown prince. Sushasana and Uncle Shakuni I had to bring in, for they were my closest aides and advisors. And I also enlisted the services of a dependable architect and two or three select spy-like courtiers, for whom carrying out the king's edict is neither illegal nor immoral, simply a royal duty to be performed, and of course a sure way to career advancement and riches.

With all the preparations in place, the die was cast. And there was nothing to do but wait for the earth to complete its jog around the sun. And sure enough, a year from the time the idea was seeded, the plan came to fruition and the Varanavata palace was burnt to cinders. The smouldering ashes contained the sad remains of the bones of Aunt Kunti and the five half-brothers; the cancer growing on Hastinapura had been surgically removed – or so I thought.

9

The life of royals is bound within narrower amplitudes of emotions and gestures than that allowed common folk ...
It is this narrow amplitude that gives them an aristocratic bearing ...

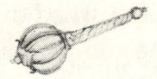

King Drupada of Panchala had arranged an elaborate swayamvara for his daughter Draupadi, also known as Panchali. The challenge for the princess's hand was one that called for the highest level of archery skills.

Word of Panchali's beauty had spread far and wide. I had been a big-time silent admirer of Panchali's, for I had fallen for her beauty ever since I had glimpsed a painting of hers – which a member of my secret service had passed on to me and which I had secreted away. The portrait had been painted by a remarkable painter who had observed Panchali sitting in her garden, entirely unmindful of being observed, and then gone on to paint her from his memory. She was known to be a dusky beauty and the painter had lent an iridescent bluish glow to her skin. If Panchali was even half as beautiful as the picture, she would be no less than a princess among the goddesses of the heavens. If ever an artist had done justice to a beautiful maiden, here was the evidence.

And then I had had a fleeting glimpse of the real Panchali in a faraway realm where we had gone to attend a royal wedding, when I was sixteen. Panchali was hardly in my mind that morning, and yet providence had us cross paths in the most unexpected manner.

We had both been on our morning perambulations, she with her friends and I with mine, she walking clockwise and I anticlockwise along the perimeter of the large garden, when someone from my retinue urgently but respectfully poked me in the rib and pointed her out to me. I lifted my head just as Panchali also turned directly towards me, and then she had passed. The glimpse had been but momentary, and yet etched permanently in my memory, as if burnt into my soul. I was not even sure whether she had looked at me or through me. I wasn't sure if the glance was arrogant or contemptuous. Was that gaze hot as coals or cold as snow? But the net result of it was that I stopped mid-track, as if I had run into a wall. My breath was taken away in one go and my heart fairly stopped beating.

Did I imagine the blue tint in the transparency of her left ear in the morning sunlight or was her skin really translucent? Did she walk by or float by? Was it my imagination or had I seen ten pearls on her feet, in two sets of fives, just drift away? Were those dainty arms of hers, parallel from shoulder to the elbows and then tapering rapidly to the wrists, for real or cast in blue copper by a most masterly craftsman? Was that a whiff of fragrance from her very person, or a puff of wind carrying the scent of flowers in the garden? This was a woman who could redefine even the heavens for the gods. Ah Panchali! She was indescribably more beautiful than her portrait! The painter had perhaps little skill. His painting did little justice to her.

That one glimpse wrenched all sleep away from my nights (though, truth be told, it was during one such sleepless night that the Varanavata inspiration had come to me). It was as if after that one glance, there was nothing else left for my eyes to behold. But then again, what else was there to see anyway? Do beautiful women have that effect on all men? Or was I especially drawn to her? Are beautiful women similarly affected by handsome men like me? What was the effect I was having that very minute on Panchali? Surely she must be going through some similar sentiments? Surely Hastinapura was a much larger and mightier kingdom than Panchala? Surely that would weigh in my favour in winning her affections? Surely she had heard of me? Surely we were made for each other? Who else would be good enough for her anyway?

It was as if with that one look, I had somehow come undone. Her recurring image became a constant distraction, allowing me little peace. Was I smitten? It was obvious that I was. Was Panchali feeling the same way about me? There was no way to know. I made rounds of the same circuit several times in the next few days, hoping to run into her one more time, but failed to make a second connect. Oh, what could I do about it?

Alas! There was nothing for me to do but wait. For one, both of us were still far too young for me to entertain thoughts of matrimony. Second, in our times, at least as far as royalty was concerned, the prerogative of choosing a partner was the woman's. After all it is she who leaves her home and accompanies her husband to his domain. It is she who gives up her parents and her people to embrace a new man, a new family and a new establishment. Hence, the social norms demanded that she have a right to choose her husband; and men waited for fair maidens to choose their partner during the swayamvara – literally meaning choosing one's own partner – the event organized for a princess to choose her husband from among a selection of suitors. This was a fair practice and respectful to women. So there had been nothing for me to do about Panchali but to wait for her swayamvara.

When Panchali's swayamvara was announced, I was nearly nineteen. In the intervening three years between then and my first sighting of her, I had had a million unsettling questions – all either starting or ending with Panchali – buzz around my head. Though I managed to keep my sentiments largely to myself, those years were my longest.

When Drupada formally announced Panchali's swayamvara and our family received the much-awaited invite, I had little doubt that at last the time for making Panchali my wife had come. After all, there aren't too many things that crown princes desire and do not get. That my yearning for her was entirely unrequited didn't bother me; so certain was I of winning Panchali's hand. How could it be otherwise? I mean, who else was there in Bharatavarsha to claim greater eligibility than me? I was the crown prince of Hastinapura, no less. I was an all-round warrior. I was handsome, I knew. All those coy glances of the women around one's palace let you know pretty early in life when you are handsome. Why, there wasn't a girl in the palace who would not try and find some excuse to catch me alone in my quarters. Besides, by now, my moustache was a luxuriant growth curving from the sides of my mouth down towards the chin and then climbing up in a swish to my cheeks, fusing with my sideburns. We had been told that the swayamvara involved exhibiting the highest archery skills. With Karna being my friend and Arjuna dead (as I thought at the time), I had little doubt that I would hold my own among the lot present at the ceremony. Yes, I knew it – Panchali would soon be my wife!

So I put my entourage together – my hundred brothers, Karna and Shakuni and I – and proceeded in grand style to the venue. The state of Panchala occupied the territory to the north-east of Hastinapura, between the Himalayas and the Ganga. We had a long journey ahead, but time simply flew, what with all the hunting, picnicking, game meat and wine arranged for the journey.

The swayamvara venue was elaborate. The air was celebratory, with thousands upon thousands of lamps lit all around even during daytime, and the smoke and fragrance of the burning oils thick in the air. It was the time of the year when the gentle warmth from the glow of the many lamps was soothing. The setting had a dream-like quality, with brightly coloured drapes for decor, soft notes of soothing instrumental music and mellow aromas of delectable deep-fried nibbles wafting through the air. I could see Shishupala of Chedi, Jarasandha of Magadha,

Bhagadatta of Pragjyotisha, Shalya of Madra, Jayadratha of Sindhu (who, by the way, had married our dear sister Sushala), and many others, both known and unknown to me, talking loudly and cracking jokes, subtly showing off their machismo just in case Panchali or one of her close friends was watching.

They were all highly placed royal suitors, no doubt, but none I needed to fear seriously. Most of them were too old, too fat, too timid or simply not good enough for Panchali. My friend Balarama and his younger brother Krishna were there too, but not as competitors, I was sure. Not only were they both too old for Panchali, but Krishna, who was a friend of Drupada, would be an unlikely suitor, and Balarama was no archer but a master of mace (and my guru of sorts in that particular weapon). I asked Balarama jovially what his brother was doing there. God knows he had enough girlfriends and wives to last ten lives, one would have thought! Balarama responded with the same jocularity, saying, maybe when it came to Panchali, other girlfriends and wives mattered little. I said I wouldn't know because, for me, this was going to be a first, and we both winked and slapped each other's shoulders in bonhomie.

Shortly, the loud hum of a conch shell blowing drew our attention to the commencement of the swayamvara. Panchali made her entry dressed in bridal red. And what an entry! Oh Panchali! She was right there walking in at last, in small dainty steps typical of beautiful girls who seem more to glide along the floor than walk. She looked more stunning than any picture; more surreal than a fantasy; more beautiful than possible!

Duryodhana

My heart was beating like an ironsmith's hammer. But when you have fantasized about an ethereally beautiful woman for long and she is nearly within reach, such palpitations are perhaps to be expected. Every part of her was bedecked with jewels and precious stones. Watching her indescribably exquisite personage, I recall a random thought crossing my mind, wondering if all the jewellery upon her was adding to her beauty or taking away from it. It was as if you could neither add to her magnificence, nor take away from it. She represented the absolute in beauty, if you know what I mean.

I was laughing much – not from the intoxication of the wine which was flowing freely, but from my confidence that at last the time had come when Panchali would be mine and mine alone. And yet, as the hour of prize-taking neared, why was the confidence curdling rapidly like milk that had received a squirt of lemon? Was I nervous? Or just expectant? Was I on top of the world? Or at the nadir of an abyss? Was I afloat? Or swimming? Drowning, perhaps? Why was I biting my nails? Or tucking the loose strand of hair behind my ear, and curling my moustache for the hundredth time? Oh, what was I going through? Or was it all a dream? A part of me laughed at myself, at what a mere girl had done to me in a matter of seconds. But then how could a man not be so affected when only a very short interval of time separated him from *Panchali*?

Panchali looked around, as if searching for someone specific. Surely she was looking for me? But here I was! Surely she could see me, recognize me? Maybe she was looking for me but could not identify me after all this time. But why did her gaze just sweep past me instead of stopping at me? Couldn't she see in my eyes that I was *the one*? Surely she realized that she and I were a natural match? Why were her eyes still searching beyond me? What was wrong with her?

I got the impression she had seen me, recognized me, read my face, and was mildly amused. Or was it my imagination? Ah, the foolish heart of the unrequited. It is only from the safe distance of time that I realize what a pathetic figure I, as a man unreciprocated in love, must have cut.

And then the contest for the swayamvara was announced in the wake of some more conch blowing. The test was elaborate and when I listened to the terms of the competition, my heart sank. The task seemed nearly impossible to crack. It involved stringing and loading an arrow upon a mighty bow – the ancient Kindhara of Shiva, no less, shaped like the upper lip of a beautiful mouth – looking down into a swirling pool of water at the rotating reflection of a furiously spinning fish high above one's head, accounting for the refraction of water, and shooting the arrow into the eye of the fish overhead through a narrow aperture cut out in a shield, without taking one's eyes off the reflection.

I had my first pang of uncertainty. I was a decent enough archer; better than many or even most, perhaps, but not, as I have already said, in the class of a Karna or even an Arjuna (who thankfully wouldn't or couldn't spoil my party). And this seemed a job for the very best. My palpitations increased thinking about failure. I began to sweat. My hands were clammy. Suddenly my fine silk robe was drenched in sweat. Would my dream be fulfilled? Would I be up to this?

Duryodhana

Predictably, not even the most valiant of the royalty present came anywhere near stringing the bow, leave alone loading the arrow, never mind shooting into the eye of the feverishly spinning fish. Shishupala managed to string the bow, but that's as far as he went before he gave up in exhaustion. Jarasandha managed to string the bow and even lifted the bow skyward and managed to release an arrow; but the arrow went nowhere, falling limply at his feet as he was hardly able to muster enough tension in the taut string of the mighty bow. Shalya fared little better. Nobody seemed to come anywhere near the task. Prince after prince, king after king – they came, they tried and they failed. What was Drupada playing at? Did he want a beautiful spinster sitting at home forever?

Presently, it was my turn. By now, I had no illusion about the task. I knew the limit of my archery skills and this boot was obviously too big for me. And yet, having come all the way, it made little sense not to try. Who knew, I could get lucky! I forced myself dejectedly to the contraption, knowing fully well that, for reasons best known to himself, Drupada did not want his daughter married. I managed to pick up the heavy bow and, to cut a long story short, fared no better than Shalya or Jarasandha. My arrow probably did leave the bow with respectable tension, but got stuck near the hole on the shield. Not much consolation, that!

The resounding crash of my dream, all that I had aspired for, memories of all those nights of sleepless fantasies, all that heightened anticipation, the shame of failure, the newness of the emotion of shame and failure – I was drowned in a vortex of emotions I did not know could be contained in the depths of one's heart. The world looked meaningless. The sun which had seemed bright earlier seemed dimmer now; the music in the background which had sounded pleasant earlier was discordant now. The sights that had looked beautiful before seemed like so many garish blotches. I wished the world would be shrouded in a vast, black blanket into which I could curl up and go to sleep and never wake up. A million sentiments and thoughts of life without Panchali tore through me in those short few moments.

Nevertheless, another part of me took charge of the situation and I urgently asked Karna, who I knew was probably the best archer, then or ever, to take his turn. I knew that the test was hardly beyond him. He was somewhat nonplussed, for he had probably already gauged my eagerness as well as the subsequent disappointment. He was as close a friend to me as I was capable of making. However, Karna seemed to hold me in special regard, probably because I had stood up for him against Arjuna. It was as if he felt in some way beholden to me, which was not necessarily a bad thing. What I had done was spontaneous and I never felt as if I had gone out of my way to do him a favour. However, I realized that such a sentiment in him was only likely to bind him closer to me, which would be of great value to me and Hastinapura. So I never saw the need to go out of my way to dispel his sentiment of gratitude. Who says mild deviousness does not play a role even in the best of friendships?

But to return to my narration, Karna regarded me

uneasily for a few uncertain moments, knowing he could probably pierce the fish's eyes with as much exertion as piercing a piece of meat with a fork. He was loath to go for a prize that I had craved but lost moments ago. I was appreciative of that sentiment, but nevertheless keen for him to win Panchali's hand. This is perhaps because (and I had not argued out all this cogently in my mind at the time, mind you) even if I could not win her hand, at least she would remain accessible – and I mean it honourably – as my friend's wife. She would not be completely lost to me. I would be able to get glimpses of her from time to time, speak with her off and on, laugh with her now and then, and so, have an infinitesimal part of her always available to me. Such is the way of a desperate mind harbouring freshly crushed love. You may tame wild horses more easily than a heart gone berserk.

Karna – the tall and handsome Karna, the Karna of the golden tresses, armour plates and earrings, the majestic and magnificent Karna – proceeded towards the bow with measured steps. The fame of his archery skills had already spread far, and many an eye gazed at him with an admixture of anticipation, envy, expectation, dejection and apprehension natural towards one who is certain to be taking away a cherished trophy. I thought I caught Krishna, sitting not too far from me, catch Panchali's eye and shake his head ever so gently – or was it entirely my imagination? Unaware of a hundred gazes trained upon him, nonchalant, Karna simply walked up to the mighty bow, paid obeisance to it with folded hands, lifted it with his left hand without visible effort, picked up an arrow from the adjacent quiver, balanced it upon the string, raised the bow skyward, bent his head and gazed into the pool of water, pulled the string all the way to his ears and took aim.

You could hear a feather drop. The music stopped. Every eye in the assembly was riveted on Karna, when suddenly a piercing voice cried out, 'Stop!'

All eyes turned from Karna to the source of this high-pitched cry, which it turned out had emanated from the throat of Panchali, who had risen from where she was seated.

'Stop, Sutaputra!' she said, then turned towards her father and continued in a strident voice, which seemed entirely inconsistent with her dainty appearance: 'Father, I do hope you have not sent invites for my swayamvara to charioteers and such? Don't you know, that man with the bow – the so-called Angaraj – is really a Sutaputra? Do you really expect me to give my hand to the likes of him? Father, this is a swayamvara of a princess. By the right that the institution of the swayamvara vests in me, I refuse to let a Sutaputra compete as an equal in this assembly. Please let him not defile the mighty bow any more with his touch. If there is no worthy king who can pick up the bow and shoot at a simple target, that's fine by me. I can wait for a worthy suitor to come along. But please do not demean me by allowing all and sundry a go at the task.'

Saying so, she took her seat again, daintily, trying to keep a serene visage, certain that she had played her part and from there on, her father would handle it all. Her words fell into my ears like molten lead. She sounded not only raucous, but also tutored. I fleetingly noticed Panchali look first at her father and then at Krishna, who wore a mysterious half-smile. The tone and tenor of her voice had suddenly taken away a lot from her desirability. And then there was the deliberate insult she had spewed at my friend. Was the entire world conspiring to break his spirit? But why? He had done nobody any harm. He was the finest man one could meet. The most honourable and chivalrous you could find. He was strikingly handsome, to tell the truth, more handsome than any of us Kauravas and all those kings present there. He was more dignified than a majestic lion. He was polite to a fault. As Angaraj, he was in fact a king. It was obvious that he would have pierced the eye of that silly fish in no time, which is what they had wanted the potential suitor to do, didn't they? So why was this woman insulting him so? What better husband was she aiming for? Was there something that I did not or could not see? Was there a meaning to that smile on Krishna's lips or was it my imagination? Was Panchali waiting for someone else, whom she secretly fancied, just as I had secretly fancied her? Who? What? Why? Why not? And a million such questions rose inside me, vainly seeking answers.

And in that single moment, all my love for that woman turned to hatred. Perhaps this is also a trait of proud royals. What you cannot or do not attain, you learn to hate. And Panchali's vicious words, spewed at innocent Karna just then, made hating her a lot easier. Wave after wave of uncontrollable rage surged within me like bile in a dyspeptic stomach. I was angry for Karna. I did not know I could get so angry for someone else. The man had grown closer to me than I had realized. Perhaps he was not just a strategic friend I had made to serve a certain state interest after all. He was a friend who could, and did, move me to emotions like sympathy and anger.

I was confused about the sum total of my emotions. Panchali's treatment of Karna had angered me like nothing had ever before, and yet this realization that Karna after all meant to me something more than a means to a selfish end seemed to evoke in me a deep sense of happiness and fulfilment I had never experienced before. Enmeshed among all these emotions was a lingering, strange and deep sadness at the loss of Panchali, albeit now a hated Panchali, whom I had adored in private for so long. It is funny how you can feel the loss of someone or something that wasn't yours to begin with!

In the meantime, Karna turned his head just a touch towards Panchali, and then towards King Drupada, retracted the arrow, put it aside, but continued pulling at the string of the bow, up to his chin ... up to his ears ... and beyond when, with a twang that would put the most deafening thunder to shame, the taut string broke and the hall reverberated in sympathy. Karna let the bow – that had suddenly lost its tension – spring out of his hold as if letting go of a live serpent, and let it clatter unceremoniously to the ground, and majestically walked back with a twisted smile on his face! This was a spectacle that would generate ample gossip for generations.

I have told you earlier, and I will say it again that, in general, royals are trained to hold their emotions in check like well-bred horses. That is, we do not even smile easily, leave alone laugh aloud. Neither do we make a public spectacle of our grief. Homages and gifts do not sway us readily, nor do fears and threats cause us visible anxiety. We do not pay tributes and compliments easily, nor are we given to more than minimal gestures. It is as if our entire life is bound within narrower amplitudes of emotions and gestures than that allowed to common folk, and it is this tight narrowing of amplitude that gives us our aristocratic bearing and lends us what is perceived as royal dignity.

The same attributes in non-royals would ordinarily make them look like stuffed snobs. But not Karna. By refusing to be provoked by Panchali's disdainful smirk, and not giving her the satisfaction of succeeding in her obvious objective of showing him down, Karna had provided the highest testimony of his royal bearing – Angaraj or not. It just occurred to me that even before I had declared him Angaraj, he had shown exactly the same refined bearing by remaining unflappable throughout Drona's rants. Had the young man reacted to the guru's needling, the round would have gone in favour of the latter. By refusing to be incited, Karna had made Drona look petty and pedestrian. Neither then nor now did the noble bearing appear put-on in Karna. It was as natural to him as a smile is to a shy maiden. Nobody present at the swayamvara would have doubted that Karna belonged to the highest class of royalty, found accidentally by Adhiratha, whatever nonsense Panchali may have uttered.

But don't misunderstand me. None of what I have said means that royalty is more tolerant of insults than the rest of the human tribe. It is not. Just the opposite, in fact. It is just that when it comes to social insults, true royal blood rarely trades insults face to face. It bides its time, preferring to address the larger picture rather than react to a narrow frame. Besides, if I knew Karna, he was far too chivalrous to show his displeasure to a lady and this resolve was obvious in his calm demeanour. I felt prouder of my friend than ever before or after. He had it in him to be my equal and I resolved then and there to shed the slightly supercilious air I had assumed as his benefactor. It dawned upon me in those few moments that Karna was royalty personified – with or without me. It had merely been my good fortune to have formally endorsed his royal aspect and gained his undying friendship in the bargain.

By now, a rumble of protest had started gathering momentum about the virtually impossible swayamvara assignment. There was also unhappiness at the great Karna being denied his chance. In the midst of all the din, a poorly dressed Brahmin quietly rose from the crowd and strode with long, majestic steps towards the podium where the whole apparatus was set up. The tall man had a sturdy build, though he looked as if he could do with a meal or two ... or even three. But his gait had a strangely familiar and very un-Brahminical swagger. The man reached the podium, calmly lifted the bow, strung it with a new string, loaded the heavy bow with the arrow, directed the whole contraption upwards, looked down into the pool of water, drew the bowstring to his ears and let go of the string, as if this was just another day at office. The whole thing seemed very anti-climactic, except that there was a ringing twang. The eye of the fish had been rendered useless for all potential use.

Surprisingly, Panchali had made no objection. The entire

hall was stunned into silence. Everything went into slow motion. It was as if time stood still or had at least slowed down. What was going on? Who was this Brahmin with such un-Brahminical skills in archery? And what was Panchali doing, rejecting the great Angaraj but deigning to place her garland around the neck of a wretched Brahmin? But she went ahead and, with a radiant smile upon her lips, did precisely that.

But realization dawned on everyone almost simultaneously. Why, this archer could be none other than Arjuna! After all, except Karna, he was the only other man capable of rising to the task set by Drupada for his daughter's hand. And that explained that swagger and the gait. But hang on, wasn't Arjuna dead? He obviously was not!

We had from time to time heard rumours of Aunt Kunti and her sons having escaped from the fire at the palace of Varanavata, which I had all along dismissed as unadulterated nonsense. But apparently it wasn't!

It would be some time before all the pieces would fall in place. I mentioned to you earlier that Hastinapura then, just as any city in Bharatavarsha today, wasn't a place where trusts could be held safe for long. Apparently, despite all the meticulous care I had taken to execute my plan, within moments of the closed-door meeting I had held on the strategy, one wise traitor had rushed to the Kuntiputras to profit from the inside information. Things haven't changed among our people even today, have they? Armed with this advance information, Aunt Kunti and her sons had evidently escaped in the nick of time, setting fire to the combustible palace themselves, leaving an old woman and her five sons, who had providentially sought shelter for the night at the palace, to burn in their stead. They escaped through a tunnel in the palace that they had furtively dug earlier for the very purpose, and eventually proceeded to live incognito, disguised as Brahmins, to save themselves from being discovered by me, in the household of a Brahmin in the town of Ekachakrapura. This incidentally had some collateral benefit to me, for no one had at the time overtly held me responsible for the fire. Had their escape been known just when it happened, I may have been suspected of having engineered the attempt. But now, with the episode safely a year behind, there was no finger pointed at me.

I spoke earlier of Vyasa's possible bias in recording facts in the Mahabharata. You can see for yourself that while the sage has been quite long on maligning me for my attempt to kill Aunt Kunti & Co., he is terribly short on commentary when it comes to the far more reprehensible act of them deliberately letting an innocent mother and her five grown sons burn in their stead. Vyasa does not trouble himself with trifling details like whether or not causing the death of an innocent mother and her five young sons – whose only fault was that they had trustingly sought shelter with Aunt Kunti and her sons on the fateful night – to save their own lives is consistent with the nobility of actions he accords in abundance to them in the epic. Whatever happened to the dharma to never harm those who come under your protection?

Which is worse: the casual killing of six innocent souls

who came to you for shelter, or the killing of six individuals who are threatening to divide your kingdom?

Not that I ever regretted my Varanavata actions. If I have regrets at all, they are merely that my excellent and carefully laid plot failed because of a snitch, and that the cowardly Kuntiputras knowingly sacrificed six innocent lives just so they could themselves live, chasing a kingdom that was never theirs to begin with.

In any case, if I had any doubt that the Kuntiputras were alive, it was removed when four more Brahmins stood up from the crowd – one of them looking like a slightly emaciated prize-fighter, a head taller than most – and joined the newly betrothed couple.

Ah fate, will I ever live this double ... triple ... quadruple tragedy down? I had lost Panchali, my first love, or rather my only love to date. Worse, I had lost her to none other than Arjuna. Worse still, Arjuna and his brothers were alive and kicking and my scheme had collapsed like a pack of cards. Hastinapura's danger, which I thought I had extinguished, was in fact burning bright. And lastly, as if in some parody of crowning glory, my good friend Karna had been viciously insulted, and that too in an open house of kings and princes – for no fault other than for being who he was.

But then again, it does not behove kings to mope for long. As I said earlier, proud kings do not long for what is not attainable; rather, they intrinsically learn to dislike what is inaccessible. Fortunately, Panchali's venomous words, her spiteful insult of Karna and her preference for

Arjuna over Karna had worked on me like a slap works on the face of a drunkard. In a trice, I shrugged off the last traces of Panchali's presence from my psyche. That the Kuntiputras weren't dead was damn inconvenient. But it had to be dealt with in time. As for Karna's insult, I was furious, but how does one hold a grudge against a woman ... and what shape does one give that grudge? But boy, would I love to see the day that arrogance was watered down a peg or two.

I held my emotions in check and waited for the commotion to die down. No one in the assembly was so daft that he did not see that the rules of the swayamvara had been bent like a cow's hind leg to keep everyone out except Arjuna. Whom Panchali wanted to marry was her prerogative, of course. But nothing gave Drupada the right to waste the time of kings and princes from all over Bharatavarsha who had travelled for days, only to be insulted with a task designed exclusively for Arjuna. Drupada had clearly used them for his own agenda by devising a filter that was impermeable to all but Arjuna, with Karna crudely excluded.

It dawned on me that Drupada must have heard rumours of the Kuntiputras escaping the Varanavata fire and devised the swayamvara only to entice Arjuna, whom he was focused on acquiring as his son-in-law. Suddenly, several pieces fell in place.

The story went back to the days when Drupada and Drona were both students in the same gurukul and grew very close as friends. When they completed their education and it was time to go their separate ways – Drupada to learn more about statecraft and eventually rule his kingdom Panchal, and Drona to pursue higher education and pursue his vocation as a teacher – the parting was emotional, and young Drupada, tears in his eyes, earnestly said to his friend, something to the effect: 'My dear Drona! Ah, how difficult it is to part from a friend. We may be parting ways today, but let us forever remember that physical parting need not imply a break in friendship, which is more about the meeting of minds and hearts. Please visit my kingdom at any time and I would be more than happy, nay gratified, to share my kingdom with you!'

Drona it seems hugged his friend for his affection and went his way. He went on to train himself as a teacher of all shaastras, especially shastra (weapons), shaastra and rajya shaastra. He married and in due course had a very able son, Ashwatthama. But Drona's career did not take off as well as he had hoped, and he and his family fell upon very bad times. There was a time when there was nothing to eat at home and the family had to go to bed hungry. It was then that his wife urged him to visit the court of his childhood friend, Drupada – of whom Drona spoke very fondly and very often – to offer his services in war craft.

Apparently, Drona tread hundreds of miles and landed, in a highly unkempt state, in the court of Drupada. He managed to get past the palace gates by referring to the king on first-name terms, thus intimidating the guards. When he was ushered into the court, he announced himself as the king's best friend before the entire assembly and offered his services to train the kingdom's entire military. Perhaps if Drona had appeared before Drupada exactly as he had looked a couple of decades ago, as a teenager, the king may have recognized him. But caught during a busy day at court, and in a moment of complete amnesia, Drupada failed to recognize, in the bearded and unkempt vagabond Brahmin, his childhood friend.

The very idea that the dishevelled vagrant Brahmin, making exaggerated claims, could ever have been his friend seemed far-fetched. The truth was that favour seekers came in all shapes and sizes, with all sorts of tall stories to kings.

Drupada patronizingly told the Brahmin that he did not recall when or how they could have met earlier, gently letting him know that friendships were possible only among equals, and that he would be very happy to give him enough gold in alms from the state treasury to support him and his impoverished family.

Drona had very good reason to be incensed. He turned around and left abruptly, but not before promising to remind Drupada of their friendship the hard way.

Looking back, I remembered that when we had all completed our education with Drona, he had, as guru dakshina, asked Arjuna to bring back Drupada as a prisoner, and had sent his disciple along with a large contingent of soldiers to fight his former friend. Arjuna managed this; and when Drupada was brought to Drona, trussed up and all, the teacher took his time jogging Drupada's memory. He finally set Drupada free in exchange for half his kingdom, and brought home the fact that now that they were equals, Drupada should have no objection to the friendship. The Panchala king, though penitent about his amnesia, never forgot the insults Drona had heaped upon him. He vowed to get even.

Aha, so Drupada must have planned to ensnare Arjuna as his son-in-law so that Drona would not be able to use Arjuna a second time against him. He was also known to be training his son Dhrishtadyumna with the single-minded purpose of assuaging the family honour by slaying Drona some day. And here was foolish Arjuna taking for a wife the woman whose father and brother breathed with the single purpose of killing the very teacher whose great pet he was! Ah, strange are the ways the dice of life fall.

I was feeling disoriented. I didn't particularly like Drona. Even less did I like Arjuna. I had been madly in love with Panchali until half an hour ago. And now I hated her. I was hurting for Karna. I was angry for him. And now I also hated Drupada, for he had denied me the woman I had loved once and, what is more, denied her even to Karna – unfairly. And, as if rubbing salt on my wounds, he had given her away to Arjuna. But if Drupada had sworn enmity to Drona, shouldn't one of them be my friend?

The visiting kings and princes were upset about the mean spirit of the swayamvara which had wasted their time and made them look like fools, and they were letting Drupada know how they felt, loudly and clearly. Wily Krishna – who had not spoken a word when noble Karna was being insulted by a chit of a girl – was at his best, cajoling and bullying the unhappy kings and princes, trying to restore order and a semblance of peace, all with a knowing half-smirk.

I will be lying if I do not confess to some vicarious sense of satisfaction at Panchali's fate when I heard what happened after she had chosen Arjuna. Apparently, soon after she had garlanded the Brahmin, aka, Arjuna, the five brothers, with Panchali in their wake, rushed back to Ekachakrapura to share the good news with their mother. Bhima, the ever-enthusiastic lout, shouted from the hallway before entering. Something to the effect, 'Ma, look what we have brought!' And Kunti, used to Bhima forever bringing home the spoils of his hunts, responded perfunctorily: 'Whatever it is, you brothers share it among yourselves as usual.'

And that's how Panchali married one and got four for free. Each of the brothers either already had, or would go on to have, several other wives. Served her right, I thought, so that even my hatred for her was considerably mitigated.

After returning from the disastrous expedition to Panchala, I was depressed for a while. But time passes and life moves on. And so did I. In due course I went on to marry and start my own family. But if you must have the details, well, it went like this. It was Uncle Shakuni who brought the news of the swayamvara to me. Bhanumati, the beautiful daughter of Bhagadatta – the powerful king of Pragjyotisha, your present-day Kashi – was hosting a swayamvara. I had not yet recovered from my embarrassment at Draupadi's ceremony. So I told Uncle that I was in no mood for any more fanciful tests of archery. Mama Shakuni smiled and told me that there was no such test in this case; that beautiful Bhanumati would be choosing her husband from among the hopefuls based on the brief of valour, wealth and versatility of each of the kings present that she will be introduced to, alongside their miniature painting. This sounded more promising and I repaired forthwith to Pragjyotisha along with Karna and Ashwatthama, if only to distract myself. As an afterthought, I asked a strong army to follow in my wake, just in case ...

We found Bhagadatta's kingdom prosperous, or rather opulent. We were welcomed most lavishly and our comforts were taken good care of. The populace looked happy and well off. The fields were green, the plains supplied with plenty of water and the forests were replete with rich game.

Asoka, Bhishmaka, Jarasandha, Kapotaroman, Satadhanwan, Shrugalraja, Shishupala, Vakra, and many other rich and powerful kings from the length and breadth of Bharatavarsha had assembled in the beautiful city to try their luck.

The terms of the swayamvara were simple. Bhanumati was free to garland the first prince or king she found acceptable, without having to check out each and every suitor. As a consequence, everyone present was dressed extravagantly and gesturing exaggeratedly in the hope of being the first one to catch her attention when she entered. The most powerful of kings were seated in the first row.

When the swayamvara commenced and Bhanumati made her elegant entry into the hall, she didn't exactly set my heart on fire. But the effect she had on me was similar to what cool spring water has on the parched throat of a man lost in an unknown terrain, who hadn't quite realized he was thirsty. In contrast, my first encounter with Panchali had been like the high you get after a quick dose of rich wine. But now that I was sober of the Panchali intoxication, and wasn't even looking for another cup of the wine, so to speak, this fresh spring water seemed to be exactly what I needed. But soon my throat went dry again. Bhanumati was entering from the far end of the hall. This meant that I would be among the last suitors she would notice. Given that there were many handsome and valiant kings and princes seated before me, why, the innocent girl might decide on one of the sods long before she saw me! The cup of wine had been denied me earlier. Would providence deny me the glass of water too? I had to do something about it.

Young as she was, she seemed overawed by the presence of so many men, all keenly boring their eyes into her. Many of them were her father's age. A few even her grandfather's. It was clear that the poor thing was completely at a loss as to whose neck she must grace her garland with. She was glancing all around her, bewildered, as she walked down the first row. Except her own judgement which just then she seemed completely incapable of exercising, there was none to guide her with the very decision of her life. By now, she stood very close to where I sat, my heart a lump in my throat.

And then it is as if a super-Suyodhana took charge of a lesser one. With the memory of rejection by Panchali still fresh, I was in no mood to become a serial discard of pretty maidens. Nor was I going to let anyone else score over me once again. I simply had to whisk her away by force. If you are shocked, rest assured that abducting beautiful brides from swayamvara scenes was an accepted royal tradition of the Kshatriyas. Why, our grandsire Bhishma himself had done it. So would Arjuna later. And so had scores of others before and after me. The justification for this came from the fact that in general swayamvaras of this kind which had no specific test-like precondition (unlike Panchali's), the bride looked for nothing but visible or proven evidence of valour from the kings and princes present. And if any of them could simply sweep her off her feet, even if literally so, in the face of opposition from anyone who may dare stop him, why, the maiden would have surely got her evidence.

So, acting from my gut, I simply stepped forth, took Bhanumati by her slender wrist, pulled her towards me, took her upon my shoulder in a single fluid movement, her weight scarcely more than a sunbird's feather, turned, and openly dared anyone to stop me and, signalling Karna and Ashwatthama to guard my back, deliberately marched towards my chariot.

It is interesting how Mother Nature loves to play out her own laws of unintended consequences. Caught in our egos and narcissism, we ascribe much of what happens or does not happen in life to our actions and inactions. In our naiveté, we feel compelled to think that the world is influenced by our deeds alone. Even when there is no causality whatever, and things happen or do not happen purely at random, we try and attribute causality to our sundry gods. And yet the truth is that much of what happens in life is random and an unintentional consequence of plain noise in the universe.

Take my circumstance at the swayamvara, for example.

Moments ago, I had been ruing my choice of seat – situated so far from Bhanu's (that's the name by which I would call my wife in due course) point of entry. But it turned out that this had also put me closest to the exit, which suited my unfolding intent admirably. On the other hand, had I per chance sat closer to Bhanumati's point of entry, who is to say things would have unfolded exactly as they otherwise did? The long way to the exit could well have thwarted my abduction of Bhanumati, and she could have ended up as someone else's wife. Similarly, it was on a whim that I had asked a contingent of my army to follow me when I had left for Pragjyotisha. And then it turned out that the momentary decision earned me my wife.

Our life is made up of so many *ifs* that even if one out of a million *ifs* did not materialize, our life could well take a very different turn! *If only Shantanu had not ventured out for his hunt that particular morning; if only Satyavati had not washed her hair that particular morning; if only Vyasa had not been passing by Hastinapura palace on the day of my mother's confinement; if only I had sat at the far end from the exit at Bhanumati's swayamvara; if only I hadn't brought Karna and Ashwatthama and a contingent of the army along …* And yet, we in our wisdom ascribe disproportionate credit or disgrace to ourselves for our successes and failures, when the truth is, we are but bit actors in a grand scheme of random events.

But let me not digress.

Many kings, led by Jarasandha, tried to stop me, but Karna and Ashwatthama blocked them with our army that was camped in the outskirts of the city, giving me ample lead time to rush homeward with my prize.

Duryodhana

Bhagadatta did not mind my abducting his daughter one bit. On the contrary, he was happy that his daughter had found a worthy husband. Thanks to our matrimony, our kingdoms were cemented closer. As it would turn out, this was one of the most sensible spontaneous decisions I had ever taken or would ever take. Bhanumati proved to be everything a man would ever want in his wife. Why, even in her lifetime they gave her the moniker Satiratna – a jewel among devout wives.

So happy was I in my marriage that even though royals were permitted multiple wives, I never had reason to look at, never mind covet, another woman – except on one occasion on Balarama's urging.

10

Kingdoms are meant to be multiplied or consolidated; not divided

I had been married. Karna too got married around the same time to the beautiful Vrushali – a choice his parents Adhiratha and Radha made for him. Bhanumati had brought unadulterated joy into my life. And so had Vrushali into Karna's. Whatever the strains and stresses of our palace intrigues involving the Pandavas or other enemies, we ensured that none of it ever affected the quality of interactions our wives had with the spouses and families of anyone else in the Hastinapura palace. Our wives may have understood the taut undercurrents of our relationship with Kunti and the Kuntiputras, but they never spoke to us about any of it. That made our wives all the more special to us.

It hadn't been easy coming to terms with the shocking discovery that the Kuntiputras and Aunt Kunti were very much alive. I spent much time with Mama Shakuni and Sushasana, discussing the escape of the Kuntiputras, who were now back in Hastinapura. Clearly, there had been some leaks that needed looking into. Bharatavarsha was always a difficult place to keep secrets in, for here secrets have a tendency to leak like water from cupped palms. With the Kuntiputras having done their best to polarize the empire into pro and anti-Kaurava camps, bribing officials wasn't difficult. I perceive that things haven't changed much even today.

If there was some glitter in the gloom, it was that Yudhisthira and his brothers behaved as if they had returned from a year-long vacation. They never broached the subject of the Varanavata fire with my father or others, and I wasn't about to lose additional sleep (their return was giving me sleep loss as it was) trying to figure out why. But no sooner had they returned to Hastinapura than Aunt Kunti's frequent meetings with my father resumed with the regularity of a metronome.

The reason for these meetings soon became evident when my father called me for a closed-door conference one morning with Bhishma and Vidhura. If he knew anything about the Varanavata episode, he kept it to himself. He reminded me of Kunti Devi's long-standing demand for a share in the kingdom. Now she had distinctly climbed down and replaced her demand with an appeal – the appeal for any patch of land at all from the kingdom which could be carved out for them. In other words, they were willing to take what was given to them and stake no more claim upon Hastinapura and leave us all in peace. This, my father and his advisors thought, would be a smart way of settling the long-festering issue.

'We have that wild west section of our kingdom, the thick forest of Khandava. Why don't we give it to the

Pandavas, your own cousins, and lay this matter to rest? In any case, they will hardly pose us any threat and will make a useful ally. After all, the forest is nothing but the den of the very devils ...' said my father earnestly, with tears in his eyes.

The claim to the kingdom had been pared down to a claim for a share in it long ago. And now even that *claim* had been brought down to an *appeal*! Kunti Devi's tactic of appearing reasonable by whittling down her demand not once but twice was clearly beginning to work. In any case, my father, Bhishma and Vidhura – simpletons all – thought so! However, I was staunchly against the idea. 'Never give an inch to the enemy' had always been my motto. Anyone who has his sights on your kingdom is an enemy of the state. Anyone trying to fragment your realm is a traitor. Give a Kshatriya an inch and soon he would seek out a yard, I had no doubt. And all this I knew in my gut.

And yet, I was also the son of a blind father, and had a *heart*. My father's eyes watered easily, and it was not always easy to tell if they were tears of joy or of sorrow. Whatever kind they may have been, I found it difficult to resist them. Also, it is not easy to be consistently stubborn, and it is not unusual for the stubborn to wish to bask in the luxury of giving-in sometimes. And when three elders – one of them your own blind father – were making an earnest appeal to you, the time for such luxury seemed just right. After all, which human being does not seek the affiliation and affirmation of his family and friends from time to time?

Looking back, I wish I had remained resolute and not given in. But I did give in against my better judgment. In a rare moment of weakness as a twenty-year-old, I capitulated. My justification to myself was that after all a poor kingdom of sorts for my poor cousins of sorts may provide a good contrast, especially since Khandavaprastha was to our immediate western frontiers. But perhaps my deeper motivation was to show off to Panchali what she had missed out by rejecting me and marrying those five brothers, and for her to know that their kingdom was a gift of our munificence. Even then, I had a premonition that this could turn out to be the one big mistake of my life. Whatever my dislike for the five brothers, the blokes were hard working and not without their share of friends, and there was no telling what they could do with Khandavaprastha. It is strange how forecasts and wishes rarely come true, while premonitions invariably do!

To my father, I said, 'Father, I beg you once again not to refer to them as Pandavas, at least not in my presence, and certainly not as my cousins. You know they are neither. Be that as it may, if you wish to gift away Khandavaprastha to the Kuntiputras, I will go along, but only for your sake. Nothing but disaster will come of this generosity. Every time I look into the eyes of the Kuntiputras, I see only ambition, not allies. But I can certainly understand your own pressures from Kunti Devi. (I was secretly glad my father was blind! He seemed quite under the woman's spell even though he was blind. Imagine if he could see ... Kunti Devi's deific personality would have thoroughly done him in!) So please go ahead.'

Fallow and forested Khandava may have been. But thanks to some hard work and competitiveness typical of the have-nots, and some powerful friends like Indra, Krishna and particularly Vishwakarma, the renowned architect of the Deva kings, Yudhisthira and Co. succeeded in building a prosperous little empire with Indraprastha as their capital, just as I had half anticipated they might. After all, it is easier to create something new, especially if you are unabashed enough to see your rich friends as white knights. So with some help I am sure from Kubera, the treasurer of the monarchs, it is hardly surprising that the brothers were able to build their tiny kingdom.

Hastinapura was an ancient kingdom with the usual taxes on agriculture and trade. While we were a pretty prosperous and functioning state by every yardstick, a large state can almost never compete with a tiny city-state in attractiveness, with all its enthusiasm of new-found entrepreneurship, new gardens, broad and well-organized pathways, tax concessions, well-planned marketplaces and what have you. Pardon my metaphor, but an old state is like a matronly wife while a new city-state is like a young nubile maiden giving the come-hither. So some imaginative incentives from Indraprastha saw many of our best artists, artisans, teachers and accountants moving there. As a civilized state, there was little we could do to stop our citizens who chose to migrate.

But this prosperity of the five brothers worried me seriously now. Nor was my worry misplaced. Rumours of Bhima and Arjuna shaking hands with some of the smaller states were already beginning to reach my ears. The hands proffered by the Kuntiputras were good old iron hands in velvet gloves, combined with some lure of the lucre. And by the time we realized how strong Khandavaprastha had grown, they were on a roll, gathering momentum.

I had underestimated the speed with which Khandavaprastha had taken root and grown in strength, all along maintaining the façade of a small city-state. My father in any case had been blind to the rise of the Kuntiputras, never considering them a threat. Well, at least he was really blind. But I? I had been caught with leaden feet and had only myself to blame for not having pushed him sooner into fortifying Hastinapura's military might and its political alliances. Bhishma was growing old and had stopped going on military excursions to continue enriching and strengthening Hastinapura.

Clearly, contentment leads to complacency. Hastinapura had become too content in its prosperity to be hungry for more – a strategic error. I was realizing a shade late in the day that you either establish your superiority over lesser states or prepare to fade away as the lesser states establish their superiority over you. The Kuntiputras had made no such mistake and it would be only a matter of time before we were threatened by them. I understand your present-day corporations speak the same language.

I had not realized how confident Indraprastha had grown until one fine morning we received an invite for a Rajasuya Yajna being organized by Yudhisthira to underscore his supremacy as a potentate. We were *cordially* invited.

The rajasuya in our days was the calling card of a powerful king to announce to the world that he had arrived and wished to be the king of kings. It was a declaration of sovereignty over surrounding kingdoms. One either had to accept the invite or prepare to wage war with the ambitious monarch.

Against my better judgement, my father had prevailed upon me to give away Khandavaprastha to the Kuntiputras, who were now consolidating their might and turning against us. Had they regarded us as allies as my father had imagined, they would have consulted my father (as the eldest Kuru) at least for the sake of formality, if not actually invited him to perform the rajasuya with their support, and not gone on to perform it on their own.

They were displaying their independence by challenging us, for a rajasuya is nothing but an open threat and an attempt at domination. We were just one of the many other kingdoms to be conquered! My worst fears were now beginning to play out.

The cordial invite that fine morning was for us to go and genuflect before the Kuntiputras to accept their dominion over us, or else fight them. Since militarily we had not been seriously working on our alliances, we were not ready enough to fight them. We had no option but to bend.

If I were to create a museum of all my memorable mornings, I would not languish for want of exhibits. Among the prime exhibits would be the morning when Kunti Devi and her five sons trooped into our palace; the

Duryodhana

morning when I set my eyes upon Panchali for the first time; the one in which I suffered the dual shock of losing Panchali and finding out that the Kuntiputras were alive and kicking; and now I add to the collection *that morning* – the morning of the *cordial* invite to the Kuntiputras' rajasuya!

I recall marching up to my father and his advisors to tax them for their bright idea of giving away the *wilderness* of Khandavaprastha to Kunti & Sons against my better judgement. Now we had to suffer the ignominy of their dominance, as if watching their growth was not torture enough. Bhishma, Vidhura and my father could not appreciate the cause of my agitation. Father's argument went something like: 'After all, Yudhisthira is the eldest of the Kuru ('Kuru' being said a little feebly) boys; they have made a grand job of the little wild patch of land we had given them; they are unlikely to attack or annex us; under their suzerainty, we shall forever remain protected – so what's your problem?'

Under their suzerainty! How could I make them, or posterity thereafter understand that these arguments were precisely my problem? Why didn't these old fogies understand the simple fact that Yudhisthira was not a Panduputra or even a Kuru, leave alone being the eldest of them? The brothers had no claim on any patch of our land – fallow, forested or fertile. To accept another's suzerainty, to compromise the pride and honour of one's kingdom, to live under anybody's protection except one's own was a destiny worse than death for any proud king. I don't know if being physically blind also leads to the blindness of one's mind. But the rest of them were not even blind physically! So why couldn't they see the obvious? Why could they not read the writing on the wall when some time ago Bhima, helped by the sly and scheming Krishna, went and murdered Jarasandha – a friend of ours – for no apparent reason?

Why, I had been extremely careless not to have seen the larger picture as well. Jarasandha was the mighty ruler of Magadha towards the east of Bharatavarsha. He ran a just and grand empire, but was known to be a tough monarch. Well, you couldn't preside over Bihar even in those days with kid gloves. So tough he had to be. He was a learned and spiritual man at whose palace scholars and sages were welcome at any time of the day or night. This good king, who was minding his own business, was murdered by Bhima by stealth, on Krishna's prodding.

We were all bewildered when the news first trickled in. However, in the clarity of hindsight, the reason for the murder is clear. Jarasandha was a bitter enemy of the Yadavas. He had been continuously pushing back the Yadava kingdom of Surasena, forcing it to retreat from central Bharatavarsha to its western limits. The Yadavas lacked the military might to defeat Jarasandha. Wily Krishna, ever game for a dash of deviousness, saw an opportunity there to serve his own purpose through Indraprastha. So the cowherd told Bhima and Arjuna that killing Jarasandha was the only way to clear the way for Yudhisthira's rajasuya, on the pretext that Jarasandha was sure to challenge it. Being my friend, Jarasandha was also on the wrong side of the Kuntiputras, and Bhima and Arjuna took the bait. And that's how Krishna's Machiavellian plan to execute the Magadhan ruler was hatched.

Krishna, Bhima and Arjuna had gone on to secure entry into the king's palace by stealth, disguised as learned Brahmins. An unsuspecting Jarasandha had gladly admitted them into his abode. Once in, in order to avoid witnesses to the murder, they invited him for a meeting at midnight. Jarasandha who would never say no to scholars, and being the gracious host that he was, had duly come for the appointment, when he was challenged to a duel and killed by Bhima with help from Krishna.

Now let me hit the pause button here. You will surely want to ask me if stealth, deviousness and sly machinations weren't the very things *I* had used when I had tried to kill Bhima many years ago, and later the entire set of Kuntiputras and Kunti herself. So what am I complaining about?

Nothing; nothing at all. I am only trying to make you see that I was after all no different from them or vice versa. To found a kingdom which was never meant to be theirs and then for its *growth*, the Kuntiputras thought the murder of Jarasandha was justified. Then why has posterity held it against me if, for the *protection* of my kingdom, I had to resort to attempting a few murders myself? Neither their killing of Jarasandha, nor my attempts to kill the Kuntiputras amounted to murder. They were but pre-emptive strikes. And this is the case I have been trying to make – I was the same shade of grey as all the rest of them in the Mahabharata. So why have I been singled out as the arch villain?

But let me come back to my humiliation at having to accept the rajasuya invite. The shame was made a million times more hurtful because the invite was from the Kuntiputras plus Panchali – the very woman I had hoped would become my wife one day, and who had instead gone on to marry an entire community of five wannabe royal brothers rather than me or mighty Karna! How, oh, how could we – the state of Hastinapura – accept the supremacy of Indraprastha? Or that of the Kuntiputras, for that matter? The world has no inkling how much this raw wound hurt the very depths of my soul.

The truth was that we had allowed ourselves to be painted into a corner. I discussed it all with Mama Shakuni, Sushasana and Karna. Under the well-known terms of a rajasuya, not accepting the invitation would amount to challenging Indraprastha's might, together with that of its allies, and we were in no position to take on this mammoth challenge, at least for now. It was clear that at least for the time being, wisdom lay in strategic retreat and in accepting the invite. It nearly broke my heart to do so, but it had to be done.

And before long I had another of those memorable mornings when I entered Indraprastha for the first time. It was evident that the Kuntiputras had taken extra pains to be extravagant. Now I am neither averse nor a stranger to pomp and show myself. But I must confess that I was impressed at what Vishwakarma had accomplished in Indraprastha and what Maya, another great mystical designer, the architect of the Asura kings, had created at the venue of the event. Clearly, the setting was intended to overwhelm the invited upon whom the hosts were stamping their sovereignty.

Duryodhana

Maya means illusion, and Maya was known to be a master of illusions. Living up to his name and reputation, he had created a palace like no other for the Kuntiputras, complete with optical illusions. Solid floors appeared like pools of water and vice versa. Walls were painted like realistic doors, while what looked like doors were in fact walls. A pool of water turned out to be a pool sheathed in toughened but transparent crystal so that when you walked on top, the effect was as if you were walking on water! The potency of the illusions and the grandeur of the palace were heightened with pillars clad in gold, gargoyles with ruby eyes, and furniture made of mother of pearl and flawless ivory. I was taking it all in without giving out overt signs of being impressed. It would hardly behove me to be overly impressed by the enemy's splendour.

The guests were sauntering in. Some of the lesser royals – less used to such splendour – stood with their mouths agape, their breath on hold. Some stood dazed – in accordance with the effect the palace was expected to produce upon its visitors. The situation got trickier as the visitors struggled to cope with the illusions, laboriously put in place by Maya for that very purpose.

It was about then that I was entering the main palace of the event, completely lost in my gloomy thoughts, determined not to be as impressed as the Kuntiputras wanted a visitor to be. Someone in the know pointed out Panchali to me, sitting at a first-floor window behind a minutely carved marble screen. Not that I had any feeling for her any more. But then why was my heart beating like hooves on a drum? Ah, it was just the occasion and the heat, I reasoned. I tried not to think. She obviously thought she was well hidden, and was amusing herself along with her friends, espying the arriving guests struggle with the illusions. Suddenly aware that she was observing me, I worked at appearing unimpressed, trying to look oblivious to the grandeur of the palace. I had a throbbing head from lack of sleep (who can sleep well when someone you detest has clearly scored over you?). Nevertheless, I intuitively brought a bit of swagger into my body language, as we men often do, when we believe we are being observed by a beautiful woman, who does not know that we know she is observing us. I may have been rid of Panchali's hold over my civil mind, but had no control over the wild heart.

Now illusions are meant to cheat the unwary; they are no respecters of kings or their moods. I kept walking, with just that wee bit of swagger, towards the carpet of flowers that had been laid out to welcome the guests and, before I could mutter a decent expletive, I was gasping for breath in a pool of water. My crown floated off my head, swimming and sinking gently, while my dhoti, woven with golden thread, ballooned upwards, rising nearly to the surface, giving perhaps a good glimpse of my hairy legs to all the fish in the pool. When I emerged, I obviously could not have cut a debonair figure. Dash Maya and his stupid childish tricks! He would never get any assignment from me, for sure.

And that's when I heard those peals of laughter, one a pitch above the others, tinged with malice – clearly, Panchali and her friends. You know all about how I felt for Panchali once. Perhaps even before entering Hastinapura after her wedding, she knew all about my relations with her husbands. As if in retaliation, she took to making her dislike for me very obvious from day one of her entry into Hastinapura. If we ran into each other unwittingly even on social occasions, while the hooves would resume beating on my chest, she would pretend that she had not seen me, so that she did not have to nod to me even out of courtesy. She seemed to gauge my innermost feelings for her – I don't know how women figure out these things – and seemed to mock me with derision.

And now, since the hooves had been quiet for a while since she had moved to Indraprastha, I had assumed myself completely cured of Panchali. Besides, I was happily married; and so, right then, beyond finding her raucous laugh irritating, I felt no other emotion.

Much significance has been attached to this incident by my grandfather and others narrating this story after him, as if it was the beginning of the epic war of Kurukshetra; as if I took great umbrage at Panchali's laughter and hence chose to exact my revenge later. In truth, I was no more and no less happy or unhappy or embarrassed or bashful than you would be in my place. Given enough time to dry up, the worst of us can laugh at ourselves. So why would I go about seeking revenge because a pretty woman enjoyed a good laugh at my expense, even if the laugh was marinated in a bit of spite?

What I did was crack a good joke at my plight with my friends, steal a look at Panchali, laugh sheepishly as if to show her that I wasn't entirely devoid of a humorous side, and hurriedly move on, as most would. One hardly nurses long grudges with pretty maidens for such things. Why should I have been any different? But yes, the episode did much to dampen my spirits and sense of humour that morning and did spoil my day; and I recall being a little more edgy for the rest of the day.

The more informed might wish to link what transpired later that day with my foul mood. They will be both right and wrong. I am referring to the melee that broke out on account of Yudhisthira singling out Krishna for the highest honour on the occasion of the rajasuya. Many of the kings present – led primarily by Shishupala, the Chediraj – vehemently opposed this since they did not consider Krishna worthy of the honour. There were many mighty warriors and learned men present who were far more deserving of the honour. Besides, Krishna was known to be a sly one; too flippant and promiscuous to be taken seriously by the elders; and not even a Kshatriya. Not that I cared much about this Kshatriya business; but after what he had done to Karna in the past for not being a Kshatriya, I saw no reason why a milkman deserved a high honour either. If a non-Kshatriya wasn't good enough to challenge Arjuna in a gurukul competition, how was a milkman good enough for high honour in a rajasuya with all the Brahmin sages and Kshatriya kings present? What is more, there was this general suspicion that the rajasuya itself had been Krishna's brainchild. He had engineered the killing of Jarasandha not only to clear all potential opposition to the rajasuya, but also to eliminate one of his key enemies. Nor had Krishna let out a single bleat to defend Karna when he was humiliated in Panchala as a Sutaputra, even though he himself was a cowherd. There were rumours of shady dealings by the Kuntiputras, under

Krishna's guidance, to browbeat some other kings into submission. Under the circumstances, the only honourable thing for me to do was to support Shishupala, which I did. Unfortunately, the situation was ripe for tempers to fly and a goodly brawl broke out towards the end of the day, resulting in Shishupala being killed by Krishna.

Whatever else may be said of the Kuntiputras, the blokes had grown strong and would not be easily challenged. They had entrenched themselves in the vicinity of Hastinapura like a particularly agonizing toothache. This was going to be the beginning of another spate of my sleepless nights.

PART IV

11

*The dice we throw are not obliged to play out
as we want them*

After returning from the demoralizing rajasuya of the Kuntiputras, I couldn't sit back and relax as if nothing had happened. My friend Jarasandha had been killed earlier. And now Shishupala. They were killed just so that the Kuntiputras' grand ambitions could be sustained. Why, at this rate I could be next! While I grudged their survival, I could hardly grudge them thwarting my attempts.

Purely from a strategic viewpoint, I could hardly fault them going for the rajasuya in order to consolidate the strength of Indraprastha. Unfortunately for me, I was stuck somewhere between being a crown prince and a king. Had I been the ruler, I would have strengthened our alliances and gone for a rajasuya long ago.

I knew I had to take up the matter with my father sooner rather than later. He wasn't getting any younger. For that matter, neither was I. A weak man, well into his autumn, with his congenital disability, he was becoming increasingly unviable as a ruler. I would just have to conduct a firm meeting with him to tell him categorically that the time had come for me to take over the reins of Hastinapura, for Hastinapura's sake. After all, he had reduced Hastinapura to a subsidiary state of Indraprastha and unless we applied the brakes, God knows what would come next. Fortunately, I knew that his weak nature would work to my advantage and I would not have to work very hard to get him to take the pillion seat.

I am not going to appeal to you not to misunderstand me as being too ambitious. You are entitled to your opinion. But if you wish to know the truth, the only reason I wanted the reins of the state in my grasp was to prevent the decline of our kingdom. I was afraid Hastinapura had stopped growing any stronger, while Indraprastha, a creation of our own folly, was cocking a snook at us, to put it mildly.

I was closeted with Mama Shakuni, Sushasana and Karna in my private chambers day and night. We simply had to find a way to stop the march of the Kuntiputras. In my scheme of things, status quo was hardly an option, for it was indicative of the decline of Hastinapura. But a direct confrontation was out of the question since we lacked the military might to take on the Kuntiputras right then or in the foreseeable future. Neutralizing any or all of them stealthily, in their strengthened state, was not feasible either.

The human mind is like a dog on a leash. Most of the time the dog is content to stay within the confines of the leash, just as the mind is comfortable thinking within a familiar framework. Occasionally, the dog struggles to go beyond the limits of the tether but fails, just as the human mind occasionally tries to break free from its conventional patterns of thinking but finds no breakthrough. And if really determined, the dog stretches a bit more, tries harder and then suddenly breaks free and finds new ground, just as a determined human mind finds the realm of unfettered ideas.

My advisors and I were in the same state and going round and round within the confines of our thinking for days. I had always set great store by evaluating the weaknesses of my enemies. So what were the weaknesses of the Kuntiputras? A sense of déjà vu hovered around me like an undefined shadow. I could recall that in the distant past, as a mere boy, I had concentrated more on finding chinks in Bhima's and Arjuna's armours as they were the most powerful of the brothers, and had finally zeroed in on Bhima's weakness for good food. But we weren't boys any more. We simply had to think smarter. I knew there was something eluding me. We strained to delve deeper into the flaws of the duo. After all, they were the ones who comprised the real muscle of Indraprastha and the men without whom Yudhisthira's power as a king was as nought.

Then, late one night, the leash snapped in Mama Shakuni's head!

I am a light sleeper, when the Kuntiputras do allow me some sleep, that is. I woke up from my fitful sleep one night, thanks to a ruckus that seemed to be working itself up in front of my bedchamber. I walked to the door and opened it to find an excited Shakuni Mama rudely trying to browbeat the sentries – who were politely trying to enquire if whatever it was could not wait until morning – to gain entry into my chamber. I always found this trait amongst those higher up on the power totem pole browbeating those lower down – who were only trying to do their duty – more than somewhat irksome. But this was hardly the time to ponder about that, and I ushered my uncle in.

He insisted that I send word to Sushasana and Karna as well to join us that very minute. Aware that Mama knew what he was doing, I had both of them sent for.

As soon as the duo arrived, one rapidly followed by the other, Mama, his face flushed, barely containing his excitement, piped out, 'I have it!' he cried. 'I have the Kuntiputras neatly bundled for you!' I looked keenly at him just to make sure he did not show any of the symptoms the mentally addled usually do. But he seemed normal, if a tad too excited.

Now, Uncle Shakuni, my mother's younger brother, was the king of Gandhar. To say he was brilliant and talented would be an understatement. But he also had a rather radical outlook towards life, for in his opinion the time we took making crucial decisions was mostly wasted. In his view, everything that happened in one's life was made up of a host of random variables. Therefore, he believed that life could be led as much and as well by the throw of dice as by reasoned choices or decisions. So firm was his belief in the random variability of life that he had confessed to me that he often took close decisions, even important ones, like – whether or not to wage a war, whether or not to make a friend of a neighbouring kingdom, trust a particular courtier or not, spend the treasury money building a particular monument or not, and so forth – by a throw of dice, rather than agonize hour upon hour trying to work out the obscure logic of equally confusing options. And he insisted in his private conversations with me that he had not been much the worse for it. And, in the process, he had come to understand dice and cowries intimately and had grown into a master thrower of them – an important asset in the royal sweepstakes.

My close friend and confidant right from childhood, he was a master strategist and a great devotee of Shiva, and was always seen in black clothes, forever rattling a pair of four-sided dice in his palms – which I am sure helped him keep his skill in good nick. Unfortunately, his reputation has been severely compromised for facilitating the Mahabharata war, and amply denigrated by posterity thanks to the customary bias of the storytelling intermediaries. It has been said that he 'poisoned' my mind and drove me to the war, that he was a cheat and evil, and then some. Well, nothing of the sort. He wasn't my charioteer and so drove me nowhere. That's what Krishna did for Arjuna, literally and metaphorically. I always remained in charge of my destiny. The Mahabharata war was foisted upon us by Yudhisthira and his brothers, aided ably by Krishna. Let no one tell you otherwise.

'Yudhisthira's weakness …' said Mama Shakuni and stopped as we waited expectantly. He was clearly in the mood to milk the moment for all it was worth. I allowed him the indulgence – after all, he was my maternal uncle, even if we were roughly the same age – without showing too much curiosity for his idea. Sushasana and Karna caught on to my tactic and played along. And then, sheepish, he came around and said, 'For days, we have been concentrating on the weaknesses of Arjuna and Bhima, while all along Yudhisthira's weakness has been staring us in the face!' He waited a moment for the information to sink in before continuing, 'And that is Yudhisthira's love for the throw of dice!'

Sushasana, Karna and I still couldn't see where my uncle was going with this. So we held our peace. And he expectedly came back with, 'Look, do you recall Yudhisthira's love for gambling? I have watched him over the years. He is a closet gambler and in reality a gambling addict who, with his sheer power of will, and other noble qualities to be fair, has managed to keep the propensity in check. But he isn't cured of the addiction. And such propensity always lurks just beneath the surface, so that an addict is never far from his addiction. It should be easy to tempt him to accept an invite for chaupar, especially when the request is so packaged that it would be indecorous not to accept it. You can be sure that when propriety teeters on the tentative, proclivity is bound to topple him towards temptation.'

With these words, he threw the pair of four-sided dice he held in his palms, which rolled on the table in front of me, both coming to rest with four dots on top – the maximum. 'So what say you? Shall we extend him a royal invite for chaupar, and when he comes to us like a deprived alcoholic invited to a wine party, we relieve him of his kingdom once and for all? You will just have to ensure that I play for the Kauravas and Yudhisthira can decide who plays for their side.'

He didn't have to elaborate on the plan. It became immediately obvious. Why, yes, Yudhisthira always did love gambling. Like all brilliant ideas, this one was so absurd in its simplicity! How come I had not thought of it?

Anyway, we had the main idea now, and all we needed was to add a few frills to it to make it work. Sushasana and Karna endorsed the plan too.

Wars are hardly the only or even the preferred tool of kings in settling inter- and intra-kingdom disputes and disagreements. Often, strategy is all about avoiding or preventing an all-out war, for it saves lives and prevents avoidable waste of economic resources. So if we could divest the Kuntiputras of Indraprastha and thus break their suzerainty over us without warfare, it was not only acceptable, but even the preferred course of action. Indraprastha's domination over Hastinapura was a loss of pride, reduction of status and dilution of liberty for the state. In this sense, Indraprastha was an enemy of Hastinapura. We were inviting them for an accepted royal game. They had the choice of turning down the invite, though a refusal would be socially awkward for them. Well, I can tell you it certainly was a lot more awkward for us to suffer their sovereignty over Hastinapura.

It may not be entirely wrong to say I was jealous of the Kuntiputras. But in all honesty, who will not feel a pang of envy if he sees someone he loathes doing well? But envious or not, I would have let status quo prevail had they not gone for the rajasuya – an act that rubbed their success into our faces. They had been brought up on our generosity after straggling in from the Himalayan forests, poor as church mice, given shelter and educated in our palace thanks to my father's benevolence. And what did they do in return? They tried every trick in the book to try and usurp our kingdom, starting with Hastinapura itself and later, as if in a great show of compromise and goodwill, *settling for* a share in it.

True, I had done my bit in trying to eliminate them early in life by stealth, precisely because I had feared what we had finally been reduced to: a fiefdom of Indraprastha. It may be possible that my attempts on their lives had set them up even more resolutely against me, leading to a vicious cycle of hardening positions. But there was little I could do about it.

Lest you harbour the notion that we were planning to cheat the Kuntiputras out of their kingdom through a fixed game of dice, it's time you know the truth. Mama Shakuni's idea of inviting Yudhisthira for a royal round of chaupar was brilliant, no doubt. The game could be played either with cowries or with dice. I had decided, of course, that he would play on behalf of the Kauravas. But, contrary to your conventional belief, there was absolutely no plan to cheat Yudhisthira at play. It would be an insult to the intelligence of Yudhisthira and his brothers to believe that he could be so obviously cheated. Besides, the game was sure to be watched by many eagle eyes – as many for us as for them. We would have been fools to try to cheat our way to victory. In truth, such a contemptible idea did not even enter our heads, which would have been below the dignity of any royal, least of all us, the Kurus, who were too proud to stoop to such lows.

The truth is, Yudhisthira was a sucker for gambling. Chaupar – the royal sweepstakes among the higher royalty – was played with extremely high stakes, on a board shaped like a plus sign. Royal etiquette required that an invite to the game not be declined, for it implied unacceptable rudeness. So it was a cinch that Yudhisthira would accept when our invite went to them – *cordially*, of course.

Contrary to popular belief, Mama Shakuni was not a cheat. He was simply a master thrower of dice.

Today you usually use the six-sided dice in many of your games of chance. In our time, we preferred a pair of four-sided dice. Each dice was a rectangular bar of bones or ivory, about two-thirds the length of an average finger. Each side had one, two, three or four shallow dimples etched on them. When you rolled the pair together, you could get any one of the results, namely: 1,1; 1,2; 1,3; 1,4; 2,1; 2,2; 2,3; 2,4; 3,1; 3,2; 3,2; 3,4; 4,1; 4,2; 4,3; or 4,4. Thus, there were, in all, sixteen outcomes. There was only one way you could throw a total of 2, namely throw 1, 1. There were two ways to obtain 3 (1,2 and 2,1); three ways to obtain 4 (1,3; 2,2; and 3,1); four ways to obtain 5 (1,4; 2,3; 3,2; 4,1;); three ways to obtain 6 (2,4; 3,3; and 4,2); two ways to obtain 7 (3,4 and 4,3) and one way to obtain 8 (4,4). So in any random throw of the two dice, the probability that you would obtain a total of two or eight is one in sixteen (6.25 per cent each); a total of three or seven is two in sixteen (12.5 per cent each); a total of four or six is three in sixteen (18.75 per cent, each); and a total of five is four in sixteen (25 per cent). Any good gambler knows these percentages intimately and keeps them in mind when playing, while an amateur plays as if all the numbers are equally likely and wonders why he gets a two or an eight so rarely and five so much more often.

A master roller of dice usually has an extreme gift of sensitivity in his palms, which he hones through hour upon hour of practice to be able to sense the position of the dimpled dice in his palms as he gently rolls them. Once he knows the position in which the two dice lie between his palms, with infinite practice, he learns to vary the force with which he rolls off the pieces, improving the probability of a desired outcome. In addition, the master is aware that even in a purely random throw of a single dice, the probability of outcome for a throw of 1, 2, 3 or 4 are not exactly equal, or one in four. This is because the face with a single dimple, for example, has less mass scooped out of it and is therefore slightly heavier on that side than the face with four dimples, so that when the die is rolled, the heavier face (the one face with only one dimple) is more likely to end face down.

Of course, even with all the knowledge and practice, the master thrower can never throw exactly the result he desires all the time. The good ones might manage an accuracy of, say, sixty to seventy-five per cent, and the best, as in case of Mama Shakuni, ninety to ninety-five per cent. When you give such a master a new pair of dice, it takes him but a few trials to get a feel for the pair and before long he gains supremacy over you. If ever genius being ninety-nine per cent perspiration was true, it was true of my uncle who was hooked to the throwing of dice from his childhood and never slept without a pair by his pillow. Mama Shakuni pottered about with his dice at least a couple of hours a day from the age of five. By his middle age, say thirty-five, he would have spent upwards of 20,000 hours to sharpen his dice-throwing skills. This was obviously enough to make Shakuni a maestro in his chosen craft. Such was his intimacy with dice (and with cowries too) that had we had a world championship in our time, one would need no award for guessing who the hands-down winner of the championship would have been.

It must also be understood that unlike a card-sharper, a master of dice does not cheat. Loading of the dice is for your amateurs and is a problem that is easily fixed by the opponent insisting on neutral dice. Even the suggestion of dice-loading and cheating is anathema to the dice *artist*.

Even though Mama Shakuni often moved about with a pair of dice between his palms, most people took this to be a mere affectation. His true level of skill with them had always been a well-kept secret. This is because if other royalty got wind of his expertise, they might pull back from playing with him, or at least hold back on the size of stakes they placed with him. In gambling, of greater virtue than expertise with dice is the discretion with which you play the game. It is your run-of-the-mill expert who shows off his skill with the dice by winning every game. A true master of gambling is far too nuanced to do this. He is not an exhibitionist of his skill. More often than not, he makes his opponent feel the better of the two. For much of the game, he throws normally, like you and me, letting the dice take its own course even if he is losing a lot of rounds (when necessary, even manipulating some of his throws to ensure he wins fewer rounds than his less gifted opponent), lulling the opponent to complacency, prompting him to not only put at stake all his earlier winnings, but even more. And then unexpectedly, when the stakes are really astronomical, he takes the opponent to the cleaners by throwing the desired numbers with great accuracy to mop up the huge booty on the table. To him, the total take is more important than the number of games won or lost. He plays for the larger stakes and not showmanship. He is the strategist focused upon winning the war, unmindful of losing a few battles. Such is his subtlety of play that the opponent never really realizes the true extent of the master's expertise. Unfortunately, nor did my grandfather, Vyasa. Or else his epic may have been scripted a little differently.

The master of gambling is also a master of human psychology. He knows that people view gold won from gambling differently from gold earned through work, and so they bet their winnings in a gamble more readily than their own capital. He knows that gamblers often believe in winning and losing streaks, when in truth there are no such streaks because each throw of dice is independent of the previous one. And the expert gambler is not beyond exploiting these beliefs of the amateur. He knows that people, even seasoned gamblers, behave differently when they believe they are on a winning streak. They bet more eagerly when they are winning than when they are losing. He also knows that people view betting cold money differently from betting an asset or a possession, like a horse, palace or a jewel, typically undervaluing the asset. He knows too the role of hubris in a pathological gambler. He can sniff a gambling addict a mile off and is quick to exploit this weakness. He knows that emotions should never be mixed with gambling. When a dice artist also masters all these abilities, he graduates into a maestro.

Well, Shakuni was a virtuoso in this department – a master of masters.

And that is where the power of Mama Shakuni's suggestion to invite the Kuntiputras for a game lay. His not-so-widely-known genius would be our main weapon in this strategy. The strength of the strategy also lay in the fact that Yudhisthira had always remained a closet gambler. Not even his closest circle may have suspected the extent of his well-guarded addiction. So when we sent our invite, no one on his side would have any serious reason to dissuade him from participating in an 'innocent' game of chaupar with the Kauravas. Following the rajasuya, the timing was just right for us to invite the Kuntiputras for a friendly visit over chaupar as a return courtesy of hospitality. Flush with the success of the rajasuya, it would be seen as petty and socially indelicate on their part not to accept the invite.

They would come as kings but leave as paupers. And then Indraprastha would be ours again, and this time forever. And Hastinapura would walk with its head held high; the Kauravas would walk with their heads held high.

12

*Addiction is dangerous;
failing to resist it, even more so*

I simply had to unroll Mama Shakuni's plan so he could roll those dice. So an invite had to be on its way. But protocol required that an invite to Yudhisthira, the king of Indraprastha, be sent from the king of Hastinapura. But I seriously doubted my father's ready endorsement of the idea of inviting them for a game of chaupar. So the time was nigh that I converse with my father about his passing on the baton to me. But it had to be done with some delicacy. It is not as if I was itching to wear the crown. But the constant threat to my diadem had made me more than a little insecure.

But my conviction that I must wear the crown and soon, as usual, was the easy part. The tricky part was to put the conviction into action or, simply put, to broach the subject with my father. Such a conversation with a king is never pleasant because it reeks of traitorous intent and palace intrigue, even if that is not where I was coming from. And the proposition itself is fraught with many a danger, with much potential for misunderstandings and exploitation by vested interests, of which there is seldom dearth in a palace, specially one presided over by a weak king.

Worse, conservative and senior courtiers never like princes who are too eager to become kings. And if I were to be king, I would need the support of all these courtiers. To make matters even worse, my father was blind, aging and increasingly indolent and feeble – all contributing to his progressive ineffectualness – a combination that could easily make him emotional; and the ensuing tears could swing sympathies further in his favour, even if I thought I had a legitimate case to hasten the transition at the helm. But the irony was, were it not for his increasing indecisiveness as king, I had no reason, desire or even need to contemplate such a course. I had no illusion that no matter how I approached the subject – for not addressing the subject was hardly an option – I was bound to be judged harshly by posterity.

When I finally approached my father, the whole thing turned out to be an anti-climax. Apparently, he too had been thinking along similar lines and, to cut a long story short, I ascended the throne of a much weakened Hastinapura, albeit as a sort of king on probation, while my father assumed the role of a chief mentor till I proved myself. On paper, if I did not measure up to my responsibilities, my father had the right to return to the throne. This of course I did not mind at all, for my true motivation – even if you do not believe it – lay more in what I *could do* as a king than *being* a king. And I had little doubt that I would use the position for the betterment of Hastinapura, and the probation was merely academic.

I was now ready to put my plan into action. But it was of great importance that we had more friends aligned with Hastinapura than we currently had, especially with two powerful allies, Jarasandha and Shishupala, dead. So I promptly started dusting up hoary relationships, mending broken fences, refreshing stale friendships, calling in old debts, bestowing favours to vitalize waning diplomatic alliances and make new ones. But this alone wasn't enough. A successful king must also bond closely with his courtiers. All these years, as a young crown prince, I had not been too close to the courtiers in my father's court. Actually, most of them had treated me with the indulgence of an adult towards a youth. I now had to build and strengthen these relationships as an adult in my own right. I also had to work towards attracting more savants, statesmen, soldiers, sages and scholars into the court.

While Hastinapura had always been a fairly well-governed kingdom, as an old and established regime, things had got both bureaucratic and jaded – a bit taken for granted. I had to speedily put a lot of new development works under way so that, as king, I could also connect with my people. After all, what is a king but the sum total of his people? How does a king flourish without his people prospering first? I therefore set about building new pathshalas, dharamshalas, parks, roads, medical centres and animal husbandry centres. I supported and encouraged the arts, artisans, scholars and sages. I improved the bureaucracy and courts for superior administration and delivery of justice, tightened the army, brought in new blood experienced in different skills and put everyone on rigorous training schedules. Above all, I gave much boost to trade and export. I ensured that tax collection was humane yet efficient, so that all the state schemes were paid for. In short, I improved every aspect of life in our kingdom and strengthened Hastinapura in every way. Merely weakening Indraprastha could never have been enough.

But, of course, Vyasa and others never told you all this, did they?

To get back to the invitation for chaupar, I had Vidhura himself carry my invite to Yudhisthira. Nobody, but nobody other than Mama Shakuni, Sushasana, Karna and I knew of the deeper motives attached to the invite. To my father, Bhishma, Vidhura and the rest of the courtiers, and even my own wife Bhanumati, this was simply meant to be a gracious invite to a standard royal pastime. Some of the courtiers – the contemptible weaklings! – even congratulated me for my *chaupar diplomacy* to keep Hastinapura on the right side of the rajasuya power! I bristled at the 'compliment', but played along. Nor do I offer any apologies for this caginess, for I had learnt a lesson or two in secrecy from the Vanaprastha episode. Some people, especially Vidhura, had his suspicions about the innocence of my invite, but hell, I was the king now and nobody, not even Vidhura, would dare question me directly. If he had any reservations, he could keep them to himself; I wasn't about to discuss them with him. The court of Hastinapura was no longer weak.

I had chosen Vidhura to deliver the invite for a reason. I never trusted him cent per cent, good man though he was. He had always been somewhat distrustful of me and a tad more sympathetic to the bowing and scraping Kuntiputras. The problem with him was, he was a good man but not royalty. He only had proximity to royalty, to a rather weak one at that. So he could hardly be blamed for not thinking like one, because it was never his crown or kingdom at stake. As a half-brother to both my father and Pandu, born to a lady-in-waiting to my grandmother Ambika, he was largely indifferent as to whether he served Dhritarashtra, me or even Yudhisthira. I never doubted the good intentions of the likes of Vidhura. They always meant well, even if they weren't clued into the reality of how the mind of a monarch worked.

He regarded the Kuntiputras as *Pandavas*. In his worldview, all that counted was for brothers and cousins to live amicably together. To a simple and good man like him, it was anathema to even think of the Kuntiputras as anything other than Panduputras. So it didn't count with him at all that the Kuntiputras were neither my brothers nor cousins really. It didn't matter that, notwithstanding the naïve uncle–nephew adoration he and the Kuntiputras heaped upon each other forever, they were nothing of the sort, unless he was a brother to Yama, Vayu, Indra or the Ashwini Kumaras, because Aunt Kunti's or Aunt Madri's brother he certainly was not. It was lost on him that cultivating the likes of him was part of the larger strategy of Kunti Devi. Higher rajadharma – that kingdoms aren't meant to be given away in gift or divided insouciantly or that there are rules that govern the passing of crown from father to son, or that there is shame in being a vassal state, etc. – sat lightly on him. It was on account of his emotional tilt towards the Kuntiputras that, in close consultation with Mama Shakuni who was a master of human psychology, I had chosen Vidhura to carry my invite across. We knew that the Kuntiputras were programmed to trust Vidhura.

Bhishma could have served the same purpose. But he had been a true crown prince of the kingdom who had forfeited the throne to enable his father to marry his femme fatale Satyavati, so that her progeny would have no obstacle to the throne. His status in the kingdom was far too exalted for him to be sent as an emissary. With Vidhura, however, I could take the liberty.

When he himself had been trusted to carry out the deed, Vidhura, being an honourable man, and being in my employ, would not openly advise the Kuntiputras against accepting our invite. And even if he were tempted to do so, he would not be able to, as he would be accompanied by other courtiers in the entourage, some of them my auxiliary ears. He would extend the invite more neutrally than most other courtiers who were bound to go overboard trying to convince the Kuntiputras to accept the invite and arouse unnecessary suspicion in the brothers' minds concerning its strategic intent.

What exactly transpired in Indraprastha upon receiving the invite, I will not be able to vouch for. But it trickled down to me from the usual crevices that Vidhura, as I had expected of course, did not go overboard in trying to convince Yudhisthira and his brothers to accept the invite. Arjuna, always the sharp bloke, interpreted Vidhura's body language to mean it was desirable to decline the invite and advised Yudhisthira accordingly.

But as I mentioned earlier, Yudhisthira was a gambling addict who – keenly aware that gaming and wagering were inconsistent with the image he wanted projected in the public domain – had kept his impulses bottled up through sheer willpower for too long. But as anyone with a sweet tooth would know, it is one thing not to go near sweets to avoid the temptation, but another to desist when a candy is waved under your nose.

Faced with a formal invite from me, I could imagine at least ten reasons why Yudhisthira would overrule Arjuna's advice. First, he was a closet gambler who would hate to forego a formal opportunity to indulge his long-suppressed addiction. Two, it was socially acceptable for royals to play chaupar. Three, it was socially unacceptable to decline such an invite. Four, though underplayed by my grandfather Vyasa, Yudhisthira had a big ego. When he thought he was on firm ground, he rarely yielded to the suggestions of his younger siblings. Five, Vidhura himself had delivered the invite to him. Six, he had little will to read Vidhura's body language which was at loggerheads with what he had been directed to convey. Seven, he could see no significant downside to a game of chaupar, barring the usual possible losses which a king of his stature could easily afford. Eight, like most amateurs, he fancied himself an exceptional player of chaupar. Nine, neither I nor anyone else in Hastinapura was known to be a chaupar player of any repute, so that Yudhisthira did not have to fear any great champion. Ten, since he fancied himself a proficient player, he probably fancied his own chances of taking me to the cleaners.

So I was hardly surprised when Vidhura, with a neutral

expression on his face, informed me that the invite had been accepted.

The day arrived for the big event and the Kuntiputras, along with their entourage, comprising family and friends, set foot in Hastinapura. Our palace looked elegant and we had not gone overboard like the Kuntiputras had with their rajasuya venue. I believed in grandeur befitting an occasion, but not in undue profligacy with public funds.

The event was organized in the main circular courtyard of our palace. A tall pole was planted in the centre of the yard, from the top of which radiated yard upon yard of silk in varied colours, going all the way to the periphery of the courtyard, creating the ambience of a giant tent through which daylight filtered in rainbow hues.

In the centre was a low table on which was spread the plus-shaped chaupar, in thick ornately embroidered cotton. Flanking it were two low divans, facing each other as if they were adversaries themselves. Mama Shakuni and Yudhisthira would occupy these divans.

Immediately surrounding this arrangement was the first circle of comfortable divans to seat our families, other higher royals and their families. I was seated right behind Mama Shakuni, with my knees all but nudging his back, from where I could observe the throws of both the players and watch the board without hindrance.

Others on my side of the semicircle of the circular arrangement were my father, Karna, Bhishma, Vidhura, Sushasana and Balarama. On the opposite side sat Yudhisthira's four brothers. In the next concentric circle sat the next level of important royalty and their guests from both sides.

The courtyard had five concentric rings of seats that gently sloped upwards, creating an amphitheatre-like atmosphere. The last circle was for the invited commoners. The spectators invited were all adults. The men mostly wore colourful headgear, coordinated with their vests and dhotis. The women were even more colourful in their best silks, jewellery and jasmine flowers in their hair, enriching the surrounding visually and olfactorily. Six aisles radiated from the centre of the courtyard to the periphery for people to move about. From the balconies overlooking the courtyard emanated soft, ethereal music, played by various sets of royal musicians assembled from far and wide. Waiters – miraculously carrying two loaded trays, one on each palm – were busily serving water and refreshments.

The arena was all set. The spectators were in place, craning their necks. A gentle breeze was wafting through the courtyard, with just a suggestion of the scent of jasmine from the bushes planted on the edges of the courtyard. The morning sun was raising its bright head over the eastern horizon. The music stopped and drums began to beat. Sounding like the hooves of distant horses galloping on mud tracks, rising to the rumbling of thunder, the drums picked up tempo all the way to a crescendo, as if portending Armageddon. And then a sudden hush! With the abrupt silencing of the drums, you could have heard a bee belch. It was as if the entire stadium had stopped mid-breath in anticipation.

Yudhisthira and Shakuni entered the courtyard from opposite ends and walked down the gangway, reaching the centre at the same time. They exchanged polite greetings and took their seats. The referees introduced themselves to the players and the spectators and announced that the tournament would last three days: from the sunrise of day one to the sunset of day three. Any party giving up sooner would do so only in disgrace. All the rules of the game were read and agreed upon. The tournament dice were inspected for fairness and selected.

I had invited a number of other kings, our friends and the Kuntiputras', just to ensure there would be enough witnesses when we won – as I had no doubt we would. Tension between our friends and well-wishers vis-à-vis the supporters of the Kuntiputras ran high.

There are many variations of chaupar. The royal variant typically involves not only getting one's own pieces around the board and back home, but also cutting down the opponent's pieces en route if your piece can occupy the precise cell of the opponent by an exact throw. Much of the game is played for enormous stakes placed on one or the other result, namely: cutting of the opponent's piece by a precise throw; returning home one's own piece on a precise throw; betting against the opponent achieving a similar feat; throwing a two or an eight, and so forth. But since this tale is mainly intended to take some of that sheen off the halo given to the Kuntiputras and hopefully blunt some of those pointy demonic horns that we Kauravas have been endowed with, and not meant as a primer on how to play chaupar, let me not digress on the nuances of ludo and get on with how the tournament unfolded.

Day One

In the first session, Mama Shakuni decided to play without any application of his keen mind, so that the game seemed fairly symmetric, both Yudhisthira and Shakuni sharing the honours more or less evenly. By the second session, the situation changed a bit. Yudhisthira was rolling with the outcomes expected of a pair of fair dice. He wasn't getting all his throws to his advantage, the outcomes being random, while Mama seemed to be getting more throws wrong than right. While Yudhisthira was betting prudently, Uncle was placing aggressive bets every time he lost his wager, as if desperate to recoup his losses. And then there would be a brief interlude when Mama would win a small sum briefly, but soon lose a much larger amount. He would again bet rashly as if to make up for the loss. By now, Yudhisthira was having fun and beginning to roll his dice with a bit of attitude and flourish, stealing a look at Arjuna every now and then, as if telling him, 'So here is to all your words of caution!'

Guessing pretty well what Mama was up to, I feigned painful emotions on my face at the losses we were running. By the end of the day, several chests of pearls and precious stones, gold and silver coins had shifted from our side to theirs. By now, even the four brothers were beginning to show some mirth. As the end of the day approached, the decibel level of their laughter at their eldest brother's frequent jokes was getting higher by the moment, and Yudhisthira himself was taking bigger and bigger swigs from the silver goblet of wine. On the other hand, I pretended to sulk, while most of the Kauravas wore genuine expressions of concern. At dinner, many of our friends and well-wishers gave Mama Shakuni assorted advice on how to bet more prudently, pointing out how Yudhisthira was proving to be the cannier player, etc., and Mama wore the expression your batsmen wear when they have scored a duck and are being advised by the press how to bat.

All in all, it was an eventful day and, while much sura drained down the gullets of both the camps, when the curtain came down on day one, the five brothers and their kin and kith were decidedly more tipsy than my brothers and I were.

Day Two

The Hastinapura end had to be replenished with several more chests of valuables from our treasury to make up for the previous day's losses. The morning session seemed like a repeat of the previous afternoon, if a tad worse. Not even one of Mama's throws seemed to be falling right. He was staking larger and larger sums and losing. Frustrated, he would place an even larger bet and lose again. The only time he seemed to win was when Yudhisthira made an obvious error miscalculating the odds, or when, due to the random nature of the rolls, some of the numbers fell adversely for him. In any case, Uncle's bad rolls seemed like Yudhisthira's lucky ones and Yudhisthira continued to win and Shakuni continued to lose on the whole. So strained was Mama's countenance at times that I almost wondered if I had overestimated his prowess, or if he had lost his touch and was really playing recklessly. And he – and more than him, I – had reasons to worry, of course, considering that by afternoon nearly two-thirds of my treasury had depleted.

Lunch was a boisterous affair in Yudhisthira's camp, with somarasa flowing unhindered, while on our subdued side, my father, Bhishma, Vidhura, et al., were giving the usual silent treatment to Shakuni and me, which is generally more painful and irksome than a swift kick in the back side. I attempted a weak joke with Mama, saying something inane like 'I hope you aren't going to make the king of Hastinapura a pauper', for which Shakuni, his shoulders slouched, chose to give me the silent treatment, with nary an expression on his face.

Midway into the second half of the day, four-fifth of our treasury had run out and my uncle was playing like a bumbling amateur, while Yudhisthira sported the body language of a competent and assured winner. He and his brothers were taking generous draws from their wine goblets. Yudhisthira could hardly believe his form. He had been a closet gambler for a very long time and here he was, showing off his hidden skill at the royal game of chaupar before one and all, and how!

With barely an hour and a half's play left for the second day, Mama Shakuni did something desperate. He repeatedly wagered absurdly large sums, bringing my heart to my mouth because, had he lost some of those wagers, our treasury would have been deep in the red. However, by doing so, he forced his opponent to wager symmetric sums, which Yudhisthira, on a roll, didn't seem to mind very much.

Bumbling though Shakuni may have appeared in comparison to Yudhisthira, he ended up winning eleven of the fifteen large wagers, while earlier he had lost thirty-six of the previous forty-five bets on the more modest stakes initiated by Yudhisthira. When the day ended, a blundering Shakuni had recouped much lost ground, and nearly eighty-five per cent of our treasury had been restored. We were still trailing significantly – about fifteen per cent short of the starting level of our treasury funds – but not as bad as mid-day had portended.

To Yudhisthira and his camp, and even to our own, it was clear that Yudhisthira was the superior player, and Shakuni had been lucky to cut his losses somewhat by some desperate gambles – after all, of the total of sixty wagers in the session, Yudhisthira had won forty. No one doubted that if Mama Shakuni continued in the same vein, we would be in deep trouble on the last day. On the other hand, having dominated two of the three-day play, the leading Kuntiputra's face was flushed the colour of vermillion; whether from frequent sips of the wine or the pleasure of the win, it was a toss up.

Day Three

A worried and unhappy-looking Shakuni with drooping shoulders took his place in front of the plus-shaped board, while Yudhisthira, smiling ear to ear, made some patronizing comment to my uncle to boost his spirits. As soon as the game commenced, Shakuni lost a little more, making some more dents in our treasury, and Yudhisthira's disposition brightened in proportion. Shakuni kept losing gradually, which kept Yudhisthira and his camp in great humour. Our own side was nearly in despair and I placed my hands on my uncle's shoulder, pressing it gently as if to say, 'Go easy, buddy.' By now, both the sides were guzzling impressive quantities of wine – the Kuntiputras celebrating their everlasting good fortune, and my brothers and I praying for some luck. If there was one sober man in the entire courtyard, it was Mama Shakuni. The man hadn't touched a drop.

Soon, Mama Shakuni's luck seemed to turn 180 degrees. His dice began to fall right. Before long, it seemed he simply couldn't throw wrong and, while his run seemed to last, he bid ever larger sums in rapid succession, doubling and quadrupling the enormous stakes on the board recklessly, with Yudhisthira having to match him wager for wager. Moreover, with his astute computational skills, Mama would roll the dice such that, more often than not, Yudhisthira would need twos or eights to win the stakes and, since they are the least probable numbers to roll, Yudhisthira would miss more often than not. At the same time, Mama Shakuni would position his pieces such that in his next move he would need a five, which had the highest probability of being rolled.

Such computational skills, aided by his skill in the throwing of dice, gave Mama Shakuni an edge that Yudhisthira simply did not possess. By the time the session was adjourned for lunch, Shakuni had not just recovered all the losses, but the winnings amounted to nearly double our treasury funds, while the Kuntiputras had had to call for more chests from their quarters and even sought some

'IOUs' from our treasury. Yudhisthira was visibly agitated. And correspondingly, he again started glugging larger and larger quantities from his goblet. For that matter, my brothers and I too were now sipping our wines freely to celebrate the relief from the anxiety of the last five sessions.

Raring to go, Yudhisthira, his eyes red, resumed his seat a little before lunch time concluded. This was the last session of the game and it was clear from his demeanour that he viewed Mama Shakuni's big winnings in the last session as a fool's fluke that couldn't last forever. With the superior skill that he had clearly displayed in four of the previous five sessions, Yudhisthira was confident of not only winning back his losses but depleting the Kaurava treasury again.

Once the session commenced, confident Yudhisthira assumed a relaxed posture but started playing more seriously. He was cracking fewer jokes, humming less to himself, and shaking his left leg vigorously, clearly trying to do some rapid mental arithmetic. Shakuni was by now beginning to play with furious rapidity, which Yudhisthira tried to match out of sheer machismo. He did not realize that Shakuni's strategy was to play rapidly so that he could throw the dice far more number of times, so that the odds of ninety per cent right throws that he was capable of would play out more and more. Nor did he realize that subtly but surely, by forcing him into rapid play, Shakuni was denying him time to think. He also did not realize that from then on, the more rapidly he played, the more he was bound to lose, because from there on, Shakuni was likely to be throwing right ninety per cent, may be even ninety-five per cent of the times, no matter what throw of number he needed. And so my uncle did.

An hour into the last session, there was some commotion in Yudhisthira's camp. Sahadeva was going about whispering something urgently into the ears of Bhima and Arjuna. And then Bhima whispered something into Yudhisthira's ears; Yudhisthira gave him a cold stare in response. Given Sahadeva's edginess, it was clear what the problem was. Sahadeva had caught on to what was happening, and was whispering into Bhima's ears. Besides, the Indraprastha treasury had been exhausted and was now overdrawn. I muttered this into Mama Shakuni's ears. Without looking at me for a moment, his expression wooden, Shakuni continued rolling the dice at a feverish pace, enlarging his bets manyfold. Yudhisthira was losing at a pace he could not fathom at first, and when he did after Bhima spoke into his ears, blood rushed into Yudhisthira's face. His eyes were on fire.

Shakuni would tell me later that this was the classic look of a compulsive gambler. This is the stage at which the gambler ceases to worry about the consequences, and wants to gamble more irrespective of whether he is up or down. Yudhisthira had reached that stage and, unfortunately for him, could do little about it. His chips were down and literally so. Worse for him, he was nearly drunk with wine. For that matter, so was I with the sheer delirium of happiness at the way my uncle had been able to command his dice during the session.

Shakuni kept slapping larger and larger wagers on the game board without respite as he rolled the dice, goading Yudhisthira to keep up with his pace. His throws barely seemed to go wrong. The stakes had risen so high that even when it was Yudhisthira's turn to roll the dice and it was his initiative to call the wager, he was no longer placing modest bets as he had been doing in the earlier sessions. It was as if he had been conditioned into placing enormous bets; as if he simply could not bear to bring the level of the game down to lower wagers: such was the psychological pressure Shakuni exerted on him to play fast and bet big – and lose bigger.

And then it happened.

Bhima walked up, asked for a brief time out, and announced that Yudhisthira had lost the entire treasury of Indraprastha, and that he had nothing more to wager. However, under the terms of game, it had to run its full course. You could hear a feather drop. Everyone held their breath. Bhishma and Vidhura, with grave expressions, whispered to me that since Indraprastha had been entirely debilitated, it was best to suspend the game. Before I could respond, Yudhisthira turned towards his brother. I could only see the back of his head and could not read his facial expression. Whatever it is he mumbled or communicated, Bhima quietly withdrew to sit by Arjuna, looking downcast.

Yudhisthira had clearly refused to concede cessation of play. And Shakuni doubled the ante on the board, with a roll of two fours, forcing Yudhisthira to bet all their palaces to continue the game. Yudhisthira's roll played out wrong, with a two and a three, while in order to win the accumulated wager on the board, he would have had to roll two ones. Shakuni quadrupled the combined wager again and his dice rolled once again to the requisite number, so that all the palaces of Indraprastha now belonged to the Kauravas. A relentless Shakuni doubled the ante yet again. Now Yudhisthira was sweating like the proverbial ice pitcher. He beckoned Sahadeva and whispered into his ears. He had the option of withdrawing from the game, but the ignominy of withdrawal would attach to him forever, like the stigma of an undischarged insolvent. It seemed to me that Sahadeva was respectfully suggesting Yudhisthira to do so. In response, Yudhisthira mumbled something in Sahadeva's ears for nearly a minute.

I would learn the contents of his mumbling much later from one of the courtiers who happened to overhear some of the chatter in their camp. Apparently, Yudhisthira was telling Sahadeva to relax because, according to the laws of probability, Shakuni could not continue to have a run of desired numbers for long, given he had already landed quite a few lucky rolls, and since he himself had not been getting two fours or two ones for a while now, his luck must break soon!

None the wiser perhaps, Sahadeva withdrew respectfully, unaware that the gambling addict was now in a state not very different from an elephant in musth. The sweat dripping from Yudhisthira's temples made the parallel all the more ironic. He was taking a few more thirsty sips of his wine. So was I.

Yudhisthira turned to the board again.

Up or down, flush or broke, excited or miserable, compulsive gamblers must continue betting. Yudhisthira was in the grip of several of these emotions. Like most amateur gamblers, he overestimated his understanding of how the dice worked, and staked his entire kingdom to match the total wager on the board. And then he rolled the dice. With a mere one in sixteen or six and a quarter per cent chance of rolling two fours, he predictably missed again. The entire hall sucked in its breath as one. Indraprastha had been lost to Hastinapura. I felt the kind of contentment and ecstasy I had not known ever before. I recall a random thought entering my consciousness: even piercing the eye of that fish in Panchali's swayamvara would probably not have given me as much happiness and satisfaction as I am getting now!

But it was now Shakuni's turn to roll the dice. Shakuni doubled the entire stake on the board yet again with a roll of five, landing a four and a one, and won!

Bhima suddenly stood up, walked over to Yudhisthira, and shook him by his shoulders, and they urgently started exchanging some words in hushed tones. Arjuna joined them too. After much deliberation, Yudhisthira turned towards me and in a soft timbre declared, 'I have lost my entire treasury, my palaces and even my kingdom. I have no possession that I can call my own except my brothers and wife. I am afraid even though the rules of the games require me to match the bet on the board, I cannot do so. What do you want me to do?'

This took me by surprise. While I had certainly known that we would wrest Indraprastha from Yudhisthira, I had not foreseen a situation where Yudhisthira, dispossessed of his kingdom, would directly seek my opinion on what he could do to honour his turn in matching Shakuni's stake. Besides, what with all the wine inside me, I could barely think clearly.

But before I could respond, Shakuni interjected, 'O Yudhisthira, you are well aware of the rules of the tournament. The game terminates only when the sun sets on the third day. Any party giving up sooner would do so only in eternal disgrace. You just declared that you have no possession that you can call your own except your brothers and wife. So, by your own admission, you have not yet lost all your possessions. But, of course, you may call for a premature end of the game. So do we take it that you abstain from completing the game and quit in disgrace?'

At this, there was much commotion. Several elders from our side rushed to me, appealing to me to spare Yudhisthira further humiliation. They wanted me to announce an end to the game as the Kuntiputras had lost everything they possessed. I was more or less in a state of shock; not sure if I was living a dream or dreaming a reality. But even in that state, I was convinced that now that I had the Kuntiputras in a vice-like grip, it would be foolish to loosen the hold. Just then, I heard Mama Shakuni referring the decision to the tournament referees, whereupon the referees read out the rule pertaining to the tournament duration once again, saying that, as per standard rules, it was for Yudhisthira to take a call.

I was happy that the decision had been taken away from my hands.

It was then that Yudhisthira staked his four brothers, himself and then Panchali in a bid to wrest back his kingdom. It seemed to me as if the earth was spinning.

Panchali at stake? This man was placing his *wife* at stake? What was going on? Was Yudhisthira as drunk as all that? Had he gone mad? Do the rules of the game permit a mad man to play? Things were happening too fast. Bhima stood and advanced towards Yudhisthira menacingly, questioning his right to treat his siblings and wife as his personal property. Arjuna seemed equally upset, but tried to hold back the impetuous Bhima. But the question marks on the brothers' faces were more eloquent than any display of muscle by Bhima. Yudhisthira, realizing that he owed them a response, stated calmly that as he was the king, they were all his subjects; that a king's right over his subjects is absolute, his honour above any personal considerations of kinship, and more such balderdash. Then he turned towards Shakuni, ready to roll his dice.

Relentless Shakuni had once again left him to throw two ones to win the entire stake. If he landed two ones, he would save his kingdom. If not, he would lose his brothers, himself and Panchali! But the laws of probability were against him. While there was a 6.25 per cent chance that he would save Panchali, his brothers and his kingdom, the odds against that were a whopping 93.75 per cent.

Alas! The percentages played themselves out as they were expected to. After all, a fifteen-to-one odd is not for everyone to beat. With vigorous shaking of his cupped palms, Yudhisthira rolled the dice again, which rolled to a four and a three.

And Yudhisthira had lost his kingdom and his brothers.

By now, he was a man in a frenzy. His eyes were glazed; his actions that of a man in a trance. He tilted the entire contents of the goblet into his throat for the last time in the tournament, and rolled twice more in quick succession, alternating with Shakuni's rapid-fire and accurate throws, only to lose first himself, and then Panchali!

Men are known to lose queens on the chess board; Yudhisthira must be the first in the history of mankind to lose a queen at the chaupar board!

And now it was my turn to empty the contents of the goblet into my throat; and it wasn't the last time for the evening.

13

One who dishonours his wife is a dishonourable man

Panchali! Yudhisthira, who fancied himself dharmaraj, had gone ahead, staked and lost his very kingdom, along with his brothers, himself and *Panchali*! In some ways, the development took away from the joy of dispossessing the Kuntiputras of their kingdom. Why, this was the very Panchali I had loved to distraction once – even if she had never even given me a glance; even if she had studiously shown nothing but disdain for me; even if she had laughed with a dash of malice at my clumsiness at the rajasuya venue; even if she had insulted my closest friend Karna, the honourable Karna, in the crudest manner possible; and even if this was the Panchali who had preferred Arjuna for her husband, getting four more in the bargain! And what does the eldest of them do? He goes ahead and gambles her away! Gambles her away, for God's sake! And now, at least technically, even if only won in chaupar, she was mine. Not that I coveted her any more.

However, my hand seemed to be tipping the goblet

towards my lips repeatedly, as if with a mind of its own. I remember being surprised at how much of the wine I was imbibing, considering I felt no joy whatsoever at the unexpected turn events had taken. A million sentiments ran through me like a million lightning bolts striking together.

My head reeled, and frankly I was confused if that was because my spirits were high from the win or the wine. What kind of dharmaraj was this? The man had just lectured his brothers on the dharma of a king. He knew enough about the rights of kings to know that a king's right over his subjects is absolute; and yet he seemed innocent of the fact that a king enjoys that absolute right only in the service of his subjects and not for gambling them away as chattel. Lecturing on the dharma of a king, he seemed innocent of the dharma of a husband or a brother. He seemed equally innocent of the elementary rule that all rights have their corresponding duties. The rights of the monarch gain their legitimacy only by how well he carries out his duties towards his subjects. Staking one's kingdom in a game of chance is the same as a king looting his own kingdom, and it certainly is not one of the dharmas or rights of a monarch.

Perhaps the dharmaraj was placing his vanity above his dharma. He had accepted our invite for chaupar against the counsel of his brothers, pretending that royal custom demanded that he accept the invite, while he knew the truth all along – that he was merely succumbing to his gambling instinct. He had all along shunned gambling through sheer willpower, and yet at the first opportunity he submitted to the royal invite when he thought he could get away with his image intact. So focused was he on the *rights of a king* that he had little thought for his *duty as a husband or brother or king*. He lacked the discrimination of judgement to see that it is one thing to be tempted into gambling and quite another to stake your own wife. Between the dishonour of withdrawing from the game prematurely and the ignominy of placing his wife and brothers at stake on the chaupar board, the dharmaraj saw the former as more disgraceful! In his opinion, a wife – the ardhangini, one half of oneself – was his personal property, to flip as a gold coin on the gambling board! So absolute did he regard the rights of a monarch that he did not even consider it necessary to consult the other four husbands of Panchali before gambling her away. He may have been king; but it did not strike the dharmaraj that he was just one of the five husbands of Panchali and, in that capacity, the other brothers were his equal and he had no right to stake their 'property', even if he considered a wife to be a husband's possession. Personally, I was of the view that a man who does not know the value of his wife is not an honourable man; leave alone being honourable enough to be a king. So was this all there was to the dharmaraj?

The bile rose inside me.

Knowing no other way to calm my nerves, I swallowed another generous quantity of the sura.

It is as if, by some mysterious reasoning and furtive decree, it has been agreed that no blame should ever accrue to Yudhisthira for betting his wife and losing her on the gambling board, but Suyodhana (or *Duryodhana*, if you please) must take all the blame for winning her on the same board – never mind that he did not even play on the board directly. I was unable to make cogent sense of what was going on. My head was heavy and mind in turmoil thanks to my conflicting emotions. It was like being caught in an ocean, both boiling and freezing at the same time. And yet, I was happy, even ecstatic. Indraprastha's dominion over us stood lifted. The Kuntiputras were off my back for good. As if in collateral benefit, even Panchali was mine. Mine! Mine? But what did I care about her any more?

But can first love ever be extinguished? It was as if my yearning for her had merely been dormant all this while and had never really died. And now the angry volcano had erupted … and set off a tsunami of emotions. It was as if I was drowning in the tsunami and destiny had thrown a lifeline at me – a second chance with Panchali. Dare I take it? Why not?

Royals routinely took several wives. Why couldn't I? But then, most royals probably didn't have wives like Bhanumati. Perhaps most of them confused lust for love. And every time lust passed, they took another wife. Or maybe in royal code, marriage had less to do with love or lust and more with statecraft, politics or the production of an heir, if not all of them.

Could I take Panchali for a wife? But Bhanumati had given me everything one could ever ask for in a wife – unconditional love, profuse care, immense concern, incredible loyalty, deep friendship, a delightful son (Laxmana) … How could I take another wife? What reason did I have to do so?

It came to me that if I had ever respected Rama, it was for one and only one act. I had never thought much of the way he looked on indulgently as his brother (though I confess Bhanumati insisted on naming our son after the brother, Laxmana) slice off the nose of Princess Surpanakha, King Ravana's sister, whose only fault was to try to flirt with the brother in the forest. The justification bandied out was that Surpanakha was an asura, while Rama was a deva. Rama had also killed Bali from behind a tree just so he could make Bali's brother Sugriva the king for all the wrong reasons. And he had banished his virtuous wife Sita because some scandalous sod pointed a finger at her. But to be fair to him, he had never taken a second wife – either before or after he had banished Sita to wilderness. In that sense, he had paid her the highest homage. And this was the one act – or was it a non-act? – of his I had always admired.

So then, how could I dream of taking a second wife and not be diminished in my own eyes? How could I brush aside years of my commitment to Bhanu and, more importantly, her commitment to me? Would that not be a dishonour to Bhanu, with whom I had been in love all these years?

Yes, I had been in love with Bhanu. But the love I had for her was never the same as what I had felt for Panchali. If my love for Bhanu was the staple of life to satiate the soul, my feelings for Panchali were like the sura that intoxicates the very consciousness. If Bhanu was a tenant who took residence in perfect harmony in my heart, Panchali had been the shadowy ghost who haunted that residence. If Bhanu was a good night's sleep, Panchali was insomnia. Bhanu was the wife; Panchali the unattained mistress. And now attainable!

And the very prospect unexpectedly made me think of what I had been missing with Bhanu. After the first few years of matrimony, we were so contented in each other, so absorbed in our son, so tied up in the affairs of the state, the palace, and the many relationships, that we never realized when romance had given way to routine. Life was so cosy, so uneventful and yet so full that it was like living in a tidy and sterilized garden of neatly trimmed plants from which the riot of colours of forest flowers had gone missing. And now as the prospect of that riot seemed within reach, my longing for colours suddenly seemed to overwhelm me. But if you ask me whether I continued to love Bhanu, I would have said, 'YES.'

Perhaps that's the colour of the face of mature love – a quiet shade of grey, unlike the bright purple, orange and yellow of puppy love. At this time of my greatest internal battle and upheaval, I had the epiphany that love is like people. It is perhaps a lot more attractive when young, but a lot more loyal when mature; a lot more volatile when young, but a good deal more stable when old; more insecure when young, but a lot more secure with age.

Ever since I had married Bhanumati, she had been the only woman in my life. Until this moment, I thought I had snuffed out all smouldering embers of feelings I may have had for Panchali long ago with the cold soothing river of tender devotion which was Bhanumati. And now it was as if Panchali was making a mockery of my years of steady loyalty to Bhanu. I was furious with Panchali for doing this to me! I hated her, as a matter of fact, for I loved Bhanumati!

Or was it that I loved them both? Is it possible for a man to be deeply in love with two women at the same time? After all, wasn't Panchali in love with all her husbands at the same time? Does that make her immoral? Is it natural? Did nature mean humans to be fundamentally monogamous? If not, why am I uncomfortable being in love with both Bhanu and Panchali? But if yes, why? After all, a mother loves two or more of her children equally at the same time, doesn't she? We routinely love more than one of our siblings at the same time, don't we? We are routinely committed to more than one friend at the same time, aren't we? So why cannot we be passionately in love with more than one woman at the same time? Why can't one love two women for two very different sets of reasons? Or is it a wrong analogy? If so, exactly where does the analogy break down?

It was as if all my contradicting emotions were coming at me in tsunami-sized waves and each wave was smashing me against the hard rock of Bhanumati. I felt as if I was going mad – stark raving mad. What did I care about Panchali ... except that I still loved her? In a way, I had loved no one else ever; and now she was mine!

Having won her fair and square, 'Why shouldn't I marry her?' was the debate uppermost in my head. Surely Bhanu would understand, especially as I had in the past confessed to her that Panchali was my first-ever love? And surely if I married Panchali with the concurrence of Bhanumati, it would imply not the smallest slight or dent in my love for her? After all, she had understood when it had come to Subhadra.

Balarama my friend had once wanted to give me the

hand of his sister Subhadra to strengthen the political alliance between Dwaraka and Hastinapura. However, Krishna, as expected, wanted her hand for Arjuna and conspired with his protégé – with some deviousness, of course – to spirit her away from the very venue where I was scheduled to wed her. But the matter had never weighed heavily on my mind. I was happily married to Bhanumati and had never even dreamt of taking another wife.

So intimate were we that when Balarama proposed that I marry Subhadra, I was reluctant and confided in Bhanumati. Actually, it was Bhanumati who counselled me that I should go ahead and take her hand, especially as Subhadra's brother was my close friend. This would cement our friendship into a relationship. She also felt that it would strengthen Hastinapura a good deal since even Krishna would then have to be less antagonistic towards me. At this point I had relented. But I had been touched and amazed at her selflessness. That's why when Arjuna played the spoilsport and abducted Subhadra from the swayamvara, I wasn't necessarily upset. In fact, I viewed it as a blessing in disguise. Arjuna may have taken Subhadra for one of his four wives, but I was happiest with Bhanumati.

But then taking the hand of Subhadra hardly appeared to be an insult to Bhanumati, for I held no particular feeling for Subhadra in my heart. But with such sloshing emotions for Panchali, even the thought of taking her for a wife appeared like a direct assault on all that was noble about Bhanumati.

And yet, Arjuna pipping me to the post not once but

twice had always rankled. And now Panchali was free. Lost by Yudhisthira in a gamble. And I had liberated her from her uncaring husbands! Now I had a right to her. I must marry her. But of course I would do no such thing. This was my chance to let that woman realize that she had made a bad choice that day when she rejected me and even Karna.

But ... here was a divine opportunity to seek Panchali's hand once again. With her husbands letting her down ignominiously, surely she would turn towards me? Why would a woman like Panchali, who had a high degree of self-worth, bordering on a large ego, have any respect left for a bunch of husbands who had lost her in gamble? Yes, I would honourably marry her! And fall in my own eyes?

My head was dizzy with all these conflicting feelings. When I surfaced from this violently churning ocean of emotions, I knew what I was going to do. Bhanumati was the one I loved. It also came to me as a revelation that hate is another manifestation of love. I recalled every instance of Panchali spurning and mocking my silent love for her, of her always looking *through* me and not *at* me even though her husbands had been brought up under our care. As these flashes of memory lashed at me, I found my love for her rapidly curdling into hate. Yes, I was now in control of myself. I had caught a long, deep breath and had found solid ground in that ocean of swirling emotions.

I was in a stupor, but I knew what I had to do. This was my moment to get even with Panchali for all those years when she had ignored my existence as if I were a mere third place in the decimal. Panchali! The haughty and snooty Panchali! The Panchali who considered herself too good for me! The Panchali who had insulted Karna! Yes I had to show her that she had not chosen right. That she should have chosen me, but she had not. She had chosen losers; losers in life and losers in this gamble, in which her husbands, or at least one of them, had reduced her to chattel, a possession to be wagered.

After all, when one loses something, *anything*, in gamble, the lost object belongs to the winner. I would show Panchali that she now belonged to me, but that I had no use for her. It was now my turn to scorn her. My turn to set her free!

After all, I was the ultimate winner: of her husbands, of *her*, of her kingdom. It would be an appropriate slap on her face, and that of the five Kuntiputras, for her to stand in the centre of the court and look into the shamed eyes of her loser husbands and see them for the wretched, helpless and pathetic creatures they were. Yes, I would like to see her ignore me now. I would like to see what Arjuna would do about it now. Surely he wouldn't look half as cocky as he had when he took first Panchali and then Subhadra from me.

I would show her that her husbands might gamble her away, but I was too gallant to accept her as a prize of that debased wager. If wagering one's wife is wrong, it is equally wrong to accept that shameful wager. Wives are to be married and loved, or loved and married; not lost or won by throws of dice; not even by kings. I would grant Panchali her freedom here, in my court, exactly the place where her husbands had wagered her away. All that remained was to get her to the very spot where her dignity had been compromised by her husbands standing shamefaced in my court.

Aha, at last the time had come to settle a long-standing account! Surely Bhanumati would understand? There was of course no question of seeking her counsel on my idea of revenge, for I knew what her response would be. It would be easier to make her come around once I had done what had to be done.

I asked Sushasana to go and fetch Panchali. 'Appraise her of the developments and tell her she is summoned to the court. Tell her, her husbands have reduced her to the state of a serf in our service. Tell her to come and take a look at her miserable husbands! Make haste, Sushasana,' I roared as Sushasana, sitting next to me, got up and hurried towards the guest quarters.

The assembly waited an eternity before Sushasana returned, announcing softly that Panchali had refused to respond to the summons. 'What? Refused the summons? Refused *my* summons? How dare she?' I thundered, unsure whether I was angry at her, at Yudhisthira, or at myself, before continuing, 'Did you tell her she is no longer a queen, and her husbands no longer kings and princes? That they don't have a kingdom any more? Go back. Impress upon her right now that her husbands are my serfs, as is she. She has been lost by her husbands in a board game and that this is a royal summons that may not be disregarded. Go back, Sushasana, and do not return without Panchali.' As I spewed out these words, I unwittingly changed my sitting posture, folding my left leg so that my thigh spread out on the divan in the space cleared by Sushasana, while my right leg rested on the ground as I leaned back for the wait.

I was expecting the proud Panchali to rush in in rage, eyes flaming, hair flying. But surprisingly, that was not the entry she made. To my consternation, I saw Sushasana all but pushing her into the assembly, in full view of the commoners and courtiers. I was momentarily blind with anger. How dare he lay a hand on Panchali! But I held my temper. Too much was happening already without my losing my cool at my own brother just yet.

It was a surreal scene – an unkempt Panchali, her wet hair askew, her sari's pallu slipping off her shoulders, the black kohl running off her eyes, making her cheeks a darker shade of blue-black, shrieking incoherently. It would be only later, much later, that it would dawn on me that Sushasana, or rather I, may have made a mistake in bringing her thus.

But that would be, as I said, later. Later, when Sushasana would tell me that when it dawned on Panchali that what Sushasana had recounted was true indeed and that the summons to her was not a bad joke, she grew nearly hysterical. She absolutely refused to believe even a grain of what he, Sushasana, was telling her. 'How dare you speak such filth about my husbands? How dare you just walk up to me – the queen of Khandavprastha, the wife of the monarch whose dominion includes Hastinapura and a man who is a venerable guest at Hastinapura – and speak such drivel, even if you are King Suyodhana's brother?' she had apparently challenged. 'Go tell your little king that my husband is the chakravarti king of rajasuya fame, to whom your brother should be paying obeisance. Or else, prepare to die at either Bhima's or Arjuna's hands,' she had screamed.

Now Sushasana was not used to being disobeyed. Nor was giving a peremptory command to Panchali just another day at office for him. So when she not only defied his command repeatedly but also rebuked him in public for summoning her, afraid of my wrath should he return without Panchali a second time, he had gently pressed his hands against her shoulders, pushing her towards the direction of the assembly. At his touch, Panchali had recoiled as if stung by a scorpion and became delirious. And it was in this state that she had entered the assembly before me, followed by Sushasana, with his hand on her shoulder.

Sushasana briefed me on all these developments and I had no reason to disbelieve him. And his narration sat well with what I myself saw as Panchali had entered the court. He had no record of misbehaviour with women – none of us had, for that matter – and I had no reason to believe that he had just sprouted a new habit of molesting women. Nevertheless, I realized that he had perhaps acted on my direction a trifle too literally. Perhaps he should have avoided bodily contact with Panchali at all costs.

Just then, as Panchali appeared in the assembly, with Sushasana right behind her, his left hand placed at her back and the right on her shoulder, my first reaction, after I got over my anger at Sushasana, was of a sense of relief that here was Panchali at last and I could play out my script and bring this unexpected, unforeseen and unseemly chapter to a close. I looked at Panchali and then at her wretched husbands. She was speaking to them jointly, singly, severally, and every which way, trying to confirm if this ridiculous piece of bull-dropping she had heard about Yudhisthira having gambled her away was true.

She asked the same question again and again in a rising pitch. She called upon them, any of them, all of them: 'O Yudhisthira! O dharmaraj! Weren't you the one at play? I know that you of all the people in the world could not have placed me at stake on the gambling board; so why are you quiet? Or have you really done what this abominable man says you have? And if you have, what right do you have to do so? Am I your wife or your property? Besides, what right do you have to bet your brothers' wife – which I am – on the chaupar board? Do you have the right to bet Subhadra, who is also your brother's wife? If not, why me, O dharmaraj? How about you, O Bhima? You do not even gamble, do you? Am I not your wife too? So why am I on the board? Why were you mute when this sacrilege transpired? And you, O Arjuna! Aren't you the one who won my hand at my swayamvara? Aren't you the one my father had devised the very swayamvara for? Can't you say a word to assure me that Sushasana has lost his mind and has been blabbering? O Nakula! O Sahadeva! Do say something!' And with every question that she spewed at her husbands, she took off each piece of jewellery on her person and flung them one by one at each of her husbands.

But when she encountered five lowered heads, she suddenly stood speechless, as if allowing time for the truth to seep in. She was trying to make sense of it all. The stunned quiet in the assembly spoke more than any words could. And Panchali abruptly twisted and turned away

Duryodhana

from Sushasana, as if contemptuous of all males, as if every male was a pus-oozing leper, and as she did so, the pallu of her sari stayed in Sushasana's fist – as he had bunched her pallu in his fist to avoid the direct contact of his hand upon her shoulder. The result was a most awkward sight as Panchali spun away, for the free end of her pallu was in Sushasana's grasp while a good part of the fabric covering her shoulder had come undone.

At this point, hell broke loose. Not just then and there in the assembly, but in all eternity. Panchali screamed in anguish. Arjuna and Bhima drew their swords and advanced menacingly towards Sushasana. Yudhisthira, who was closest to where Panchali stood, tried to stop them. Had he realized that what had happened, though unseemly, was not deliberate? My own advisors, counsellors and virtually the entire assembly was on its feet in consternation. Things were just unrolling, as if of their own accord.

Krishna suddenly materialized out of nowhere – he had probably just sauntered in to catch the final moments of the tournament – and rushed towards Panchali, crying 'Krishnaa!' (that is how he always addressed Panchali) and, snatching her pallu from Sushasana, he wound it around Panchali, who was sobbing inconsolably from the combined indignities of being gambled away on the chaupar board by her own husband, from the humiliation of the peremptory summons to the assembly and the manner of its execution, and from the mortification of the fall of her pallu in public. Everything was happening so fast that it was difficult to make sense of the events.

Before the game of chaupar, I had carefully planned what I would do once Yudhisthira lost his kingdom. But not even in my wildest imagination had I envisioned the surreal scene unfolding before me.

In my tangled state of mind, I wasn't sure what I ought to say or do. I realized that even through all that was unfolding, with her husbands humbled by me, she had not spared one single look – even one of fury or loathing – in my direction. And that sparked a flame of anger in my belly. And that is when a small part of me, I am ashamed to say, was almost happy that the haughty Panchali had been humbled. She had been stripped of her arrogance and haughty airs, and her superior husbands now stood, heads bent, at my mercy. She had insulted Karna – who later turned out to be yet another of Aunt Kunti's sons, and so the eldest of the Kuntiputras, so to say – in public as a low-born; and as if in divine justice, the eldest and the best of the Kuntiputra siblings, who had been spurned by her, was on my side too.

I looked towards Karna. But his expression was inscrutable, bordering on the grim. I tried hard to look for some signs of approval in his countenance but found none. And then I suffered a twinge of uneasiness and felt a wave of anger surge inside me that Panchali had not evoked the same reaction in Karna as in me.

And then I felt the anger turning into a strange sympathy for her – the sympathy one feels when an elephant trips. I wanted to smirk, but reach out to her at the same time, to tell her that her husbands were not worthy of her grief. I also wanted to scream at her that she had all along been blind not to have seen my love for her in my eyes. My tender emotions rose to the surface once again.

'Have you been blind not to have seen my love for you in my eyes? I would be happy to seek Bhanumati's consent to take you for my wife. There is no reason why you should not accept me for your husband, now that your husbands have forsaken you. From now on, your place is by my side ... here ...' What I thought were my thoughts turned out to be my words, uttered at the full pitch of my voice!

Oh no! What had I done! I had truly gone mad! I had actually uttered my confused thoughts. That was not all either. In a state of stupor, I had been completely unconscious of having folded my left thigh beside me; and my pat had unwittingly glanced off my left thigh. The gesture, at some stretch, could be interpreted as if I had indicated my thigh as the place for Panchali. But that was not my intention at all. Why, such an action would degrade me, and hardly her, as posterity, alas, has ended up doing anyway. But before I could correct myself or say another word to Panchali in explanation, there was pandemonium.

The world chose to see that gesture and record it for eternity. The Kuntiputras and their friends chose to interpret the developments as it suited them best. They ensured that their artists captured the moment in colourful detail, without ever realizing that they were doing their own wife, leave alone me, no favour by depicting the moment thus. Nobody ever asked me for my take on the matter since it suited everyone to have an epic with an arch villain.

14

*Gambling may not be a crime,
but wagering your wife certainly is*

What happened from that point on, leading all the way to the great Kurukshetra war, was mostly a foregone roll of events and is well documented in a million versions of the epic and there is little that I want to add or contradict.

Posterity has dubbed the unfortunate episode 'Panchali's vastraharan' and sees it as the final trigger for the war. It has been made out as if, between Sushasana and me, we had attempted to disrobe Panchali in the Hastinapura court, with all the respectable elders in mute attendance. I have been portrayed everywhere – in illustrations and films alike – as a leering tyrant who looks on as his brother pulls with both hands on one end of the sari of a helpless half-naked Panchali who is trying to shrink into herself even as she pirouettes like a top, with Krishna supplying the other end, faster than Sushasana's pulling.

For millennia have I wondered: assuming I was the

arch villain who compromised the dignity of a chaste Panchali, why would a truly caring posterity want Panchali's honour compromised again and again with that pathetic depiction which keeps the memory of her humiliation forever alive, unless posterity has merely been a voyeur, vicariously leering at the very half-naked picture of a hapless woman being molested by a fiendish man which it pretends to decry?

What one believes reflects upon oneself. A society itself is diminished if it thinks that in such cases the shame is upon the victim rather than upon the perpetrator of the crime. A victim is a victim precisely because he or she has no control upon the fate that visits her or him. But the control is entirely in the hands of the perpetrator and hence the responsibility of the misconduct and the resultant shame, disgrace and dishonour must accrue to the perpetrator as well.

There is nothing in my conduct, either before or after this imagined vastraharan episode, to portray me as an ogre generally injurious to the dignity of women. On the contrary, unlike Krishna who cavorted with anyone in a pleated skirt, and who had over a hundred wives and partners, I was wedded and attached to just one woman, and that was Bhanumati. Unlike Rama who put his wife through agni pariksha to test her chastity, I had always deeply respected Bhanumati.

I hate to tell you this story involving Bhanumati, Karna and me after all these millennia, but with the reputation I have been given by generations of *Duryodhana*-baiters, how else do I set my record straight? Clearly, leaving it to the victors to write history hasn't helped.

Once, returning from court after a long day, I walked into our private chamber to find Bhanumati and Karna keenly engaged in a game of chaupar with substantial stakes. Karna had his back to me, while Bhanumati sat facing me. Seeing me enter, Bhanumati tried to stand up, which we both usually did for the other out of respect and affection. But as she was trying to get on her feet, Karna just grabbed for her clothes in a spontaneous move, in a bid to prevent her from rising (I would learn later that she was losing heavily and Karna thought she was trying to get away without completing the game; and hence he was trying to stop her from escaping). As he reached out to prevent her from leaving, her waistband broke and pearls rolled out in all directions. I noticed that Bhanumati stood half bent in mortification as blood rushed to her face, and it took Karna a few moments to realize why Bhanumati was perturbed. And then, as realization dawned on him, he turned towards me, looking no less distressed and embarrassed. I had a hearty laugh at the two – both of them my best friends – and helped Bhanumati pick up the scattered pearls. To be honest, I was not even aware that I had done anything noteworthy. When you love your wife and trust a friend, you don't do so conditionally. But Bhanumati would somehow always regard my reaction as indicative of my love and trust for her and for Karna, and saw the whole episode as remarkable. She would often tell me that I innately respected women and that was reason enough for her to be proud of me.

As it turned out, when I unburdened to her the culminating events at the conclusion of the game of chaupar, narrating the conflicting emotions that had waged a veritable war in my heart that day, Bhanumati had understood me entirely. True, had I revealed to her my strategy to dispossess Yudhisthira of Indraprastha, she would have thoroughly disapproved of it. But then strategy always has an element of oblique deception to it, and good innocent people like Bhanumati seldom approve of deception – direct or indirect (but then nor can innocent people rule kingdoms). But she also had a cardinal rule not to interfere in matters of state, except when I sought her sage counsel explicitly. On this occasion, I had thought it prudent to interpret the chaupar as a matter of state and chosen not to discuss it with her. I have no doubt that by the time of my confession, she had fathomed my real motives, but since I had not broached the subject directly, she nobly held her counsel.

But she did understand my sentiments and actions concerning Panchali and, though she would rather I had not summoned Panchali to the court, she said that she understood the conflict inside me. When I sought her forgiveness for having asked Panchali to marry me, though I really had not meant to do so consciously, and did not even know until those moments that I had any feelings for Panchali at all after all those years, she said, 'But what is there to forgive, O Suyu? What do I care whether or not you had any feelings for Panchali? And if you did, good for you, for it only speaks of your good taste.' She laughed naughtily as she said this. 'I know you have always been devoted to me. But even today if you desire Panchali and take her hand – which, unfortunately for you, is not to be – why, I do not for a moment think that would take anything at all away from your devotion to me or my love for you. I know that in that case you would simply be equally devoted to us both, just as Panchali has been equally devoted to her five husbands, all at once. Love alone has the power of infinity. Just as infinity loses nothing from its immensity even when you divide it into many parts, so does love remain boundless even when you divide it.'

To me that is enough. I don't care what anybody else thinks of me. I don't care what the entire posterity, with its gods and non-gods and hordes of humans, thinks of me. To me it is enough that Bhanumati did not think me evil. In short, I did not mean any dishonour to Panchali. There was no vastraharan. There is only one truth: if Panchali was dishonoured that fateful day, it was at the hands of Yudhisthira, not mine.

~

At another level, do you think Krishna – who was Panchali's long-time friend and well-wisher and her father's friend from her childhood – would have just sat there watching Panchali's honour compromised? Well, according to popular script, he nearly did.

But let me tell you why Krishna did not act – because there never was any threat to Panchali's honour. He knew that what had happened with her pallu was accidental, even if Sushasana could have conducted himself better. He did however have the presence of mind to do the right thing by immediately helping Panchali cover herself; and an equal presence of mind to use the episode strategically against us. And yet, you seem to forget that this was the same Krishna who was known to steal or hide the clothes of bathing girls and watch their nubile forms stealthily as they dashed around trying to recover their garments.

How come Krishna did not try to dissuade Yudhisthira from violating the dignity of womanhood and the dignity of the very definition of a wife when he was wont to go nosing around everywhere, dispensing his crafty advice and conniving plots, at the drop of a peacock feather? He would, in time, with two huge armies arrayed on two sides for the mother of all wars, in a largely sensible discourse, lecture the brothers that it was all right to kill even one's loved ones at the altar of rajadharma. Yet, he did not see the necessity of counselling Yudhisthira that the supreme dharma demanded that he accept personal disgrace by withdrawing from a game of chaupar rather than lose his rajya (and wife) on a throw of dice. After all, nothing prevented the disgraced king from passing on the kingdom to the next of kin, so that the honour of the kingdom was in no way besmirched. But it is ironic that the dharmaraj should have needed such counsel in the first place, and worse, should not have received it with Krishna in the immediate vicinity. Was someone playing to the gallery?

~

Was it my fault that Yudhisthira chose to accept my invite? Was it my fault if he chose not to heed his brothers' advice against accepting the invitation? Was it my fault that Yudhisthira had a gambling addiction? Was it my fault if he was delusional about his prowess at chaupar? Was it my fault if he had a warped understanding of a king's rights – that he could wager his kingdom on the board? Was it my fault if he wagered his own brothers on the board? Was it my fault if Yudhisthira considered his wife to be his property and wagered her? Was it my fault if Shakuni was a better player of chaupar than Yudhisthira? Am I to be faulted for agreeing to give away Indraprastha to the Kuntiputras in the first place? Am I to be blamed for their conducting the rajasuya which also subjugated Hastinapura as their dominion? Am I to be faulted for winning back Indraprastha by strategic statecraft rather than open warfare with a state more powerful than mine? Am I to be faulted for having an unrequited crush on Panchali? Then why have I been so vilified while the Kuntiputras continue to shine blameless?

~

After Yudhisthira had lost his kingdom, lost himself, his brothers and wife to us, I could have legitimately maintained the status quo for good. However, my scheme had been to dispossess Yudhisthira only of his kingdom, not his personal liberty and that of his brothers and wife. I had no intention ever of taking Panchali away by force if she still wanted to be with those good-for-nothing husbands of hers who had gambled her away. As a matter of fact, I was not even sure if I had really wanted her hand, though indeed to my dismay, I had asked for her hand in my stupor.

That is why I returned them their personal liberty even if I banished them from my state for twelve years to prevent any more smooth machinations by them. At the behest of their well-wishers, including my father and the other elders, I even gave them a gamely, though improbable, chance of getting Indraprastha back if they managed to live their thirteenth year incognito. In retrospect, this was a childish condition we could have done without, and stopped at permanently extraditing them. But I wonder if even that would have averted the war.

As it transpired, with Krishna's connivance, they tried to cheat themselves out of the agreed conditions (by refusing to accept that we had trounced their attempt at incognito existence) and came back to claim Indraprastha. When I refused to fall for their bluff and hence refused to return Indraprastha, Krishna tried to mediate a compromise, asking for at least five tiny villages, if not Indraprastha itself, for the Kuntiputras. But I was in no mood to carve out our kingdom yet again and start the cycle all over and famously refused to part with 'even enough land to be accommodated on a pinpoint'.

They say that I could have averted the war if I had compromised my rajadharma once again. But isn't there a saying in your present time that goes 'You fool me once, shame on you; you fool me twice, shame on me'? Well, I had learnt my lesson after giving the Kuntiputras Indraprastha the first time, when they had gone on to perform the rajasuya and establish their dominion over us. It was clear to me as daylight that Hastinapura's pride was safe only as long as the Kuntiputras remained without a kingdom, which in any case was never their legitimate due to begin with. I was not going to earn the ignominy of committing the same mistake a second time.

From here on, events took on a life of their own and inexorably moved towards the war. Exactly how the inevitability of the war gathered momentum; how it all panned out; how near and dear ones – friends and relatives, teachers and students, uncles and nephews – fought each other; how both the sides cut corners; how they both lied, cheated and killed; how both the sides showed uncommon valour; how both violated the rules of warfare; and how an entire generation of women and children were widowed and orphaned on both the sides; and much more is documented in great detail in mythological history.

Years ago, my father had accepted the Kuntiputras into Hastinapura as Kuru princes, even if they weren't Kurus by a long shot. In keeping with this gesture, I would never have dithered if all that the Kuntiputras wanted was a generous privy purse worthy of princes and had agreed to live quietly under my rule. Of course, given their abilities, I could have used Yudhisthira as my minister for justice, or Bhima and Arjuna as my generals, et al. But the mother and sons were never prepared to accept anything less than either the Hastinapura crown or a slice of it. And this wasn't something I was ever prepared to accept. Not then; not today.

That is why I have never felt the burden of Kurukshetra on my conscience. I have never regretted not giving in to the unreasonable demands of the Kuntiputras.

There have been times when I have wondered if lady luck had always remained a shy maiden to me. After all, my parents never set their eyes upon me. My childhood was barely enjoyable as the machinations surrounding my crown started rather early in life. Not only had I been unlucky in love, but I had lost the girl to my most hated rival too. My well-planned but covert strategies to secure my kingdom for good had failed. My adult life remained perennially distracted by the constant gnawing of the

Kuntiputras at my kingdom. Somehow it became my fault that Yudhisthira had his priorities mixed up and decided to wager his wife on the chaupar board and lost. I had been accused of being complicit in the so-called disrobing of Panchali, even though those who witnessed the proceedings should have known better. The war at Kurukshetra was thrust upon me, leading to large-scale death and devastation. Posterity treats me with utmost contempt and condemnation.

And yet, I can hardly say that the shy lady never winked at me. Winning the ovarian lottery as the crown prince of a flourishing state; getting Bhanumati for a wife; having Karna for a friend; my affectionate brothers and sister Sushala; caring and loving parents; to have been able to live life on my own terms; to die in combat – well, I had enough to be thankful for in life.

Yes, perhaps I was headstrong. But weren't the Kuntiputras equally so? I may have been greedy for not letting go of even a fraction of my kingdom. But I had done it once and realized the greed of the pretenders to the throne at my cost. I may be called evil for the many plots that I devised in the course of protecting my kingdom. But weren't the Kuntiputras equally evil in their own plots in trying to wrest away what was legitimately mine? Well, I have no regrets about what or who I was.

However, as I had said earlier, if I have one regret today, after all these millennia, it is this – that Panchali never gave me eye contact; if she had, she would have known that I could never have dishonoured her. But alas, she did not! And God, did I pay for it ... And so did she, did she not?